THE VENGEANCE OF LEGION

Helen Fields

First published by Wailing Banshee Ltd in Great Britain in 2012
18 High Street, Overton, Hampshire, RG25 3HA

ISBN 978-0-9571246-3-9

In memory of Brendan Andrews
Quick to smile, slow to judge, forever in our hearts

And to my darling Gabriel, for being so proud of me
I'd write a thousand books just to see that smile on your face

Prologue

When Eve MacKenzie finds an adoption certificate with her name on it, her world begins to spiral out of control. Eager to find the truth about her parentage, she travels to Slovakia to meet the midwife who delivered her, but the baby she recalls had Down's Syndrome. Whilst Eve is defending a soldier in a rape case in Krakow, she is approached by Perun who claims to have the key to unlocking the mystery surrounding her past. After surviving a horrific train crash in the Tatra Mountains, Eve decides to give up her old life and travel to San Francisco to pursue the few clues Perun gave her about her true family. Whilst there, she meets former actress Sabina Roman who takes her in and gives her work. A ranch hand, James, seemed to be interfering unnecessarily in Eve's plans until she discovers that he has his own score to settle with Perun.

In an attempt to draw Eve back into his own world, Manitu, Perun finally reveals the truth of how she came to be adopted. Eve is a demon from the Vilya family, swapped with a human child, Zora, at birth. Too late, Eve realises that Perun has been feeding her information for his own purposes, just as her family are about to take power in Manitu. Perun wants to get her there to stop Zora from ascending to the throne. Whilst James rescues Zora, Eve turns up unannounced at the ascension ceremony to buy her family the time to organise themselves against Perun and his tribe. When Perun realises he has been manipulated, a bloody battle begins which is still raging as Eve and James leave Manitu. Eve's mother, Anousk, reassures her that they will be able to return their world to its former peace. James and Eve part ways as they try to put the past behind them and reclaim their normal lives, but the shadow of the things they have seen and done is ever present.

One

Pulse racing a little too fast, I was struggling to control the power beneath me and the vibration between my legs was on the borderline between pleasure and pain. I opened the throttle a fraction more, overwhelmed by the exhilaration of speed, and felt the bike begin to slide. It wasn't sudden or harsh, in fact the movement was remarkably smooth and I could see the faces of children in a passing car, staring at me with open mouths and round eyes as my body came away from the seat and I flew spinning into the air like a gymnast.

I was weightless, breathless and there was no panic, only a burning desire to keep going, catapulting up into the clouds above me. It came to an end, of course, and there was only the unforgiving ground waiting to break my fall. As I closed my eyes on the return journey, I had time to hope this wasn't the end and that fate would be kind. In the split second before gravity welcomed me home, I heard my mobile ringing in my pocket and wondered, vaguely, who could possibly be calling at a time like this?

I thought the rolling would never stop and, when it did, I looked at the scars I'd left in the grass with something approaching awe. I must have hit the ground at the top of the slope, well cushioned by moss and other soft foliage, and just tumbled over and over until the bank at the bottom broke the motion. I could see flattened leaves in a trail above me with plants pulled out by the roots where my boots had dug in. I tentatively moved my legs, then my arms, waiting for the inevitable onset of pain but it didn't come. I was unhurt, apparently, although I doubted the same would be true of my motorbike. I sat up and took off my helmet, a slow grin spreading across my face as I realised I'd been given a reprieve and that, for once, I'd been dealt the lucky hand. The sky was still blue, my body was still attached in the same sequence of parts as when I woke up this morning, I had four weeks of vacation time stretching ahead of me and I was very much alive. The only thing marring the moment was the persistent ringing in my pocket, which I answered with nothing more than an intention to silence it.

'Eve, where are you?' Sabina's voice was shaking so badly, I could barely make out what she was saying. When she got upset her Slovakian accent kicked back in.

'Out on my bike. What's wrong?'

'It's Naomi. We've been trying to contact you but you weren't answering your phone. You have to come home.' Sabina was babbling and I wasn't sure if it were her not making sense or if I was concussed.

'What's happened to Naomi? Is she alright?'

'No, she's not. She's been arrested.'

'There must be some mistake. What could Naomi possibly have done?' I walked back up the slope looking for my bike, stretching my neck and not liking the grating sand sensation inside.

'They're holding her on suspicion of murder.' Time stopped. A stabbing pain punched into my chest.

'I'm on my way back to the ranch, okay? If she calls again, take the number and tell her I'll phone her as soon as I get home. And try to get hold of Tim, see if he can give you any more details.' Sabina sobbed. 'It'll be okay, I promise. This is just some crazy misunderstanding. I'll sort it out.'

'You don't understand,' she choked. 'Tim's dead.'

I hung up without saying another word. A chill coursed through my body, numbing me as I flagged down a passing car and explained that I needed a lift into Carmel, leaving my bike in its crumpled state at the side of the road. An hour later I was approaching the house, wondering if I'd imagined the conversation with Sabina.

Naomi's my best friend. She lives in England and is about the only thing I miss from my life there. She is the sweetest, kindest person imaginable and the idea that she could've committed any criminal offence, let alone a violent one, was absurd.

I had a constant slide show running through my head; Time spent with Naomi and Tim from the day they met at a friend's birthday celebration to shared weekends in country cottages, the way they'd looked after me at my adopted mother's funeral and their beautiful wedding in Scotland, just two months ago. He was everything Naomi had ever wanted and they were more deeply in love than any two people I'd ever known. He couldn't be dead. More than that, he certainly couldn't be dead at Naomi's hand. By the time I reached Sabina's front door, my numbness had turned to denial. I burst in without knocking, storming straight through the hall towards the living room.

'Sabina?' I shouted. There was no reply and as I walked in I could see why. Sabina was sat holding a telephone to her ear, tears streaming down her face. I paused in the doorway, knowing there had been no mistake. It was very real.

'Alright, my darling, Eve is here now, I'll pass you over to her. Let me know if I can do anything else.' Sabina held the phone out and for a second I didn't want to take it, knowing that when I heard Naomi's voice the shared pain of her loss would be intolerable.

'Naomi, it's me. I'm so sorry, honey. I'm so sorry.' There was no sound at the other end except a quiet keening. I sank to the floor on my knees and carried on whispering meaningless words to her as she cried. Sabina's secretary had entered the room and was passing her a piece of paper, talking in a hushed voice. Little by little, Naomi's sobbing trailed off. I focussed on the only thing I could, to get through the conversation. I had to get Naomi out of whatever trouble she was in.

'Naomi, where are you right now?' I asked.

'Kingston police station. I'm waiting for my solicitor, Mike Fletcher, to arrive before they interview me.'

'Tell them to send him home,' I said. 'I'll call Bryn now. Say nothing until he's with you, you understand?'

'Okay,' she whispered, the tears starting again. There was no way I could talk to her about what had happened over the phone. 'Eve, I can't believe he's dead. I don't understand what's happening.'

Sabina appeared next to me with the piece of paper her secretary had handed her. It was an internet flight booking under my name. I grabbed Sabina's wrist and kept hold of it whilst I read.

'I'm coming, Naomi,' I said. 'Sabina's booked me a flight. I'll be with you late tomorrow night. Bryn will keep the police tied up 'til then. I love you.' She was quiet for a while and I thought she was about to put the phone down. I waited to hear the receiver click then her voice whispered.

'James said you'd know what did this. He told me to tell you it was them. He wouldn't say any more. I love you too.'

'James?' I asked, but I was talking to a dead line. Sabina took the phone from my hand and replaced it with a glass of whiskey. I stayed where I was on the floor, sipping it slowly. What Naomi just told me made no sense at all.

Six months ago James and I had agreed to part ways. We knew that if we stayed together it would end in disaster. He'd slipped away at the end of the opening performance of the play I was appearing in and I hadn't seen or heard from him since. Now, I find out that he's in contact with my best friend and somehow involved in her husband's death.

'He asked me not to tell you,' said Sabina. 'He wanted you to be able to get on with your life.'

'You knew?' I cried, getting to my feet. 'You knew he was with Naomi and you didn't tell me?'

'Eve, I don't know what happened between you and James last summer, but when he left I watched you close that particular door and make the decision to start again. You haven't so much as spoken his name since he went and yet every time you walk across the paddocks it's as if you're still looking for him. I didn't want to upset you.'

'Fine, I understand and I'm sorry I shouted but I'm getting on a plane tomorrow and I need to know exactly what I'm walking in to.'

'Alright.' Sabina patted the couch and I sat beside her. She'd been a constant support to me since I turned up in Carmel last year trying to find my birth mother. She'd given me a job and somewhere to stay. I knew I could trust her and that whatever she'd done, it was with the best of intentions.

'When James left the ranch he decided to go travelling. He asked if he could leave what possessions he had here in storage until he settled somewhere. Naturally I said he could. Occasionally I would get an email or a letter, just a few lines, telling me where he was and that he was well.'

'I wish I'd known' I whispered.

'If you had known, you'd have spent every day waiting for the next contact, wondering where he was, not moving on. I didn't want to see you suffer like that.' I didn't say anything, she was absolutely right. The only way I'd managed to get through the last few months was by forgetting all about James and throwing myself head first into a new life. I'd done it quite convincingly as well, until now.

Sabina continued. 'About a week ago I received a telephone call from the American embassy in London. James was there and had given my name as a reference. He'd been mugged at an underground station and all his papers were gone; passport, credit cards, driving licence. He had no money and no ticket to get home. I knew he'd left copies of all his papers here in case there was an emergency. He wanted me to scan and email them to the embassy. It was as simple as that.'

'So how did he end up with Naomi?' I asked.

'He needed somewhere to stay and she's the only person I know in London. I phoned her, she took him back to the flat until his new papers were issued and I'd been able to wire some money. I don't understand what this has to do with Tim. Is James involved somehow?'

'I don't know,' I said, feeling a deep unease that I didn't want to transmit. 'Naomi mentioned his name but I don't know what she meant. Thank you Sabina, I know you were trying to protect me. I'd better go and pack.'

I kissed her on the cheek and made my way across the gardens to the guest house where I was staying. At my porch, I paused to look across the acreage to the staff cottages where James once lived. Before the memories could overwhelm me, I did what I always did; got busy with something else. Right now I had Naomi and Tim to worry about. I needed to contact my old friend to help Naomi out. She was a respected barrister, so I hoped it wouldn't prove difficult to persuade the police that she was innocent.

As I threw clothes into a suitcase I thought about the one thing I'd been trying to ignore. Naomi had said I'd know who killed Tim. If that was the most James would tell her then we were in very serious trouble. In my heart, I knew that James' oblique message meant that the Perelesnyk were back in our lives. What I couldn't comprehend was what they could want with my best friend and her husband. As hard as I'd tried to ignore it, this part of me was just not going to stay buried.

Two

At three in the morning my plane touched down in London, thanks to an eleven hour flight from San Francisco and the eight hour time difference. I'd had a message from Bryn to say that Naomi had been released pending further enquiries but needed to be back at the police station again the next morning for further questioning. She'd gone to Bryn's house for the night as the little flat we'd once shared was now officially a crime scene. By the time I got there it was nearly four. Bryn told me that Naomi had just fallen asleep and asked me not to disturb her. He showed me to the study where he'd made up a sofa bed and I settled down for the night. I'd been in bed about half an hour when my door opened a crack. A figure slipped into the room and slid into bed with me.

'Oh, Naomi,' I said and put my arms around her as the sobbing began. I held her like that as we cried together and I have no idea how much time passed. Eventually we both fell into an exhausted sleep and when I awoke she was seated at the window, staring out into the London fog. I got up and slipped a blanket round her shoulders.

'Lock the door,' she said. I wasn't going to argue with her so I leant a chair under the handle and, when she was satisfied that we wouldn't be disturbed, she began to speak.

'Tim had just got back from a business trip to Tokyo. I picked him up from Gatwick, everything was fine. We went out for fish and chips, thought we'd show James what proper English food was like; Tim's idea. He spent the evening boring James with the story of how we got engaged. We had a couple of beers and went to bed early as he had jet lag. James was in your old room, all the doors were locked, you know how security conscious Tim is.'

I put my hand over hers but she didn't even register I'd touched her so I just let her talk.

'He kissed me goodnight and then he was out like a light, exhausted. I guess I lay awake for a while, thinking about a few thank you letters I still had to write for wedding presents and ordering photographs, stupid stuff. I heard a noise in the living room but assumed it was James so I rolled over, closed my eyes and then our door flew open. There must have been lights on in the kitchen because I could see their faces and the first thing I thought was that it was a dream, you know, that I was just having a nightmare. Before I could scream they were on top of us and even then I couldn't figure out what was happening. There were three of them, so strong I couldn't move a muscle. I don't know what they were, but I don't think they were human.' For the first time since she started talking, she looked at me. 'Is this what it's like when you lose your mind? Eve, please help me.'

She reached out and I took her in my arms as she carried on telling me what she'd seen and when she touched me I began to feel almost detached from my own body. Her voice seemed to be coming from inside my own head and after a few seconds I could see everything through her eyes, as if I'd been right there.

Tim lay on his back with one of them leaning across his chest, holding his arms and preventing him from fighting back. Another one had Naomi. She'd managed to sit up but he'd slid behind her on the bed and wrapped his arms around her chest, immobilising her right next to where Tim was being attacked. It was only then that I saw their faces clearly. They were pale, slimy skinned with huge lifeless eyes that were weeping constantly. Their mouths were gaping holes with engorged lips although I couldn't see any teeth. They had no hair and their bodies were clothed in leathery rags but what I could see of their bodies showed sinew and muscle rippling beneath almost translucent flesh.

The third creature stripped the bed covers off Tim to reveal his naked body. A scream erupted from Naomi, met with a hand slapping hard over her lips and a warning hissed into her face, blowing foul breath over her. Tim was shaking uncontrollably and throwing his head left and right. The creature spread Tim's legs wide apart and slithered down between them. He put a fist into the air and then shot out his fingers, producing a deathly sharp set of nails, several inches long. Naomi started to kick at the bed as if she were trying to run away, futile with the beast behind her. As much as I wanted not to see, I watched the creature slice Tim's inner thigh with his claws and duck his head to cover the wound with the lower half of his face. The sound of voracious sucking smacked around the room. Even Naomi stopped protesting and just stared in stunned repulsion, all the fight gone out of her.

It only took a minute, one and a half at most. Between the injury to Tim's femoral artery and the force of the sucking, his life was drained from him as he lay there, helpless, tears running from the corners of his eyes as he gazed at Naomi. When it was done the creature sat up, rubbing at his lips with slimy hands and giving a gulping cry of victory and pleasure. The others joined in and together they began to pull Naomi down onto the bed on her back.

Then the bedroom door burst open, smashing hard against the wall. James shot into the room and I caught the flash of a blade in his hand as it sliced through the air and into the neck of the one who'd held Tim down. Naomi was suddenly free as the other two began a counter attack but James was frenzied and had taken them by surprise. He pulled the blade out, plunging it into the belly of the next creature then ripping it upwards in an arc, exposing its guts and dropping it dead in a single move.

The third had more time to prepare and exposed its claws, standing on the bed to get the advantage. James whipped the blade across one of its hands, taking the tips off the nails and it screeched furiously. James grabbed at one leg whilst it was distracted, knocking it off the bed and onto the floor on its face. Before it could move, James forced the knife under its neck and sliced cross-ways as it gurgled a protest from its open throat. The thing stopped kicking its legs after a few seconds and James fell to one side, dripping with sweat and panting to get air. Naomi, who'd been frozen in a corner, finally came round enough to throw herself onto Tim's unmoving body, shouting his name over and over, as if she could bring him back to life through sheer bloody will.

When Naomi pulled back out of my arms, the vision I'd shared with her ended abruptly and I came back into the present to find her whispering, as if scared we might be overheard.

'They killed him, Eve. Whatever those things were, they came into our home and killed my husband and I don't even know why. If I tell anyone what I saw that night they'll lock me up, think I'm insane. Only James can back me up and he's gone. That's why I called you. You have to find him, bring him back, he's got to tell the police what he saw.' She was crying again but I needed her calm enough to tell me the rest of the story.

'Naomi, listen to me. I need to know how it ended. I promise I'm going to help you, but just for a minute focus on what happened then. After James killed them, what did he do?'

Naomi looked confused for a minute then took a deep breath, swiped the tears from her cheeks and carried on.

'The next thing I knew he was pulling their bodies out of the door. I expected there to be blood all over the floor from where he'd cut them but there was just this clear sticky liquid. James pulled me off Tim's body, I fought him to start with but eventually he persuaded me to let go. I think I must have fainted. The next thing I knew I was in your old bedroom, on the bed. I tried the door but James had locked me in exactly as you just did with that chair. I started to panic but then saw he'd left me a note on the floor. He'd put the phone with it and told me to call the police, act like the attack was happening right then. I heard a window smash in my bedroom and I read the rest of the note as I waited for the police. I had to pretend I'd been locked in by the attackers, act like I didn't know Tim was already dead. James said he had to leave, that I should contact you straight away and that you could explain what was going on. That's everything.'

'Did he say where he was going or leave anything else behind?'

'No, his passport had come through that morning and Sabina had sent money so he was planning to leave the next day anyway, but I don't know where he is now. Why did James think you'd know what those things were? I keep running it over in my mind and the one thing I realised is that James never seemed shocked by them. Not by the way they looked or what they were doing. He just carried on as if it was all perfectly normal. I don't know what I'm trying to say. Sorry.'

'We'll get through this. James did the right thing, locking you in the bedroom. Whatever the police suspect, you couldn't have put yourself in there. Did you give them James' name?'

She shook her head. In a moment of pure selfishness I was relieved. The last thing I wanted was James facing a murder charge.

'I can't describe them, Eve. I've got to go back for questioning later today. All I've said so far is that I saw three men but how am I supposed to give detailed descriptions?'

'You're not and it won't seem odd at all. How many victims have you and I cross-examined who couldn't give any information about attackers? You were in shock, you're still in shock and you're grieving. They woke you up, took you by surprise. It was dark, they bundled you into a room and that's all you can tell them. Keep it short and simple. The less you say, the fewer questions they can ask.'

At that moment Bryn knocked gently at the door asking if we wanted breakfast. I replied that we'd be out in a few minutes and started to get dressed so that Bryn and I could agree a strategy for handling the police. Naomi remained sitting at the window.

'They won't let me see his body. I can't even go and say goodbye,' she said. 'They're doing an autopsy. He's going to be taken apart. It's not fair, he's been through enough.'

I walked over and took her hand to get her up. 'You still have to eat,' I replied. 'One step at a time. Let's just get through today, okay?' She nodded, still looking at the floor. I walked to the door and held it open for her. As she shuffled past me she paused to look me in the eyes.

'I want the truth, Eve. Whatever that is, it can't be as bad as feeling like I'm going crazy. If you know something then you have to promise to tell me. Not right now. But when I ask you again I expect to be told everything.' She stared at me and I couldn't tell the lie that I desperately wanted to. I couldn't tell her I knew nothing. 'Say yes,' she said.

It was my turn to look away and I wished with all my heart that she would never get around to asking the question. 'Yes,' I said. 'I promise.'

Three

Bryn was a determined bachelor in his early sixties, married only to his job. He had the extraordinary knack of being everyone's friend; he rarely raised his voice, never let police officers bully his clients and wouldn't tolerate snobbery. I crossed my arms, leaned against the doorframe and watched him fry bacon.

'You do know that frying bacon in that much salt and butter is like ordering a take away heart attack, right?' I smiled at him, realising how much I'd missed my old friend.

'Shut up and earn your keep, MacKenzie. Make a pot of tea. Just because you're a big star now doesn't mean you don't have to muck in with the rest of us.' His words may have been gruff but when I stood next to him to boil the kettle, he patted my hand in a gesture so familiar it brought tears to my eyes. I dabbed at my face with my sleeve.

'Now don't bloody start crying, that won't help anyone.' He ruffled my hair and kissed the side of my head like an indulgent father. He was right. I took a deep breath and put my lawyer head back on to deal with the problem at hand.

'What've they got? If they've taken Naomi in for questioning they must suspect something. Did you find out anything at the police station?' I handed him a mug of tea as he sat at the table and pulled documents from an envelope.

'It's more what they haven't got, love. There's no murder weapon, no forensic evidence, a smashed window but no footprints or fingerprints and no other witnesses. That's the official version.'

'And unofficially?' He took a long gulp of tea but didn't answer. 'Oh, come on Bryn, I didn't get you involved in this just for the hospitality. What you can't find out isn't worth knowing. What are they saying behind closed doors?'

'The forensic pathologist isn't happy. Apparently he's got a body completely drained of blood.' I slumped down onto the chair across the table from Bryn. 'Which might be understandable except that the police reports say there wasn't a single drop spilled at the flat.'

'So they don't think that's where he actually died.'

'At least life in California hasn't totally addled your brain. That's right. Naomi's problem is that her version of events doesn't make any sense. Nobody's saying it yet but I'd put money on them trying to pin a conspiracy on her. Given that it looks like he was killed elsewhere and then his body was brought back into the flat, she'd have to be lying, presumably because she's involved in the whole thing.'

'So that's where this is going, is it? They'll say I paid someone to kill my husband. I may as well just confess right now and get it over with.' Naomi appeared barefoot in the kitchen doorway.

'Honey, I'm sorry, we didn't hear you coming through,' I said.

'Don't apologise but if this is the reality of my situation then I ought to be in on the discussion, don't you think?'

'Now look here, Miss Anthony, why don't you let Miss MacKenzie and I handle this, you've got enough to think about...' Bryn trailed off mid-sentence and Naomi busied herself pouring coffee.

'Actually, Bryn, I need something to stop me from thinking. And for the last time, I'm staying in your flat, eating your food and relying on you to get me out of this fucking mess. So would you please just call me Naomi?'

I could count on one hand the number of times I'd heard her swear in the last ten years. If ever she was entitled to, it was now.

'Bacon sandwich, Miss Naomi? It's all ready.' Naomi laughed at him and for those few seconds the tension broke. We ate together, without speaking, until the doorbell rang. Bryn went to answer it, but reappeared just a few seconds later with a brown envelope in his hands.

'It was the junior clerk from your chambers. They had an urgent delivery for you, thought they'd better send it straight over.' Naomi held out her hand to take the post. 'Sorry, I meant Miss Eve.'

'But I haven't been in chambers for the best part of a year. Why would there be a delivery for me?' I ripped it open, thoroughly confused until I saw the scrawled handwriting on the single sheet of paper inside.

'Anything important?' Bryn started to look over my shoulder and I instinctively thrust it back into the envelope.

'Is it from him?' Naomi asked. I nodded but said nothing. Bryn hadn't been told anything about James yet.

'I'd best get ready, we need to leave in fifteen minutes.' Bryn said. 'You don't need to tell me what's in that envelope and I'm starting to think I don't want to know but just remember this: I can't help you unless you trust me. I'm going to need something to get the police to back off. I can't lie and I wouldn't even if I could. But I know Miss Naomi didn't do this, so when you decide what I should or shouldn't be told, I'll be ready to listen. Alright?'

'Sure,' I muttered. He wiped his hands on a tea-cloth and excused himself to give Naomi and me some privacy. I felt awful asking Bryn to help, then keeping things from him, but it was for his own good. Enough damage had been done already. When he'd left I took the note back out of the envelope to read it. Naomi was washing up the plates in the sink. The letter was from James. He hadn't signed it in case it was intercepted by the police, or someone worse, but I knew it was him.

'Eve, I'm so sorry for what happened. I left as I think my being around was putting her in even more danger. There are a couple of things Naomi doesn't know and only you can decide how much to tell her. The night before the attack we went out for dinner in Soho. We were in a fairly dark restaurant but after about an hour I noticed a woman staring at me. She was some distance away but I'm sure it was one of the Perelesnyk. She had the look, you know what I mean and she wasn't making any attempt to hide the fact that she was staring, so I made an excuse and we left. Until then I'd thought it was a coincidence but when we left I believe we were followed.' I stopped reading and rolled my head to the ceiling. These were exactly the words I hadn't wanted to hear. The Perelesnyk were a tribe of demons who'd tried to overthrow my own family last year and a bloody war had broken out as a result. I thought I'd left it all behind. Apparently, I was wrong.

'Eve, you okay?' Naomi was looking concerned.

'Yeah, I'm fine. Why don't you go and get ready. I'll come and talk to you when I've finished reading.' She disappeared off to her room but time was pressing so I picked up the letter and continued.

'By the time we got back to the flat I'd seen the shadow of a man once or twice, always keeping a good distance behind us but not trying too hard to stay hidden. Once we were inside I checked all the doors were locked and looked out of the front window. He was stood under a street light across the road, staring back at me. I'm certain it was an incubus but more than that, I'm sure he wanted me to know he was there. It was a message and my gut tells me they assumed I would contact you to let you know they'd found me. I think that when they came the next night they were after me, not Tim, that's why they were so surprised when I burst in. At least it gave me the chance to save Naomi. They were sent with a single purpose and that was to kill. I don't know how much Naomi was aware of and I left before she could ask me more. I hope I did enough to keep her out of trouble but I'm sure you'll be able to help her. I wanted so much to stay and see you but you know why I couldn't do that. I'll do what I can to keep you all safe. Look after Naomi and tell her I'm sorry. Be careful. I don't know what those things were.'

When Bryn walked in wearing his suit I remembered to look at my watch. Naomi was due back at the police station and I had to tell her something before she went.

'Later, okay Bryn? I'll tell you whatever I can, I promise.' He simply nodded his head and put his papers in a briefcase ready to go. I went to Naomi's room to start a conversation that was going to be one of the hardest of my life.

'You ready?' I asked her.

'Ready as I'll ever be. Is James safe?'

'I guess so. I don't know where he's gone but he managed to stop long enough to write, so that's something.' I didn't know what to say, how can you tell your best friend that you think you're responsible for her husband's death. I held out the envelope to her. 'Do you want to read it?' I asked.

'Will it make any sense to me?' Naomi asked. I shrugged my shoulders, the letter would probably just make things worse. 'Then it's best I don't, not yet. What am I supposed to say to the police today?'

'Stick to exactly what you've said so far. They have nothing except unanswerable questions about where Tim's blood is. I'm going to ask Bryn to get me access to the post-mortem report.' Naomi's eyes filled with tears as I said it, conjuring an image she really didn't need. 'It'll be a long day and they'll ask you the same questions repeatedly. Don't deviate, don't try and fill in the blanks. By tonight I'll have figured out how to handle it.'

'Tonight, then.' Naomi walked towards me and I held out my arms to hug her but she put one hand up in a gesture that told me she'd had enough. She picked up her bag and walked past me to Bryn.

'Off we go then. We might be some time, Miss Eve. I'll text you when we're leaving the police station. There's a key on the table in case you need to go out and I'll email you the report if I can get hold of it.'

'Thanks Bryn. See you later.' Naomi didn't say goodbye or turn round and I didn't blame her. I had one day to do what little I could to help but what she really wanted was beyond my power. If I couldn't bring her beloved Tim back, I had to make sure she didn't pay the price for his appalling death. I dressed and set off for the apartment we'd shared happily for several years. When I stepped outside it was raining and although the London streets were familiar they no longer felt like home.

Four

My phone started ringing just as I reached my former home and was staring up from the street at my bedroom window. I took it out of my pocket without looking at the dialler identification, assuming it would be Bryn with an update.

'You've decided to dump me then, have you, you witch?' The Irish accent with the Californian twang was a shock.

'Aedan, hey, I wasn't expecting you to call.' I was incoherent for a while as I tried to figure out what time and day it was in San Francisco.

'So, I'm guessing you hadn't remembered that last night we'd arranged to go to Xander's birthday party and that I would be calling to pick you up, oh, about six hours ago.'

'Oh, hell. Aedan, I'm so sorry. I'm away for a few days.'

'I know that, you crazy woman. I was a bit curious about where you'd got to, though.' Aedan was as good natured as ever. I couldn't believe I'd forgotten to cancel our date before climbing on the plane. I had some explaining to do.

'I'm in England. Something happened and I just forgot all about our plans. Xander's going to kill me. Listen, can I call you later? I'm standing out on the street and it's really bad timing.'

This time the voice on the other end had lost its bounce and was filled with a gentle concern. It felt good to have someone worrying about me. 'Of course, darlin', just tell me you're alright. You sound a bit out of sorts.'

'I'm fine. I'll explain everything later. Can you tell Xander I'm sorry, Sabina can give him all the details. Speak to you tonight.' I hung up. Aedan and I had been dating casually for the last two months. I'd met him at the Pacific Repertory Theatre where I was working as an actress, to my everlasting surprise. He'd come along to a party Sabina was throwing to attract sponsorship; he recognised the English accent and had come over to introduce himself to a fellow expatriate. I'd spent the next few weeks avoiding his calls and making excuses every time he asked me out, until one day he simply turned up at the bar Xander and I frequent after rehearsals. Xander sloped off looking guilty and I knew I'd been well and truly set up. It was no bad thing though: Aedan was great company, light-hearted and bright. When I gave Xander a telling off about it the next day he explained that Aedan had spent an evening telling him how brilliant he was in the last show, following which Xander would have done almost anything Aedan asked. The most worrying thing about the situation was that one of my closest friends could be so easily bought.

'Miss MacKenzie? I thought you'd moved away. How nice to see you again.' My train of thought was broken by the familiar voice and through the rain I saw Jimmy, the building's security guard, leaning out of a ground floor window and waving at me. I returned his greeting and ran across the road to talk to him properly.

'Hello, Jimmy. How are you?'

'Oh, could be worse, still got a job which is better than most these days. Sorry to hear about Miss Anthony, lovely young lady. Just can't believe it. That why you're back?'

'It is. I know I can't go into the flat but I had a couple of questions, nothing the police won't have asked you already, I'm sure.'

'I wasn't on duty I'm afraid, so I doubt I'll be able to help. Bill Sparks was on that night although I can tell you he didn't see or hear nothing. Couldn't help the police at all. He was dealing with a water leak in Miss Scofield's bathroom most of the evening, didn't even know Miss Anthony was home.'

'Is there any CCTV footage, Jimmy? I know there used to be a camera.'

'No, Miss, been out of commission some time, I'm afraid. There's so many cameras out on the streets now that the residents committee didn't want to spend the money replacing ours. I wish I could help.'

I asked after his wife, thanked him and made my excuses, walking out of his office into the lobby area just as another resident came in to speak to him. Whilst Jimmy was distracted I took the stairway up one flight to our apartment. Police tape was stuck across the door in a large X but there was no sound from inside and the lack of closed circuit television meant I could go in without anyone knowing. I slipped my old key into the lock as quietly as I could, ducked below one piece of tape, stepped over another, and crept in. The flat was eerily silent except for the occasional buzz of traffic passing below. The heating had been turned off and the place felt icy although that might have been more to do with my imagination.

I couldn't delay. If I were caught in the apartment I'd be arrested so I forced myself to walk straight through into Naomi's bedroom. There was little sign of the drama that had taken place. The bed clothes and mattress had been removed for forensic testing and sections of the carpet had also been cut out and taken. I grabbed a suitcase from the back of Naomi's wardrobe, shoving in enough of her clothes to make her stay at Bryn's more comfortable. Once I'd thrown in all the shoes, jeans, tops and lingerie I could find, I pulled out the tiny box of treasures she kept hidden away in an old box. The police had obviously decided it wasn't relevant to their case so I decided that taking it couldn't hurt.

I lugged the case out of the bedroom into the hallway and from the corner of my eye saw a lone hat hanging on the wall pegs. I dropped the case and walked over to take it down. It was a well-worn Carlsbad, better known to me as a cowboy hat before I met James. He was rarely without it and the small, simple fact that he'd left it here was testament to the horror of that night. I held the hat against my chest, caution forgotten. I was in my old bedroom before I knew what I was doing, curling up on my bed in the last place I knew he'd been. I was doing quite well until then but when I started to cry it was as if a dam had broken.

I wish I could say it was all for Naomi but the tears were for myself in equal measure. I was crying from the unbearable guilt that I'd brought these monsters into my friend's life, and for the loss of a time when I just got up, went to work, saw friends and slept without nightmares. Most of all, I was crying for the loss of a man who I'd fallen in love with and had to let go. Years before I met him, James had been cursed by the same demons who were taking revenge against me now. James and I knew we'd made some bad enemies although we could never have anticipated this. As hard as I tried to control my emotions, they brought rage along on their tide and my self-control disappeared. The rain that had been no more than a persistent drizzle began to beat against the windows and as I hit my fists against the wall the water turned to ice, hail stones battering the glass like shrapnel. This is what happens when I lose control of myself and if I didn't get a grip I would slip right out of this world, the only world that exists for most people, and go back to Manitu. There, my blood family was trying to govern a land that was being torn apart by war when I left. I bit down hard, catching my tongue as I did so and the pain helped me focus my thoughts on calming down.

When I opened my eyes there were shadows flickering across the walls. I turned my attention to the windows expecting to see hail or snow causing the effect but what I saw made me shrink back to the bed in terror. Hundreds of tiny bat-like creatures were scraping at the glass with their wings except they weren't like anything I'd seen before. Pale pink and hairless, with wings that looked like webbed human hands, I could see them peering in through the glass, watching me. Their mouths were open and as they snarled I could see rows of teeth designed to lacerate flesh. I had no doubt how much harm they'd do if they got in. Trembling, I forced myself towards the door. The storm had stopped but it was all the demons needed to alert them to my presence. I'd been so stupid to let my emotions get the better of me. They'd been waiting for exactly this moment.

The wailing of police sirens along the road outside distracted the flying mutants and, as one, they swooped away from the window. I ran to the window and opened it just enough to get a better view of the street directly below. The police were on their way back to the crime scene and I needed to get out now. As I went to shut the glass, a stray bat sank its teeth into my finger. I seized it with my other hand and pulled it back inside as I slammed the pane shut. My fury was enough to end the creature's life. I didn't need to exert any pressure on it: all my hatred and anger flowed into it and I felt its fight drain away. I turned it over in my hands, noting with a shudder the second mouth on its belly, presumably so that it could grip flesh with one and eat with the other. I couldn't leave something so obviously alien lying around here, so I shoved it in my pocket and hoped I didn't get stopped. I ran from the bedroom grabbing James' hat, then picked up the case and let myself out of the flat. Taking the stairs, I went up instead of down, exhausted by the sixth floor, then caught the elevator back to ground level. I slipped out without seeing Jimmy again, but kept my head down until I was a good distance away.

I stuck to the side streets until I thought it was safe to stop and hail a taxi. By the time I was back at Bryn's, my mobile was buzzing a text alert. He had pulled whatever strings he'd spent years cultivating and it had paid off. He had access to the pathologist's preliminary report and told me to wait for an email. I just had time to stow the suitcase under Naomi's bed, throw my coat down and put the kettle on, when it came through. Most of it was in medical terms I barely understood but the crucial facts were there.

The police had arrived about half an hour or so after Tim died, as far as Naomi could make out, and the medical examiner turned up roughly thirty minutes after that. Tim's core body temperature, taken internally, was recorded at 95.2 degrees Fahrenheit. He showed signs of primary flaccidity, with all his muscles still relaxed and there was no evidence of rigor mortis which I knew from previous cases I'd done, typically starts about two hours after death. There were no injuries other than the slash across his inner thigh and no unusual fibres or marks had been found that indicated he'd been bound, wrapped up, or hauled in and out of a vehicle. The toxicology screen was negative, so the police couldn't claim he'd been sedated or poisoned. I stood by Bryn's printer tapping my foot impatiently as the paper chugged out, then wrenched the last sheet from it and ran for the door. Bryn wouldn't thank me for what I was about to do but I'd just have to make it up to him later.

Five

At the police station, a young female officer went to fetch Bryn out of the interview room for me. It took a few minutes but he finally appeared, looking more flustered than I'd expected. The police were going hard on Naomi and I knew that if they questioned her long enough she'd let something slip; anyone would after what she'd been through. I had to stop this right now before she mentioned James, setting off an international manhunt and making it obvious she'd been lying this far. Bryn updated me and I told him to go back in with Naomi to formally notify the police that she wouldn't be answering any more questions. He disappeared and it wasn't long until my instructions had the desired effect. An unmarked door opened to one side of me and the detective in charge of the investigation stormed through.

'Miss MacKenzie, I suppose I should have expected you.'

'Nice to see you again too, Inspector Pearson.' We didn't have a happy history. I'd been defending in a drugs case which had been thrown out after a year of police work, when it had emerged that some officers had falsified evidence. It had caused a barrage of negative publicity for the police force and I'd made some enemies.

'You have no right to interfere in this case, you know. You're not working for Miss Anthony's solicitors and from what I understand you're not even practising as a barrister any more. Now why don't you go home and wait for your friend there? Although I'd better warn you, it could be some hours.'

'Don't you want to go somewhere a little more private to discuss this? It doesn't have to be quite so unpleasant, I just want to have a reasonable conversation about the state of the evidence,' I said, trying to stay calm in spite of his hostility.

'When I want to have a conversation with you, I'll arrest you and do it in my interview room. I don't know how you can do your job, defending those scum that my officers and I sweat blood to put away. Well, you're not touching this case. Your friend in there knows a lot more than she's telling and I intend to find out what really went on.'

I lost my cool, unable to tolerate bullying from people in positions of authority.

'Alright Inspector, you want to do this here, where everyone can listen then that's fine by me. You've got nothing in this case and you know it. The reason you've got nothing is because Miss Anthony has done nothing wrong. As tiresome as the prospect might be, you need to get your officers back out onto the streets to find the real perpetrators instead of pinning it on the easiest scapegoat. You know you can't charge her or you'd have done it already. What you do have is this: one dead man who was idolised and adored by his new wife, a fact that everyone will attest to. You have no motive at all for her to kill him. The woman you are questioning was found by your officers in a room locked from the other side and there is absolutely no evidence of a conspiracy or you'd have put it to her by now.'

Pearson walked closer to me and stuck his face into mine. 'I've got a dead body with no blood left in its veins and not one single drop anywhere in that property. Try explaining that.'

'I can't and neither can Naomi. But just because you don't understand what's happened doesn't mean she had anything to do with it. What I do know is this: from Tim's body temperature and lack of rigor mortis you can't put the time of death at any more than half an hour before your police officers arrived at the scene.'

He sneered at me. 'The body's core temperature had fallen about three degrees, putting time of death roughly two hours earlier. If you're going to rely on leaked information at least get your facts right. If that's the best you've got then I have work to do.' He turned to leave so I stepped after him, putting a hand on his arm.

'That might be right in a case where somebody dies from a blow or a heart attack but when all the blood is drained from a body, cooling happens at a much faster rate, something you haven't factored in. The pathologist will tell you that given the lack of blood, the core temperature was still remarkably high, indicating that he passed away shortly before your officers arrived.' He shook off my hand but was finally listening, so I carried on while I had the advantage.

'Naomi called it in from the flat about ten minutes before the police arrived. It's just not feasible to suggest that she could have killed him elsewhere, got him back to the apartment, into bed, stripped him and ensured there was no evidence on him from wherever he was supposedly killed, in the time between his death and calling the police. There's always a security guard around in the evenings and if he'd reported seeing anything suspicious we'd know about it by now.'

'You'd better not have been interfering with this investigation, because if you have I'll...'

'Oh stop! You have absolutely no basis to suspect her and you know it.'

'Just because your mate's a barrister doesn't mean she's not capable of murdering someone. I'm not being told how to run my own investigation.' He was red in the face, becoming more bullish and I was losing my patience.

'I'm not telling you what to do, I'm making you a promise. If you have something on Naomi then you need to charge her right here and right now. If you do, and it ever makes it into a court, I will conduct the defence case myself. When I cross-examine you I shall make it clear to the press how you made an assumption about her guilt because you didn't understand the forensic evidence, thereby letting vicious killers roam free. And when they strike again and you've done nothing to stop them, your career will be well and truly finished. If, on the other hand, you want to take a moment to think about this more carefully, and perhaps telephone the pathologist to check what I've said, then I'm sure you will come to your senses and release my friend. Not because she's a barrister and not because I'm asking you to, but because you have no reason to believe she was in any way involved. This is one mistake you do not want to make.' He didn't answer me, just glared furiously then stomped off, slamming the door behind him. The small crowd of observers that had gathered behind the glass panel at the back of the station scattered as he went. I forced myself to sit on the metal bench and look unworried as I waited. It didn't take as long as I'd anticipated to get results.

Bryn appeared first and told me he was waiting for Naomi to be checked out and have her possessions returned. He wasn't pleased I'd made it so obvious that the pathologist's report had been leaked but he knew why I'd done it. The Inspector didn't appear again and I was grateful. I'd had enough confrontation for one day. When Naomi was released she looked pale and tired. I put an arm gently around her shoulders and led her out. She hadn't been charged and her only status in the ongoing investigation was as a witness, as if this could ever go to trial. One miniscule part of her nightmare was over.

Back at Bryn's I busied myself making tea, until a bottle of whiskey and three glasses were plonked down next to the kettle.

'Think we all need something a bit stronger, Miss Eve. And can I recommend that you don't break any laws round here for the foreseeable future. I think they might just throw away the key!'

Naomi appeared in the doorway. 'Thank you both, I don't know what I'd have done without you.' She tried to smile but her heart just wasn't in it.

'How you holding up?' I asked. She shrugged.

'Tim's family still don't want me to see the body and they've asked that I don't attend his funeral. I understand, they need someone to blame. I don't think the police tried very hard to convince them I wasn't involved.'

'I'm sorry, sweetheart.' My mobile buzzed just as I was about to give her a hug. It was a text from Sabina. I looked up at Naomi without thinking what I was saying.

'At last. Sabina's heard from James. He made it out of the country safely. She didn't say where he was, only that he hadn't been stopped at the airport.'

'Who's James?' Bryn asked. Naomi and I stared at each other. 'Forget I asked,' he muttered handing around glasses fuller than was sensible so early in the day. 'To those we've loved and lost.' We raised our glasses and thought of Tim, and I was grateful that James was safe, wherever he was. The mood certainly wasn't celebratory but we finished our drinks and enjoyed the fact that some of the earlier stress was gone. Bryn was ready for some space and went out food shopping.

Naomi drained her glass and held her hand out to me. 'Come on,' she said. I put my hand in hers and she led me to Bryn's lounge where we huddled on the couch. 'Tell me,' she said. 'Everything, no protecting me, no editing. I want it all.' I have loved Naomi since I really got to know her. We've been best friends for years, work colleagues and flat mates before I moved to California. She supported me through countless failed relationships, looked after me when my arm was broken, comforted me when my adopted mother died. More than that, last year after I moved to Sabina's ranch and went through the worst time of my life, she was on the first plane out to be at my side. I think she probably saved my life with her calm, constant presence. Whether she believed me or not, she deserved the truth and it wasn't my place to decide if she could cope with it.

'Last year, after we found my adoption certificate naming Adela Karas as my birth mother, I identified the midwife and went to visit her. The child Adela gave birth to had Down's Syndrome. It couldn't have been me. Adela's husband, Branimir, was from an old, superstitious family in rural Slovakia. He found me in the cot one morning, saw that my face wasn't the same as the baby he had grown to love, and convinced himself that I was a changeling and his baby had been taken. In a crazed moment, he held me over a fire and burned my feet. According to myth if you burn a changeling child they fly away and the original baby will return. It's called immolation. Adela saved me then put me up for adoption to protect me.' Naomi was perfectly still and quiet. She wasn't questioning what I was saying so I continued. 'I'm not human, Naomi. I can fill in all the blanks and take you through each step of the journey but my real mother, the one who gave me to Adela Karas, is the matriarch of a tribe of demons called the Vilya. She lives in a place called Manitu. That's where I was with James when I came back so distraught and you looked after me. It's where we'd been when James ended up in a coma last year.'

I waited for a reaction, for some sort of response. What I didn't expect was the explosion that I hadn't even known Naomi was capable of. 'That's it? My husband is dead, I've spent days being accused of slaughtering him and you're telling me this crap? How dare you treat me like that! Are you completely deluded? I want the truth, Eve and I want it right now.' She was screaming and crying and I didn't blame her. It pushed me completely over the edge when I found out that everything in my life was a lie. How could Naomi possibly believe it in a matter of minutes? I looked down at my hands, ashamed that I'd brought so much despair into my friend's world and wondered how I could help her. 'Nothing? No response? Get out, Eve. If that's the best you can do, then just get out!' She meant it and I wasn't going to argue. She was entitled to be left alone if that's what she wanted. As I pulled my coat off the back of a chair, picking up Bryn's spare key and slipping it into my pocket, my hand brushed something limp and rubbery. I shivered at the hideous double-mouthed freak I'd taken away from our old flat and, as much as I didn't want to touch it again, I forced my hand back into the pocket. I walked back into the lounge where Naomi was sat on the couch, weeping and put the lifeless body down on the coffee table in front of her.

'You need to look at this,' I said. Naomi didn't pick her head up straight away but when she did I caught the look of repulsion on her face.

'What is that?' Naomi reached out a finger to touch it then changed her mind.

'I don't know exactly. There were a large group of them beating against the window of our flat today. I think it was a mistake for me to have gone back there but I didn't know they'd still be watching.'

'How did it die?' she asked, leaning over to inspect the eerie, pink body.

'I opened the window when I heard police sirens, I needed to know if they were coming into the building. This one got in and I caught it. I was in a rage and when I'm like that it's as if everything I'm feeling flows into whatever's around me. It died in my hands. I'm starting to think I'm as much of a monster as them.' I put my head in my hands, the dreadful reality of what I was telling my friend hitting home.

'Don't talk like that, Eve, it's not true.' The Naomi I knew and loved so well had reappeared. I smiled at her through my tears.

'You always said I could make you better when you were ill and I told you it was just your imagination. Well, it wasn't. I can heal people, the ones I care about, when I'm here. It doesn't work in Manitu. I couldn't even save my sister.' My voice trailed off as I thought about Ellette, who I was just getting to know when she was killed protecting me in battle.

'Alright. I'm listening. I won't shout or scream and I'll do my best to believe you. Start from the beginning, okay?' Naomi took my hands in hers and I felt her opening her mind, not even for her own sake, but to share my pain. I gripped her hands tightly in return and told her all I could. I described how the tribe of incubi and succubi use humans to procreate and the way they'd tried to trick me into joining them. I told her about the human child with Down's Syndrome, Zora, with whom I'd been swapped and how the incubus Perun had plotted to get me back into Manitu to replace her. I explained how James had been cursed by a succubus when he betrayed his wife on their wedding night and how he'd saved me from Perun when he first saw me in San Francisco. Finally I told her James' theory, that it was him they wanted to kill that night, and how that attack was retribution for my intervention in their attempted coup in Manitu. When I finished talking, it was nearly an hour later and Naomi had barely made a noise except to encourage me when I faltered. When my tale came to an end, she raised her hand and stroked my hair like a mother would a toddler.

'Poor you. How could you have been through so much and not told me?'

'You believe me? I don't know why, I scarcely believe myself.' I wiped away the tears running down my face. I hadn't even realised I was crying.

'I saw those things drain the life out of my husband. I knew they weren't human. And it all makes sense, the state you were in when you came back with James that first time. Then there's this thing here, like nothing I've ever seen. I can't really process it all right now but, yes, I believe you. I can't stand to hear you call yourself a demon though, Eve, that's not right.'

'Perun said it's a label put on us over thousands of years by humans, that it originally meant a state between a god and a man. As man's fear grew and their minds closed, they put all the things they didn't understand into a single category and decided they were evil. It's not like that, though. Manitu's a world just like this one, as if we share the same space. Everything we do to this planet impacts there. Every race is different physically and in their customs but they have a social system, politics, laws. They have good and bad amongst them just like us.'

Naomi laughed and I looked up at her amazed. That was the last thing I expected from her. 'What?' I asked.

'It's incredible, in the middle of all this, I find it wonderful and reassuring that we're not alone. Why would we be? Why would humans be the only race in such an unfathomable universe? Is it scary?' She was looking at me like a child seeing a rainbow for the first time.

'Yes,' I said, honestly. 'But beautiful, unspoiled, surreal. I spoke with my mother, Anousk, for just a few moments. It was enough.'

'Will you ever go back?' Naomi was looking more worried than awestruck now. As I was about to answer, a key turned in the lock and Bryn came in laden with bags.

'Miss Eve, there was a young man waiting for me outside the building. He asked me to give you this. Didn't like the look of him myself, didn't look real somehow. Gave me the creeps.'

'They followed me,' I said, half to myself. 'From our flat. I may not have a choice about whether or not I go back. This is going to get much worse.'

Six

Inside the package was a lock of dark cherry red hair, the same as my own. Before Naomi or Bryn could stop me, I raced out of the flat and down the stairs to find the man who'd delivered it. He was long gone of course, their plan wasn't anything as low key as an altercation on a London street. I trudged back up to Bryn with a feeling of dread settling in. I knew I wasn't safe and the worst thing was that Naomi wasn't safe either, not now they knew who she was and could follow her. If the Perelesnyk's plan was to take away the people I loved one by one until I went back to face them, then I'd provided plenty of targets.

I made my excuses and went for a shower, needing some alone time. When I got back into the lounge I found Naomi on the phone to Sabina. They'd become friends when Naomi stayed with me last year and had been in close contact ever since. Sabina must have been worried sick, waiting to find out what was happening. It reminded me that I owed Aedan a call back but it would have to wait until after dinner as Bryn was already calling us. Naomi said her goodbyes to Sabina and I added my own quick shout of 'love you' over her shoulder. Anxious not to keep Bryn waiting when he'd been so kind, we sat down to eat.

'How's Sabina?' I asked as I helped Bryn serve up pizza with salad and put a large forkful in my mouth just before Naomi answered me.

'She's had your motorbike picked up and mended. And she's looking forward to meeting us both at San Francisco airport tomorrow' she replied. I choked and Bryn gave me a hard slap on the back. Naomi ignored it and carried on. 'She's booking our tickets now and Bryn's sorted out a taxi to Heathrow.'

'Naomi, I'm not sure that's wise. I don't know,' I paused, unsure how much I should say in front of Bryn. I didn't want to put him in danger as well. 'It might not be safe with me.'

'I wasn't safe with you thousands of miles away,' she said, quietly. 'Listen, I can't go back to the flat while it's still a crime scene. Bryn will formally notify the police of my new address. Now that my status has been downgraded from suspect to witness, they can't stop me from leaving the country. I can't face going back to work. Sabina said I can stay at the ranch as long as I like and I've been wanting to go back anyway. Also, I have a funny feeling you'll be needing me. Don't you?' I couldn't answer her. I thought I'd be needing something more like an army, but my best friend would be a good start.

'If that thing you left on the table when you ran out is any indication of what you're facing, then I'd say you should take whatever offers of help you get.' I stared at him. I'd completely forgotten the bat creature I'd shown Naomi. I opened my mouth to make up some excuse but he cut in before I could say anything. 'I don't want to hear it, MacKenzie. Shut up and eat.' I did as I was told.

I know when I'm beaten. After dinner and clearing up the kitchen we took coffee in the lounge. Determined to come back with me, Naomi had just realised that she was short of a suitcase and spare clothes. The chaos of the day had made me forgetful. I produced the case and she opened it at once, pulling her box of treasures from within the jumble of clothes.

'Now I know it was the right decision. This is everything I need. All my letters from Tim, my photos, jewellery. Thank you, Eve.'

'Don't thank me,' I said. 'It's all my fault.'

'You didn't choose this' she whispered, kissing my cheek as she disappeared off to bed, taking the box of memories with her. For the first time since I arrived a fraction of her normal composure seemed restored. Bryn handed me a gin and tonic. I didn't often drink this much in one day but it had been twenty-four hours of hell and I figured it was fair enough.

'You two going to be alright?' he asked. I just raised my eyebrows at him. I was done lying to my friends and I suspected the truth wasn't the answer he wanted. 'That man downstairs earlier, is he responsible for what happened to Tim? Because if he is, you need to be very careful indeed.'

'Bryn, please don't.' My hand was shaking as I raised the glass to my lips. 'I don't want you involved. You've done enough already.'

'Eve, listen to me.' The simple fact that he'd used my first name without its usual prefix of "Miss" was enough to get my attention. 'I've known you for what, six years? Together we've sat in rooms with murderers, rapists, arms dealers, you name it we've seen it, right? We've looked in men's eyes and seen every emotion I can name. When that man, if that's what he was, handed me the package and said your name, there was nothing. Nothing at all. It was like he was dead. He smiled as if he'd been taught to and looked like he'd walked out of a painting but I felt like I was about to meet my maker. You can't fight creatures like that. When men have no fear they don't behave the way you expect, don't follow any rules.'

'Then what can I do, Bryn? Because I think someone's about to bring this war to me.'

'Keep hold of your humanity, outthink them. Never forget that you're something better. I fought in two wars before I left the forces and I learned the hard way that sometimes the only way to win is to put your weapon down. And if that doesn't work, then run as fast as you bloody well can.' I laughed.

'I've missed you, Bryn. I wish you were coming with us.'

'California, Miss? Not sure I'd fit in there. That said, if you ever need me,' he didn't have to finish the sentence.

'I know, Bryn. I know you'd come.'

'Like a flash. You just remember that.' I would. For now, though, the thing I needed more than anything else was eight hours solid sleep. I fell into bed thinking I'd be out like a light but when it came to it I just couldn't settle. It was late in London but mid-afternoon in San Francisco. I decided to call Aedan, let him know I was heading home and explain what'd been happening, or at least an acceptable version of it. I dialled his office number and a young woman picked up, greeting me in her usual super-perky way.

'Hey Cat, it's Eve. Is Aedan busy or can he speak?'

'Oh, hello there. Dr. Verne is just finishing another call but if you wouldn't mind waiting I'll put you through.'

'You know what, I'm calling on my mobile from London so I shall,' but I was already speaking to some tinny electronic music. Aedan's personal assistant, Cat, wouldn't engage in anything other than meet and greet politeness, no matter how many times I spoke to her or how chatty I tried to be. A little uncharitably, I thought she resented other women in Aedan's life and then chastised myself. My overactive imagination has always made me believe that unnaturally cheery people are harboring some deep, dark secret.

'I thought you'd forgotten all about me and decided to go back to your old life in England without so much as a farewell.' Aedan's warm Irish accent was booming down the phone and I could tell he was grinning as he spoke.

'Actually, I'll be on my way home tomorrow. Just thought I'd let you know.'

'Home? So that's what Carmel is now? I'm pleased to hear it.' I'd surprised myself but when I thought about it, I realised it was true. After quite a short time living there, it did feel like home.

'How was Xander's party? Is he going to forgive me for missing it?'

'I think he'll probably make you grovel for a few weeks but he was so inebriated by the end you could tell him you were there all along and he'd probably believe you! Sabina told me about your friend's problems. Is it sorted then?' The jocular voice turned to genuine concern and I felt a pang of missing him.

'As much as it can be, for now. Naomi's coming back with me. She's going to stay at the ranch for a while.'

'It'll be good to meet her. Listen, I've got a patient waiting so I'd better dash. Do you want me to pick you up at the airport?'

'No, don't worry, Sabina's got it all arranged. I'll give you a call when I'm home.'

'I'll be waiting.' He hung up. Dr Aedan Verne was one of the most popular orthopaedic surgeons in the San Francisco area, as much for his natural charm as for his medical skills, I suspected. His mother was American and his father Irish and although he'd been born and raised in Belfast, when his parents divorced he went with his mother to California where he'd studied medicine. He'd maintained the roguish accent that allowed him to get away with almost anything, as far as I could see. He was good looking, perhaps not in the traditional American sense but with a little roughness around the edges.

I recalled his first line to me at the party where we'd met. He'd pretended to struggle to find a word to describe me and, after a few moments keeping me waiting, said I was "callipygian". I wasn't sure if it was an insult or a compliment and asked him what it meant. He'd said it was a technical term, invited me to have dinner with him the following night and handed me his card. I'd declined, politely, and he said it was a pleasure to meet a woman who knew how to say no, knowing I would be intrigued enough to go home and look up the meaning of the word he'd used.

Callipygian, apparently, means having beautifully shaped buttocks. I'd laughed out loud and would be lying if I didn't admit I enjoyed the compliment, but I threw the charming doctor's card in the bin. He was a player and a well practised one at that. After all I'd been through with James, the last thing I needed was another entanglement.

The next day at the theatre a bouquet of flowers arrived with Aedan's card. I kept the flowers but his phone number joined the last one in my bin. That went on for two more weeks until Xander betrayed me and told him where to find me. I found out that the roguishness was mostly front and that Aedan had much more depth than he'd originally shown. He loved the theatre and all types of music. He would rather be outside walking in the wind and rain than sitting in front of a television and he only dated women who would stand up to him. The lawyer in me, who always loved a good debate, found that last quality completely irresistible and we'd begun dating. If nothing else, it took my mind off James and made me contemplate a normal future where I could blend in with normal people. I wondered what Naomi would make of him. I could use the plane journey tomorrow to tell her about him. With that last thought, I drifted into sleep.

Seven

Sabina was waiting for us at the arrivals gate in San Francisco International. She opened her arms to Naomi like a long lost niece and seeing the two of them together was confirmation that it was absolutely the right thing to bring Naomi here, in spite of my earlier reservations. She and Sabina would be good for one another. We took a leisurely drive back to the ranch, south of Carmel. As Sabina had suffered for years with Parkinson's disease she had a driver, which meant we could all settle back in the car and enjoy the scenery. We made small talk most of the way and then Sabina asked about Tim's funeral. It was a subject I'd been avoiding but Naomi had already come to terms with missing it.

'His family don't want me there. I'm sure they know it was nothing to do with me but after the police investigation and my being unable to identify the killers, I don't think they want to see me, not yet anyway. Eve brought me my wedding photos, our old letters, the keepsakes that mean the most. In some ways I don't want to see him buried, I'd like to remember him the way we were happiest. That's one of the reasons I wanted to come here: at least this far away I have no choice but to get on with grieving instead of trying to hang on to what we had before.' Naomi's one of the most sensible people I know. Sometimes people mistook her gentleness for weakness, but I knew better. She has an inner calm that masks extraordinary strength and resilience. Sabina covered Naomi's hand with her own.

'Though I am more sorry than I can express that you've returned because of such a tragedy, my dear, I am thrilled to have you back. There's a little jeep on the ranch and I have put your name on the insurance. I spoke to that lovely man Bryn who helped you both so much. He's arranging to have the rest of your things shipped over. This is your home for as long as you want it and I personally hope that will be a very long time indeed.' When I looked at Sabina's shining eyes I knew this was no comfort speech; she meant every word of it. She and Naomi had connected in a way that I'd always found difficult and for half a second I was jealous. Then she took my hand with her other free one and added. 'I was never blessed with a family. Now I have the two of you to fuss over and I shall treasure every minute of it.' Naomi smiled in spite of all she'd endured and I was glad to be back.

At the ranch we moved Naomi into the second bedroom of the guest house where I was living. It was easily big enough for us both and, although Sabina had offered to have her stay in the main house, I wanted Naomi close by where I could keep her safe. She knew her way around already so it wouldn't take her long to settle in. She'd confided on the plane that she'd been considering taking riding lessons so this was the perfect opportunity. In return I'd told her about Aedan and it was just as well, as he turned up out of the blue that evening bearing gifts of food, alcohol and movies. Even though Aedan was more than ten years my senior, he was so energetic and irrepressible that in many ways he seemed younger than me. He kissed Naomi on both cheeks when I introduced them, bypassed the depressing and useless expressions of sympathy and got straight on with telling us all about Xander's party and the most recent Carmel gossip. Naomi relaxed, able to sit and listen without having to join in, all the happier for not being the centre of attention.

After a while she made her excuses and went to sleep off the fatigue from the journey. The second her door closed Aedan raced towards me, picked me up and whirled me round, kissing me before I had a chance to get my balance. It made me giggle and it was good to have a carefree moment after everything that had happened.

'Put me down. I'm tired and I need a long bath before anyone gets that close to me.'

'Silly girl, I couldn't give a damn whether you've washed or not. I missed you.' He kissed me again then realised that I was more worried about Naomi coming out of her room and seeing us.

'You've told her we're dating, haven't you? I'm sure she wouldn't be shocked at seeing us kissing.'

'It's not that, I just don't want her to feel awkward. It's too much of a reminder of Tim, too soon.' I put some distance between us to make the point but he held on to my hand.

'Sure, I get it, but it'd be nice to spend some time together. There's still a bit of light in the sky, let's walk down to the horses, it's a fine evening.' I looked at Naomi's closed door. She wouldn't surface again until morning and I was certain she was secure here. A walk would be good. I locked the door behind me and we wandered down through the meadows to sit on the paddock fence, watching the sun as it melted on the horizon. The landscape always took me by surprise; the rugged hills, lush greenery, and the sensation of timelessness away from all the hustle and bustle. Aedan slipped a warming arm around my shoulders.

'Are you alright? You sound a little, I don't know, melancholy if that's not too ridiculous a word in the circumstances.' He smiled gently and I watched as the corners of his eyes crinkled, lighting up his face. When he did that, I defied any woman not to smile back.

'I am,' I replied. 'England was awful and as for what happened to Tim, I can't talk about that yet. But I hadn't understood how much I'd come to love it here. I spent my whole adult life in London, working every waking hour, plodding through traffic and endless people. Then, after just a few months, this has become the place I'm most at peace. It's the first time I knew it for sure, but I don't ever want to go back.'

'Well, I for one, am very glad to hear it,' he whispered. He brushed his lips across my temple and we sat there, perfectly still, gazing at the sky until there was nothing left to see. Just as we were climbing off the fence I heard footsteps behind us. It was one of Sabina's ranch hands and he reminded me of James, who I'd first met when he came to work here. I pushed the thought away, feeling guilty thinking of another man when I was with Aedan.

'Sorry to disturb you, ma'am. Miss Roman has been trying to find you, she's asking that you go and have a word with her in the main house if it's no bother.' He dipped his hat and walked away quietly.

'I guess that's my cue to leave. Come on, I'll walk you up there and get my car.' Aedan kissed the palm of my hand as he left, promising to call me in the morning to make plans for later in the week. I watched him go from Sabina's porch, thinking how lucky I was to have met him. After I lost James I thought it would be impossible to feel comfortable with another man. It wasn't the same, but how could it be? I knocked on Sabina's door and opened it when I heard her voice.

She was sat in an old leather arm chair in front of the fire, looking frailer than she had for some time. I went and sat at the hearth by her feet, enjoying the warmth of the flames. Sabina coughed, breaking me out of my daydream.

'You seem very distant, my darling. The last few days must have been awful, both for Naomi and for you.'

'Yes,' was all I could say. How could I tell her about it? The only possible explanation was the one we'd given the police but I was loathe to lie to the woman who'd taken me in and treated me as her own. 'Have you heard any more from James?' I asked, to change the subject.

'No,' she shook her head. 'I know he wasn't planning on coming back to the States. When he last called, he asked if I wouldn't mind holding on to his things a while longer. I don't expect we'll be seeing him any time soon.' Her eyes held the question she'd been kind enough not to ask me since he'd left. 'Is there any chance that the two of you can work this out?'

'None,' I answered. 'I wish there were. It's complicated.'

'Will Naomi be alright, do you think?' Sabina leaned forward and poked at the embers with a fire iron. It meant I didn't have to look her in the eyes when I spoke and I was glad.

'I'm sure she'll get stronger, in time. I don't suppose any of us can imagine what she's been through.'

'Do you want to talk about it, so that I can help? I'm not a fool and I have no intention of meddling where I'm not wanted but if the version you gave to Bryn and the police was correct then where was James? I care about you, Eve. You and Naomi both. I only want to keep you safe.' She didn't look frail now, her eyes shining with fierce tears in the firelight, but still I didn't know how to answer her.

'I think that what happened to Tim was meant for James. I hoped that by bringing Naomi here I could keep her out of it, but I'm not certain about that. If you want me to leave it might be for the best and I'll understand.'

I was surprised when she responded with a short laugh. 'Leave? Eve, I'm an old woman, not at the end of my life yet I hope, but old enough to have left fear behind. What I cannot stand is to see the people I love in pain. I lived with Adela long enough to see how it breaks you down. I don't want that for you.' I took her hands in mine, aware that I'd already revealed more than was wise.

'Sabina, I'm so indebted to you and I hope you know that I've grown to think of you as family in the last few months but I'm fine, please don't worry about me, there's really no need. I'd better get back over to Naomi and you should get some rest. The last few days have been hard on us all.' She reached to the side of her chair, picking some note books up off the floor.

'What's that?' I asked, but even as I spoke I recognised Adela's diaries, given to me by Sabina when James left. I knew they might hold the key to my past; the reason why my mother had given me to Adela to raise instead of keeping me with her in Manitu. I'd spent so much time coming to terms with what I'd found out already, that I hadn't been able to take the next step and have the diaries translated from their original Slovakian so I could read them.

'When you were packing to go to London I saw the box of diaries unopened. I apologise for invading your privacy but I had no idea....' She didn't know how to finish the sentence and I wondered just what she'd unearthed. 'I found her diary for the year you were born and I translated it. I got it into my head that I could help you somehow, feeling useless when you charged off to look after Naomi. Much of it, I have to confess, I didn't understand at all so I've just done the best I could.' I took the notebooks from her with a trembling hand.

'Thank you,' I said but I wasn't sure I meant it. I stood up to leave, the chill I felt rendering the effects of the fire useless.

'If you want to talk about it, if I can do anything, I'm here for you. And if what is happening now is anything to do with what is in those diaries, then I believe Adela would have been glad I read them.' I nodded. I hadn't seen this coming and until I knew exactly what Sabina had translated then there was really nothing to add. I closed the door behind me and made my way back to check on Naomi.

Inside, I poured myself a gin and sat down with the diary on the floor in front of me. The translated version was balanced on my lap, and I could imagine Sabina sitting down to write it for me, opening up those first few pages and wondering if she'd wandered into the ravings of a mad woman or a work of fiction. I remembered her telling me once that Adela used to disappear off on her own for days with no warning and no mention of where she'd been on her return. I suspected that Sabina finally had the answer to the questions she'd kept to herself for years. I put one hand on the book meaning to open it, but my will failed me and I closed my eyes for a few moments to rest. It had been a very long day and every time I thought it was over, something new cropped up. I decided to take a break before I started to read the diaries. The next time I opened my eyes it was morning; Sabina's translation had slipped to the floor and I awoke freezing cold with a crick in my neck, to the smell of frying bacon.

Eight

Naomi had taken refuge in the kitchen and was back in her ritual of cooking for whoever she could find. If it had been anyone else, I'd have told them to put their feet up instead but I knew this was what Naomi needed to do and could understand that she was better off keeping busy.

'Good morning,' Naomi murmured, staring intensely at the pan. 'You didn't look comfortable but I thought if I disturbed you there'd be no chance you'd get back to sleep. You've got about five minutes before this is ready. Why don't you take a shower? Might make you feel better.' As I still had the taste of gin in my mouth and the staleness of long distance flight on my skin, that was an excellent idea. The hot water soothed my aching neck and the clean clothes were a therapy in themselves. I brushed my hair in front of the window overlooking the forest and noticed movement just behind the tree line. On closer inspection, I saw nothing and put it down to oversensitivity but as I went through to the kitchen a flock of birds rose up out of the trees. Whatever had disturbed them was foreign to their environment but Naomi was calling and I didn't want to put her on edge. I swallowed my suspicions for the time being and went to eat. Two huge plates of bacon and scrambled eggs were on the table and Naomi was pouring tea. My mouth was watering before I sat down.

'So Aedan seems really sweet,' said Naomi. 'Very charismatic, isn't he?'

'And persistent. I did try to say no when he asked me out, in case you're wondering.' Naomi laughed.

'I wasn't, but in any case, I can't imagine the lovely doctor is used to hearing the word "no" coming out of a woman's mouth. It was probably the most excitement he's had in a long time, having to fight for a date.'

'He's lovely,' I said. 'But he's not James.' Naomi put down her cutlery and rested her chin in her hands.

'When he first met me in London, James tried not to mention your name, didn't say a thing about you,' she said. 'Then the night we went out to dinner and he'd had a glass of wine, that was it. All he spoke about for, I'd say, maybe two hours was you.'

'I miss him so much,' I said and then it dawned on me how crass and selfish I was being. 'Oh Naomi, I'm sorry, I've got no right to sit here whining after your loss. Let's talk about something else, okay?'

'If I have to go through the next month only discussing cooking recipes and the weather, I shall go insane,' Naomi responded hotly. 'And whilst my darling Tim may be dead, you and I are still alive and I'm not sitting around weeping while the world keeps turning. If I understand anything more clearly now, it's that you should grab every chance at happiness that comes along. So if that's with James or Aedan or anyone else then I don't want to avoid talking about it; I have to believe that there's still something good left out there.'

'You're right,' I said, humbled by my friend's extraordinary view of life. I put the plates into the sink, our appetites satisfied. Naomi continued to surprise me by saying that she'd already been on the phone to Sabina and was having her first riding lesson that morning, giving me time to check out whatever had disturbed the forest. I put on some hiking boots and a jacket, made sure Sabina knew I was out for the day so she'd keep an eye on Naomi then set off along the pathway towards the foot hills. I followed the river until I reached a clearing. This was the first place from which I'd entered Manitu with James, and I was hoping to find some clue about what was happening there now. Without warning, a body jumped out of a tree directly in front of me and I screamed. Before I knew what was happening two arms were around my neck, hugging hard. I came to my senses enough to know this was a greeting rather than an attack and, as the figure pulled back, I recognised Serenta, a member of my tribe, the Vilya. She had the tell tale deep red hair and pale skin.

'Eve, you came. How did you know it was me?' she asked.

'I didn't,' I said. 'I saw movement in the woods and decided I couldn't hide from this any more. I thought it was better just to face up to whoever was watching me.'

'That was dangerous,' she said. 'Could you not sense me?' I shook my head but an old sensation was reawakening even as I did so and suddenly I felt a current buzzing through me, like static electricity. I remembered how I knew when my sister Ellette was close by, and times when it seemed as if we'd connected in our minds.

'Serenta, why are you here? Tell me what's going on.' I sat down on a log and she perched next to me, so graceful it made me feel ungainly.

'Your mother sent me. Anousk thought you should know that Zora is ill. We are doing all we can but we do not know what causes the sickness. The Perelesnyk say that if Zora is not well enough to rule in your absence then they should take authority as next in line. We do not know what to do for the best.'

'How serious is this illness?' She was slow in responding. 'Serenta, I must know!'

'We are not certain how long she can survive. We cannot use our healing powers in Manitu, they only work in the human world and yet if we bring Zora here, because she was changed with you, she will not be able to return with us. Anousk is beyond comforting.' I thought of beautiful, innocent Zora fading without medicine and the image was unbearable.

'What happened Serenta? Zora was so sure that she and mother could cope, that once I left things would calm down. Has the Council not regained control?'

'The Council cannot control those families who have declared themselves beyond their rule. Manitu has been ravaged by war. In just a few months, the world we knew has disintegrated.'

'Take me there,' I said, getting to my feet. 'I have to see for myself.'

'No, Eve. Anousk said you were not to come back with me.'

'Have you forgotten who I am?' I asked. I wouldn't have behaved so pompously if I wasn't desperate but I wanted Serenta to do as I asked, and if pulling rank was the way to achieve that, then so be it.

'You are ruler of Manitu,' she said. 'No-one has forgotten.' I felt awful. Of course she hadn't forgotten. I'd tried to ensure that the Vilya had their turn to rule and stop Zora from being ousted but all I'd done was destroy a place that had previously been a peaceful idyll. 'I will do as you ask.'

She took my hand, walking slowly enough to begin with and then we were trotting along the pathway under the canopy. Before I could plead a lack of fitness, Serenta grabbed my arm and sprinted off at full speed, leaping across the fallen tree trunks in our path, ducking under low branches and avoiding obstacles with a deftness I had no hope of achieving. Yet somehow, miraculously, I willed myself into action, did my best to keep up, and what I lacked in grace I made up for with effort. I couldn't focus on the forest around us, it was flying past in a blur. I felt the surge of adrenaline burst through me and wondered when I'd feel the first crippling pain of a stitch in my side. On and on we ran until, in the distance, I finally saw Serenta stop and wait for me to catch up. I let my legs relax and slow until I was next to her, panting and exhausted, while she looked as if she'd taken a gentle stroll.

'Why did you stop?' I asked.

'We're here' she said simply. 'Anousk said you would need to forget yourself completely. If I have to find space inside my own thoughts, this is what I do.' I stared around me. She was right. I'd crossed over into Manitu without temper or trauma and it was wonderful.

'Thank you, Serenta. I had no idea that would happen, although I'm not sure I could do it alone. How long will it take us to get to Anousk? Last time I was here it took a few hours walking to reach the Vilya's camp.'

Serenta looked crestfallen after the high of sprinting through the woods.

'Forgive me, I forgot that there is so much you do not know. The camp you came to last time was only temporary as we were on our way to the Rock of Ages. Our people used to live a nomadic lifestyle and could often be found around here. Since the war, we have retreated back to our homelands. It is too far for you to travel to see Anousk. I brought you back only to witness what has happened in Manitu since you were last here.' She walked out into what looked like a clearing ahead and I could see that the landscape dipped dramatically. Before today everything I'd seen of Manitu was stunning, wild and perhaps even dangerous, but nature at its best. The colours were brighter than in the human world, the trees taller, foliage thicker. The people who inhabited this land embraced nature, existed without building harsh structures or using up the resources around them. What I saw now was nothing short of devastation. The frame of a wooden pyramid stood in the earth crater with half decomposed bodies, some skeletal, hanging from ropes secured to the peak.

'What happened here?' I choked.

'The mountain dwellers went back to the Rock of Ages after the fires and floods had gone. They picked up the bodies of their fallen enemies, alive or dead and brought them here. They cut down the trees, which is forbidden under our laws, and with the wood built the pyramid you see there. They strung up each body and left them, food for birds and animals. They burnt the earth around the base so that nothing could grow to cover the horror of what they had done. When we found it, we knew this was their declaration of war. Any hope we had of reuniting the families of Manitu was gone. What you see here was just the start: these structures are everywhere, the burning of the ground, pillaging the places we consider sacred. Those families who oppose the Perelesnyk are subjected to raids, even hunted and the laws by which we have lived for centuries have become meaningless.'

'It's chaos,' I said. 'But Zora was so sure that she would be able to bring peace.'

'Zora is so full of goodness that she cannot conceive of the evil around her. If she had come to rule without opposition, it might have been possible. The hatred the Perelesnyk have inflamed in the other warring families runs too deep to heal. And it is not chaos, far from it. It is being carefully organised.'

'By whom? Mandalina?' She was the matriarch of the Perelesnyk family and I knew she'd been dealt a bitter blow when I left someone of human blood to govern in my place. I had no idea she was capable of this sort of carnage, though.

'Not Mandalina, although she watches and consents. It is Perun.' My knees felt weak and I didn't fight the desire to sink to the floor.

'He's alive?' I asked. 'I thought that perhaps he had died. As I left, he attacked James and me. I saw him fall. I thought that because I hadn't heard anything, his death had resolved the power struggle.'

'He was badly hurt. His scars don't show, of course, an incubus cannot be marked physically, but injuries weaken them. For a long time we had no news and then he returned, mad with humiliation. Anousk is scared that he will not rest until he has destroyed the Vilya. Zora would not be safe, even if she were not so ill.'

'Where is Anousk now?' I looked down into the clearing below at the bones hanging from the wooden scaffold like medieval London and knew Perun would stop at nothing. I wasn't going to let him destroy my family without doing all I could to protect them.

'Medicine Lake Volcano, Modoc: it's many days walk from here, north east. I can ride back there so I should be able to meet you tomorrow, we do not break horses as humans do.' I nodded to show I'd understood but I was all talked out. The scars left on the landscape were etched into my memory. At least now I understood why Tim had been slaughtered. The Perelesnyk wanted me distracted, out of the way and as scared as possible. Had Serenta not come to find me it would have worked, too.

'I'll take you back,' Serenta said. We ran again as we had before only this time there was no feeling of elation, only the nasty sensation that something was chasing me and catching up fast. It took longer and I was exhausted when we stopped but I knew we'd come back through. Moving between worlds was getting easier and, fairly soon, I'd be able to control it myself.

We agreed to meet at the most southerly point of Little Medicine Lake the following day, so I needed time to prepare for the journey and warn my friends that I'd be away. The walk back to the ranch was uneventful but I felt a mist descending that had nothing to do with the end of day. Last time I did this James was with me, lending me a strength of which I was barely aware. This time I felt vulnerable and lonely. Perun was formidable before, utterly ruthless in his attempts to obtain power and this time he was out for blood. Any happiness I might have felt at the prospect of seeing my mother and Zora again was overshadowed by the sickening sensation that everything was already lost.

Nine

I saw Naomi and Sabina before they spotted me walking through the paddocks. They were sat out on the back porch of the main house, drinking tea and looking as if they'd been there forever. The horses ran to see if I had food but left just as fast, disappointed at my empty hands. If James had been with me they'd have walked along next to us, just to be near him. I felt an ache inside that I'd managed to ignore for the last few months. When I reached the porch I didn't know how to explain what was happening. The less involved they were, the better.

One look at my face must have told them all they needed to know. Sabina handed me a mug of tea as I sat down.

'I have to go away for a couple of days,' I said. There was silence for a few moments. They both knew I wouldn't leave Naomi right now unless it was unavoidable.

'Can you at least tell us where? That way, if you get into trouble,' Sabina's voiced trailed off and I figured that telling them roughly where I'd be was a sensible thing to do.

'Medicine Lake. I should probably go tonight, save an early start tomorrow. Naomi, if you don't mind, I think it'd be best if you stayed with Sabina while I'm gone. Probably better for both of you.'

A booming voice from behind me broke the tension. 'No problem, I shall be here to entertain you beautiful ladies. And, young woman, if you're planning on leaving town it's courteous to inform your hard working agent!'

'Daniel!' I put my arms around the man who'd come round the side of the house so quietly, white beard neatly trimmed and cane in hand, as ever. 'Gosh, it's good to see you. You're right, I apologise, do you mind if I have a brief change of scenery?' He went to kiss Naomi, then Sabina, on each cheek.

'Doing anything exciting?' he asked with his slight southern accent. He'd spent a lifetime working in an industry where almost everyone had some affectation. The accent was his, although in a very charming way. Somehow I always noticed it more when he was talking to women. When he was negotiating money you barely heard it at all. Daniel Fortune was one of the shrewdest men I'd ever met. He and Sabina had known each other for years but only got back in contact when I started working at the theatre with her. I was convinced they were in love, but suspected that neither of them was aware of it quite yet.

'Just a bit of sightseeing, nothing too adventurous. Daniel, it's the weekend. I think it would be much more fun for everyone if you stayed over. What do you think Sabina?' Sabina raised her eyebrows at me. I had just invited a man to stay in her home without asking her permission first but she knew me well enough to understand that I wouldn't have been so rude without cause. In a flash, she turned on the vivacious Sabina Roman charm.

'Oh, Daniel, would you please? There is plenty of room and Naomi and I will only talk cooking all weekend if left to our own devices.' That was settled. I felt better knowing there would be a man in the house with them. I made my excuses to go and pack whilst Sabina made a call to book me a hotel room in the nearby town of McCloud. I programmed the bike's navigation system and was putting on my leathers when Naomi came in.

'I know I can't ask you not to go, but please be careful.' As I looked up I could see that she'd been crying. I felt dreadful, adding to the burden she was already carrying. I hugged her hard then turned back to my packing to hide the upset on my own face.

'You know I wouldn't go if it weren't absolutely necessary,' I said. 'Please don't worry about me, I'll be with friends. I pulled on my boots and picked up my backpack. As I did so Naomi handed me a thin, sharp object wrapped in a handkerchief, but I could still feel the edges through the cloth.

'What's this?'

'It's from one of them,' she replied. 'Before James could haul their bodies out I stamped on one of their hands to snap it off. I shoved it into the box you brought out of the flat for me. I wanted to keep something so I knew I wasn't going crazy. Take it with you. Maybe it'll help you figure out what they were.' I unwrapped the nail to get a better look. It was impossible to tell if the talon was deliberately filed into such a sharp point or if it grew like that, but it was lethal either way. Several inches long, with a pinprick point, it allowed them to slash flesh in a perfectly straight line and make the wound as deep as possible. Whatever these things were, they were born killers. I tucked it carefully away in a compartment of my bag and kissed Naomi goodbye.

'Back in two days,' I said. Naomi left the room before I could, without a word. As I left the house I saw Sabina's translation of the diary on the floor where I'd dropped it last night. I had a long evening ahead of me in a hotel room so I shoved it in my pocket, took my keys off the table, and set off.

It was mid afternoon. One of the things I still hadn't become used to in California was the scale of the place. McCloud was about four hundred miles away and I wouldn't reach my hotel until late evening. I stopped just twice for coffee and to get the blood flowing back through my stiffening legs, so by the time I reached McCloud I was ready for a hot bath and some food. The hotel had a small restaurant on the ground floor but no room service. Feeling self-conscious about eating alone, I took the diary with me as a distraction. Now was as good a time as any to start it and I thought I should find out what Sabina had read.

I was starving and wasn't sure what I'd be eating for the next couple of days so I ordered butternut squash soup, mushroom risotto and treated myself to chocolate mousse for desert. I fiddled with the menu and cutlery for a while until I figured out that I was delaying starting to read. Sabina, perfectionist as ever, had even written the dates on the cover. The period of this journal was from March to August 1983.

When the waitress brought me a whiskey I took a large mouthful and opened the first page. It was strange, reading the words of someone I'd never met; I had no voice to put to it. I could hear the Slovakian accent that Sabina sometimes slipped back into and tried to put myself in the place of the forty year old woman who'd been a nurse all her working life, finally having the chance to care for her own baby. I started from about a week after Zora was born. As that date was supposed to have been my own birthday, it was easy enough to find.

'March 29. It's so good to be out of the hospital and home. Zora is doing well, she hasn't put on any weight but the midwife said that's normal at this stage. When she slept today I meant to get some washing done. An hour later I found myself still sitting by her crib watching her. Tomorrow we have a consultation with the Down's Syndrome specialist. Branimir doesn't want to be there, he isn't taking it well. I'm feeling better already, the tiredness of the first few days is wearing off. Zora sounds hungry. Off to sterilize yet another bottle.' The waitress arrived with my soup and I waited until she'd gone to read on. After that, there were markings about the baby's weight and length, so I skipped to her notes about the meeting with the doctor the next day.

'March 30. I saw the doctor this afternoon. As predicted, Branimir did not come. The doctor was very professional and did his best to be reassuring. He said that Zora might do very well for a few years and that those years would be ones I should value and enjoy looking back on. I asked him what he meant and he looked at me with real pity. I'm sure he didn't mean to, but it was the most awful thing. Seeing such regret in a stranger's eyes, as if they know what you're feeling. He told me her life expectancy is quite limited. The Down's Syndrome is severe. I said he couldn't possibly know that already, when she is so tiny and he became very strident. I don't think he expected me to challenge him. He said he's dealt with hundreds of such cases and that I should not expect her to see her twentieth birthday. I tried my best not to cry and I nearly managed it, too, only he patted my shoulder as I was leaving and that was it, the tears just wouldn't stop. How can this be right? My beautiful baby girl, already serving a sentence, with no prospect of enjoying the excitement of her adult years? I'm glad Branimir didn't come. He would have either punched the doctor or told me he knew this would happen all along. I'm just not going to tell him what the doctor said. If he finds out, he won't even try to bond with Zora. I have to get through this evening without him seeing anything is wrong. I'll cook him steak, that always puts him in a good mood.'

Poor Adela.   The desperation in the text was so understated yet I felt every bit of her anguish. My soup had gone cold. I pushed it aside and an eager waiter whisked it off to the kitchen.   Instead, I sipped whiskey and waited for the risotto, eating it the minute it arrived, knowing that if I started reading again I wouldn't get any dinner at all. I asked to take dessert up to my room although I wasn't sure I'd get round to it. I made a coffee, tipped the remaining whiskey into it and settled on my bed, reopening the diary with the feeling that I was intruding upon someone's privacy. I had no trouble hearing Adela's voice now, all too close and real.

'April 2. Yesterday I was out pushing Zora in her pram down to the river as it was the first warm day of the year. I thought the fresh air might brighten her up as she's looking jaundiced. Out of nowhere Castevan appeared. I haven't seen him for more than a year and I'd assumed he'd moved further away. He said he'd heard about the baby and had been looking for a chance to talk to me. It was wonderful to see him again after so long. He looked as if he hadn't aged a day but I knew straight away that he was worried about something. He asked after Branimir and how we were getting on with Zora. He even held her and she seemed perfectly content in his arms. Then I noticed another person, hiding in the trees and I wouldn't have seen her but I heard the tiniest cry, just a gurgle really. Before Zora, I might not have picked up on it but when you have a baby around you hear everything. Castevan called out and a woman stepped from the trees. She had a baby in a sling across her chest and even though she was walking towards me, saying hello she was really only focussing on the child, cooing and stroking its cheek. It was another baby girl, just a few days older than Zora, Castevan said. He introduced the woman as Anousk. She was beautiful, long red hair and gentle eyes but when she held my hand it was like a man's grip, strong and confident.

'I told them about the Down's Syndrome and they were so sympathetic. No child suffers from it where Castevan is from, they seem healthier than us in lots of ways. Castevan always appears so vital, almost bursting with energy. Then Anousk told me that she was just as worried about her own baby. They said their child, Eve, is perfectly healthy but that if others find out that her grandfather was a cambion she won't be safe in Manitu. They don't know if she'll grow up with Anousk's traits or Castevan's, but if the cambion side of her nature is active, she'll be a valuable commodity to some other tribes. They were obviously scared. We talked a little longer and then they explained why they'd come to see me. They wanted me to consider exchanging the babies. Eve would be safer growing up here and Zora would have a chance to live a much better life, somewhere she wouldn't suffer so much illness and have the prospect of an adulthood. They said I could go and visit her occasionally. At first I thought they were insane, talking about giving my baby away but then I realised I was thinking about myself, not what would be best for Zora. I told them I'd sleep on it. They accepted my need for some time and said they would come and find me in a few days. I don't know what to do.'

I put the book down and reached for my phone, flinging it onto the bed furiously when I realised there was no signal and no internet access. I had no idea what a cambion was; I'd never even heard the term. There was no guest computer in the hotel, only connections for laptops and I didn't have one. I certainly couldn't call Sabina at this time and have her do a search when I had no idea what would turn up; she was worried enough already. I stared blankly across the room for a moment before seeing the chocolate pudding next to the kettle. Frustrated and tense, I did the only thing left to do: I crammed as many calories into my mouth as quickly as I could.

For a few minutes it actually worked and the sugar rush took my mind off what I'd just read. I stared in the mirror and took a long, hard look at myself. I had confirmation for the first time that when my mother gave me to Adela, she did so out of love. I wasn't given away: I was sent to the protective arms of another. Any remaining questions were best answered by Anousk herself. I slipped off my clothes, closed the diary and dimmed the lights. Maybe it was reading about how my mother had stroked my face, and maybe the sugar helped, but that night I slept dreamless and contented.

Ten

Having spent the night at the hotel, I arrived at Little Medicine Lake with plenty of time to spare before I expected Serenta. I'd bought a map and compass from a camping supplies shop in McCloud after wondering how I would find the most southerly part of anywhere without them. Medicine Lake is in the Modoc National Forest and the volcano which gave the lake its name had been active for half a million years. I was awestruck by the place. Pine trees stretched as far as the eye could see, the lake looked as if it had a sheet of polished glass on its surface and I could hear nothing but the cries of water birds and the rustle of wind in the leaves. In the distance, Mount Shasta's snowy peak was visible amidst the layer of cloud surrounding it. It was the most serene place I'd ever been, somewhere a time machine would have no effect: You could wake up here and never know what year, what century even, you'd landed in. I hoped it never changed and understood completely why the Vilya had chosen this as their retreat. I felt the vibration of hooves thundering towards me and from the east I saw a tiny figure speeding across the plain, sensing Serenta's exhilaration as she came nearer.

'I didn't know you could bring animals through with you,' I said, running my hand along the horse's neck.

'These horses are from this region, in your world,' she replied. 'There are herds inhabiting the reserves although they are not all so willing to be ridden as this one. Come, take my hand.' She motioned for me to pull myself up behind her but I hesitated when I saw there was no saddle.

'How will I stay on?' I asked.

'Hold on to me. The horse will not let us fall, at least if you are careful not to kick her. Don't be scared, Eve, the wild horses can sense the Vilya. It knows you are one of us.' I gave her my hand and she hoisted me on with little effort. It was easy to be fooled by the petiteness of the Vilya women, but they were extraordinarily strong warriors.

'Can we pass through to Manitu on horseback then?' I said, wrapping my arms tightly around her waist.

'We can, the same as running yesterday, open your mind and let go of your sense of time and place. You must be unafraid or it will not work. Anousk is waiting.' She reached down and patted the horse's side. Suddenly we were off at a gallop. I couldn't even try to rise with the rhythm of the horse's movement without stirrups to push against, so I concentrated on moving my body in time with Serenta's. The horse was moving up onto higher ground. For a second I thought I'd slip off, then we were level again, racing across the ridge of the hill into the sunlight that was streaming through the morning clouds. It was like riding through the sky, the air cold and fresh, my hair whipping my face and neck. I yelled out loud feeling the blood coursing through my veins and Serenta joined in. As we rode, the pale, early light glowed more golden and the leaves began to glisten a deeper shade of green. The sharp scent of pine engulfed me and gradually the horse slowed. Serenta dismounted before me and I took a moment to lean against the horse's back and whisper a thank you before swinging a leg behind me and jumping down. Serenta was watching me carefully and as I hit the ground, I knew why. My legs buckled beneath me and I grabbed her for support. I hadn't realised how hard my muscles had been working but I suspected that walking might be an effort tomorrow morning.

'Nearly there,' she said. 'Follow me.' We took a path so lightly trodden that I'd have completely missed it on my own. After about five minutes walk, I saw a hole in the ground, roughly two metres across. Serenta knelt next to it, dragged ropes from under the ledge and held one out to me.

'You've got to be kidding,' I said.

'I do not understand,' Serenta replied, looking confused at either my language or my reaction, I wasn't sure which.

'We're abseiling in the pitch dark? I'm not sure I can do this.' I peered over the edge into the blackness. 'What's down there?'

'The Vilya are living in the old lava tubes. The volcano has not erupted for two centuries. It is unique in having many small chambers instead of one large one, with thousands of cave systems spreading under the ground. Only those who know them well can navigate the tunnels to find us. It was the safest place we could go. There is nothing to fear, Eve. Once we reach the bottom there will be lamps. I shall climb down first and keep the tension on your rope to make it easier. You must lean backwards as far as you can, keep your legs straight and your back level with the floor. All you have to do is walk.'

I wasn't convinced, but I couldn't stand at the top and refuse. I watched as she secured the rope around herself then fastened mine before disappearing. Darkness obscured my view of her in seconds and, too late, I wanted to ask how deep it was. After what felt like an age I heard her call back up. I felt some stress on the rope around me and realised she was pulling it taut so that I could start climbing down. My rope was looped around a tree root embedded in the rock and I prayed it would hold my weight.

'Trust me, sister. I will not let you fall.' Serenta calling me sister made me think of Ellette, my younger sibling who'd died in the battle at the Rock of Ages. She gave her life saving Zora and me, not hesitating when we needed her. Although I'd only known her for a short time I felt the loss terribly and, if only to honour her memory, I needed to show a little more fortitude. I kept my eyes on the light outside the cave, shouted a warning at Serenta that I was on my way, and started to lower myself backwards to walk down the cave wall. The worst of it was going from standing to lying back but once I'd become used to the position, it wasn't as bad as I'd imagined. It took me a few minutes, some heavy breathing and the odd moment where I was convinced I'd slip or get stuck, but I did it. Unlike my journey on the horse, this was one experience I never wanted to repeat. Serenta was trying to light a branch bound with hemp by sparking a flint on the rock but she was having no success and I suspected that the walls were too damp for the stone to spark. Finally, something I could help with.

'Here,' I said. 'Let me.' At the shop where I'd bought the compass they'd suggested a basic survival kit which included a lighter, torch, flares and water purification tablets. I'd had my mind on other things and just said yes to the lot, so I was astounded that it was actually going to come in useful. I took out the lighter and flicked the thumbwheel. The hemp was ablaze in seconds and Serenta looked at me with something close to admiration. 'It's just a lighter,' I said. 'It's cheating really. You have it.'

'No,' she said. 'Keep it. Something that useful should be with you all the time. The Vilya are not like the Perelesnyk, we do not go into the human world unless it is necessary and we never bring anything back with us. I see that you have some objects of value, after all.' I handed her a lit torch and we set off along the maze of underground tunnels. It was like a scene from a science fiction movie, these rounded caves, branching off here and there, running for countless miles deep under the earth. If you stumbled down here accidentally you'd have no hope of being found or finding your own way out. The space was big enough to avoid any sensation of claustrophobia and at the point when I sensed we were moving deeper underground there were the first signs of life. Occasional lamps were fixed to the walls and wooden beams spanned the ceilings where the cave split into multiple tubes. Serenta explained that they were for navigation and showed me the faint carvings in the wood that only the Vilya could understand. It wasn't damp, as I expected, but it was cold. Finally we crossed a long bridge, constructed of wood and rope, over a deep chasm that must have been one of the main lava chambers. On the other side I heard the echo of voices. I'd been so overwhelmed by my surroundings that I'd all but forgotten I was about to see my mother and Zora for the first time in months. I felt a surge of excitement at the thought and picked up my pace as we moved into a large hall, filled with small fires for warmth and hung with hides and skins. I smelled meat cooking and suddenly my mouth was watering. This was obviously the main living area. It was the largest cave imaginable, several storeys high with stairs and ladders up the sides to where small tunnels led off to other areas. The rock inside was a rainbow of different reds, browns and chalky white with streaks of yellow and blue.

When Serenta gently tugged my arm to get my attention I saw that every man, woman and child was bowing their head in my direction. I felt humbled that these people should recognise my authority when I'd deserted them within hours of the ascension ceremony. The idea was that Zora should govern in my absence and at the time it had seemed like the perfect solution. Now I knew that I had plunged this world into a bloody war that had left my tribe cowering underground and still they showed deference.

'Please stand up,' I said, my words echoing around the rock face. 'You don't need to do that. The crown I took belongs to Zora, all I did was buy her some time.' I looked at Serenta, lost for words. She took my hand and led me towards one of the small fires, dipping a ladle into the pot above it and pouring me a cup of hot herbal tea. I sipped it gratefully as conversation started again and people got on with their tasks. A young man came over and inclined his head to me.

'Mother is ready to see you now, if you are rested.' I stared at him. I guessed he was about sixteen, tall and pale, and he reminded me so much of Ellette that I couldn't respond. He filled in the silence for me. 'I am Anton, Anousk's youngest son.' I smiled at him but he looked terrified. I knew from Ellette that I had other siblings although we hadn't been blessed with enough time together for me to find out any details.

'You're my brother?' I said. He nodded and I stepped forward to hug him. He remained like stone and it was oddly reassuring that teenage awkwardness was the same in both worlds. Some things would never change. 'I'm so pleased to meet you, Anton. Would you mind taking me to our mother?' He relaxed, probably just relieved that the hugging had stopped. We went down a small lava tube into a ring of chambers at the end. In the furthest one a fire burned but there were no other lamps on the walls. A comfortable bed had been constructed in the middle of the room, covered in animal hides and linens. A small body in the middle stirred as I walked into the room. There was a squeal of excitement and, with a bit of a struggle, the body pushed up from under the covers.

'Zora!' I cried. I knelt at the bedside to put my arms around the young woman who was beaming with complete abandon. She kissed my cheek repeatedly and I stroked her hair. When she started to cough I helped her lay back on the pillows.

'I missed you, Eve, I'm so glad you've come back.' She tried to continue talking but the words were lost in the spluttering of a debilitating illness. She was markedly thinner than last time I saw her, her face had lost its healthy glow and her eyes looked sunken.

A figure in the doorway spoke softly. 'She needs to rest. Zora, you can see Eve again later, my love. Try to sleep.' Anousk walked forward and pulled the covers over Zora who didn't fight to stay awake. That alone made me aware just how ill she was. The Zora I remembered had unlimited energy. I sat watching her for a few moments as she slipped into sleep.

'Do you know what's wrong with her?' I asked. My mother shook her head and put a finger across her lips. She gestured for me to follow her and I did so at a cautious distance. We walked into a stark chamber with a pelt mat on the floor for a bed and piles of scrolls against the walls. She invited me to sit down. I couldn't touch her. It was the result of her changing me with Zora. If I made physical contact with Anousk in Manitu, Zora would be cast back into the human world forever. She wouldn't survive, of course, the shock and heart break at being ripped from her family would be too much. It was the reason I'd worked so hard to stop the Perelesnyk from taking power. We maintained a safe distance as she sat to talk.

'It warms my heart to see you again, daughter. It is a shame it has come to this after the sacrifice you made to save Zora.'

'I am sorry, Mother. If I'd known the devastation it would cause I would have stayed out of the situation.'

'And if you had not brought James here to help Ellette find Zora, she would have died in the caves where Perun left her. This is not your doing child. Power maddens those who desire it. The Perelesnyk could have chosen to wait the four years until it was their given time to rule. Only their hatred for Zora's human blood made them desperate to overthrow us. This would have come to pass with or without you.'

'Thank you,' I whispered, hoping she meant it and that she didn't hold me responsible for the terrible state the Vilya were in now.

She leaned towards me, face shining in the firelight, eyes bright and fierce. 'You came when we needed you and proved that, for all those years in the human world, you are still one of us. I have held your face in my heart and thought of you every day since then, proud of the woman my daughter grew up to be. Even though I cannot touch you, I carry you with me everywhere I go. Do not lose hope. A more peaceful time will come.' I dashed the tears from my cheeks, embarrassed that she should see me cry. This was the first time we had spoken privately. I didn't want her to think of me as weak.

'I had to come once Serenta showed me what was happening. Why have the Council not acted to stop the Perelesnyk?'

'There is too much division between the families. Without a ruler here the Council has no one to follow and, without Zora well enough to go out amongst the people and convince them that she can lead, the Council members have fallen prey to the vicious whisperings of our enemies. Zora is well loved by most. Almost all the Council members agree how wise she is, in spite of her differences and her human blood. They accept her as one of us. But if she cannot appear as a figurehead to unite the families, then the Council will look for someone who can.'

'Can you not heal her?' For the first time I saw her extraordinary strength faltering.

'You know we cannot heal people here, it is a power we have only in the human world. In Manitu we let nature take its course. We can give her medicine to revive her, reduce her fever but no more than that. We do not know what makes her ill and without that knowledge our intervention is limited.'

'What can I do to help?'

'Nothing, at the moment. The Council meets next week and I shall address them. Your appearance might only make things worse. We have to resolve this situation for the long term. This is about the breaking of the families' pact of peace. There should be careful and considered debates in which everyone should have a voice. We cannot resolve it until the Perelesnyk and their allies come to the table to talk. You are better off at home looking after your friend. Serenta told me what happened.'

It made me think of the talon I had in my pocket. 'The creatures who killed my friend's husband drank his blood,' I said. Anousk closed her eyes. She seemed saddened rather than shocked. I pulled the object from my pocket. 'This is from one of them. Can you tell me what it is?'

She took it hesitantly from my hand. 'It is a claw from one of the Moroi. They live almost exclusively on blood but rarely go into the human world as they can exist on animal blood, and their appearance makes it dangerous for them outside of Manitu. They cannot pass as human. They are very dangerous. If Perun sent them as a warning you should stay away. I cannot protect you in the human world.'

'It was James they were after; he was staying with my friend at the time. What's their connection to the Perelesnyk?

'The Moroi live in the Carpathian Mountains. I have rarely seen them but the last time I did was in the forests when we were waiting to talk to Adela. That region is also the home ground of the Perelesnyk. When all the families were at peace and the Perelesnyk complied with the pact, no-one was supposed to bring humans into Manitu. Although we knew they had to breed with humans, they did so in the human world and would only bring the incubus' children back here, leaving their mothers unharmed. Before the pact though, they would impregnate human women then bring them back to Manitu, holding them prisoner until the babies were born. Once they had no further use for the mothers, the stories say that they gave the poor women to the Moroi who would feed off them. In return the Moroi acted as their soldiers, a sort of private army to the Perelesnyk, providing protection and using force on demand. If the Moroi have started to work for them again then I fear they are being paid in the same way as before. This is grave news.'

She handed back the claw which I slipped carefully into my pocket. 'So they're like vampires?' I said, feeling stupid using the word out loud.

'No, child. Human tales of vampires, charming and lustful, are fantasies to entertain children. The Moroi are cold hearted killers who are not capable of anything other than fulfilling their own needs. They are more animal than anything else. You cannot reason with them; if they are in battle, either they die or you will. I would not like you to be misinformed. These are brutal predators, nothing else.' I nodded to show I understood then decided to ask the question that had been on my mind since last night.

'And a cambion. What's that?' I said. Anousk paused, rapped hard on the floor with a stone and a young woman appeared in the doorway almost immediately.

'Would you bring us food please? My daughter must be hungry after her journey.' The girl disappeared without a word and I knew Anousk had wanted extra time to prepare her answer.

'Let us go and eat in Zora's chamber. Our voices may awaken her enough that she'll eat a little with us. Come.' She would answer in her own time, there was no point forcing the subject. I wasn't even certain I wanted to know. I followed her back through to Zora's room where she was exactly as we'd left her, eyes closed but breathing more erratically than I liked.

Two women brought us in trays of thick stew and flatbread to dip in it. It helped revive my flagging energy and we finished off with slices of dried fruit. With it, we had fresh water, so cold it made me choke with my first mouthful.

'I apologise Eve, I should have warned you. The water comes down a well from the nearby lake. It is freezing at this time of year. We have become used to it and I did not think to tell you.'

Zora began to babble in her sleep and Anousk put a cool flannel across her forehead. 'It will make her feel better, knowing you visited,' she said. 'She talks of you often. James, too. How is he?'

'I don't know. He left, soon after we last saw you. You know of his curse?' She murmured that she did. 'It was too risky, us staying together. The first I heard of him was when Naomi's husband was killed. Now he's gone off travelling again. Probably for the best.'

'He's a brave man. Like your father.' I put my bowl down. She was ready to tell me more. 'His name is Castevan. Given the question you asked before, I assume you found out more about Adela. I met Castevan at the first ceremony I attended with my family. He is one of the Polevoi. You may remember seeing them at your ascension, they were the last family to rule. It was Castevan's niece that passed you the throne.' I nodded. The Polevoi are field spirits. They had struck me with their concern for the environment in the human world. The ones I had seen were fair and willowy. Perhaps I wasn't going to be hearing bad news after all.

'We fell in love without realising it; he was a free spirit, he loved to travel, sometimes he would just disappear and turn up again weeks later with no word. But I always knew he'd come back to me. We were very young and I thought there was nothing in the world that could hurt us. When I fell pregnant I was so full of joy. I thought we could marry the next spring, I would stay living with my family, I knew by then that he'd always be a wanderer but it was not too much of a sacrifice, the times when we were together were so happy. And I was the matriarch's eldest child, I had duties to the Vilya that would keep me busy. When I told him my news I thought he'd be thrilled but he just looked broken. I'd never seen him like that before. He asked me if anyone else knew. I had told my mother, of course, but other than that it was still a secret. It was very early in the pregnancy.'

'What was the problem?' I asked. Anousk was lost in the memory, almost as if she'd forgotten I was there. When she glanced up her eyes were filled with tears.

'I knew his mother, Reema, from times when our family had mixed with the Polevoi. His father was dead and I had never asked about him before but once I fell pregnant, Castevan told me he was a cambion.'

'I don't understand what that means,' I said, curious about how upset she seemed.

'A cambion is a genetically exceptional offspring of an incubus and a human woman. They don't have that sheen of perfection that the normal incubi have, they age more visibly and can scar. In cambions, human blood is the more dominant, unlike normal incubi, so they can live in the human world almost undetected. But they have the incubi's powers and can seem strange, almost magical, in your world. The cambion's name was Gregor. He had been brought into Manitu by the incubus who bred with his human mother but at some point he'd left the Perelesnyk and wandered off to live alone. When Reema met him he was living a solitary life in the mountains and she believed him human. By the time she found out differently, she was already carrying his child.'

'So my grandfather...'

'Was half incubus,' she finished for me. 'The Perelesnyk have never been able to breed with the Vilya directly so children of mixed tribal blood are very precious. In rare cases, they inherit the powers of both the Perelesnyk and the other race they were bred from. You have a mixture of Perelesnyk, Polevoi, human and Vilya blood. We knew they would make every effort to take you from us, especially as you were the first child of the matriarch. When you were born a girl, destined to take the throne as our time came, you became too valuable to keep you here. That's why we exchanged you with Zora. It broke me to give you away but we didn't think we had any choice. Even back then the Perelesnyk were desperate for power, willing to use anyone to better their position. Children from cambions bred with other tribes are unpredictable; they sometimes have unexpected powers, ones that cannot be traced to any of their known ancestors. How did you find out?'

'Adela kept diaries,' I said. I was reeling from the shock of knowing that in my distant blood line I was related to the monsters who had ordered Tim and Ellette's deaths. 'Did they ever find out about me?'

'No. We had to tell them I'd had a child, it was obvious when I brought Zora back but we said the father was from a different family altogether. We told everyone that we did it to save the human baby, that we were trying to do some good in the world. As far as I know, the Perelesnyk have no idea about your history and we must make sure they never find out or next time they won't let you go back to the human world at all.'

'Why Adela? How did Castevan know her?'

'Many years later Castevan's human grandmother had another child with her husband, a daughter. That child was Adela. Although she was Castevan's aunt, at least in half-blood, they were close in age. He would sometimes visit her when he was travelling. She was very accepting of him, never questioned the things he told her. The Slavic people believed things that humans today think are only myths.'

'Where is Castevan now?'

'He disappeared, after I brought Zora back. We knew it would be too much of a risk to stay together. I think he went to live in the human world but I haven't seen or heard from him since. I suspect that his life has ended, I know the Polevoi have had no news of him. Usually your family has a sense of a continuing life, and yet no-one can feel anything from Castevan. Ellette and the rest of my children are your half-siblings. They would all like a chance to know their sister better.' She smiled and I thought she was imagining how it would be to see her children all together. 'Does anyone else know what you have found out about your bloodline? It is dangerous knowledge Eve, I wish it had never been put in writing.'

'Sabina,' I said. 'Adela lived with her for many years. The house where I'm staying is on her land.'

'Then you must take care she does not tell anyone, even if she does not understand the importance of the information. Destroy the diaries, for your own sake.'

'I will,' I said, although the thought of doing that was awful after the comfort I'd taken from them last night. 'I should go, if Sabina is in danger then I need to be at the ranch.' Anousk didn't argue but as I stood up, a wave of nausea came over me that made me stagger back to the ground. I must have groaned because Anousk grabbed a nearby pot and handed it to me. I vomited forcefully two or three times. Anousk had picked up a towel and set it down on the bed for me to wipe my face.

'I did not know you were unwell. The journey was too much for you.'

'No, I was fine until after I'd eaten, really.' I picked up the towel off Zora's bed and saw how pale her face was. 'Has Zora been sick too? Maybe there's been a problem with the food since you've been living down here?'

'But we all eat the same things. No-one else is ill.'

'She's the only one with human blood, though. Can you be sure her body reacts the same way as yours?' Anousk didn't answer me, just picked up one of Zora's small hands and held it in her own. 'Maybe there is something I can do. Let me take some blood back with me. I have a doctor friend, I'm sure he'll arrange to have it analysed. It may take a while but I think I could get an answer within a week. Can you arrange for Serenta to meet me behind my house, seven days from now, at sunset?'

'Of course, do whatever you can.' Zora's nurse came in and drained some blood which she poured into a small bottle. I pushed the plug in tight and thrust it into my pocket.

Anousk walked me back to the main cavern where Serenta was waiting. Although we could not touch she looked me in the eyes so intensely I felt my heart pounding in my chest.

'I should have kept you with me,' she said. 'I wish I had not been so afraid. I'm sorry.'

'Don't be. You did it to protect me, I understand. Now that I've found you again there's nothing to regret.' I followed Serenta into another of the cavernous tubes to make our way out. We left the caves by a different path and I wished we could have come in that way, but appreciated the need for caution. Outside, it was already night-time. Serenta took me out of Manitu to the place we'd met at Little Medicine Lake on horseback again. It was almost seamless, moving between worlds; it must have been, because I certainly felt none of the exhilaration during the return journey that I'd experienced getting there.

Eleven

Back at my hotel in McCloud I walked straight into the restaurant. I didn't care what anyone thought by then, throwing my bike leathers and backpack down on one chair and seating myself next to the window. The waitress came over and I ordered a double brandy and an espresso, still feeling queasy and wanting to kill whatever bug was churning up my stomach. When it arrived I tossed down the coffee and sipped my brandy, hand in pocket running my fingers over the bottle of Zora's blood. As much as I wanted to get back home, I was in no fit state to ride tonight; I'd have been a liability on the road. I needed to sleep for a few hours and planned to leave first thing in the morning but first I had to phone Sabina and let her know I was safe. I took the remains of my brandy with me, grabbed my kit and was imagining the welcome of a comfortable bed.

I put my key in the door and had to jiggle it around a few times before it clicked in. When it finally opened I saw why: my room had been ransacked. My spare clothes were thrown everywhere, toiletries were flung about the place and my phone was on the floor by the door. I dropped everything from my hands and rushed to the bed, desperate to find Adela's diary. If they had that, then I could be in serious trouble. It wasn't in the backpack where I'd left it this morning and I couldn't see any sign of it with the rest of my things. A cough just outside my room reminded me I'd left the door wide open and a couple of passing guests were apparently curious about the state of the place. I muttered something placatory, picked up my leathers from the hallway and kicked the door shut. My glass had smashed so I grabbed a bin from the bathroom and carefully put the larger pieces into it. As I was on my knees mopping up the spillage, I caught a glimpse of something under the bed. I slid a hand in and pulled out the diary, realising it must have fallen on the floor when whoever did this was ripping everything apart. There was no sign it had been read or even noticed. I checked through all my belongings, nothing had been taken and no written message had been left although the warning seemed clear. I was supposed to know that I was being watched, that I was vulnerable.

I used the phone in my room to call Naomi. They were all fine, had spent the day in front of the fire, playing cards and comparing favourite books. I made my excuses, in no mood for small talk and said I'd be back with them by lunch time tomorrow. Next I called Aedan. I managed to disturb him at a fundraiser for a children's hospital and had to make my apologies for forgetting he was busy this evening. It was getting increasingly hard to separate the two distinct parts of my life and I was finding it a strain to pretend everything was normal. Luckily Aedan was too much in demand at the function to be able to chat, so I got straight to it.

'Actually, I'm after a favour and it's kind of urgent. I have a blood sample that needs checking.'

'Checking for what? If you're ill you should have told me, I'd have made you an appointment with a specialist.'

'It's not me, it's a friend. She's terrified of anything medical so she asked me to deal with it for her. I know it's a bit unusual but she's not well and I need to find out what's wrong. You know, viruses, infections, I'm not sure what tests need doing.'

'Where's the blood sample now?'

'I've got it with me. Could I give it to you tomorrow?'

'I'm in surgery all day but let's meet up in the evening. Tell you what, I'll sort this out for you if you'll have dinner with me tomorrow night. Come to my boat, we can watch the sun go down, maybe even have longer than just ten minutes together? What do you say, eight o'clock?'

'Sounds perfect. Thanks Aedan, I'll let you go.'

'See you tomorrow.' As he put the phone down I was already tugging my boots off and getting ready to take a long shower, double locking the door and checking the windows before I climbed in. I wouldn't be able to get onto the internet until tomorrow afternoon to do some research, but in the meantime I'd started to make a few connections in my head that had never made sense before. I hadn't seen any of the Vilya cause the sort of freak storms that happened when I was upset. I'd always assumed that was because they had better control of their emotions than I did but now I wondered if that part of me came from my incubus great-grandfather. Perun was a storm demon and I'd witnessed the damage he could do first hand in a horrific train crash in Slovakia. I felt ill at the thought that I shared blood with creatures capable of so much evil.

Too shaken to sleep, I picked up Adela's diary again. If I was going to have to destroy it then I wanted the opportunity to read a bit more first. I pushed a bedside table in front of the door and opened Adela's diary at the point I'd left it last night. The next date she'd written was April 7.

'God help me but I've agreed. I wasn't going to. I'd decided to let nature take its course and look after Zora myself, however many years we might have together. Then two days ago I could see that her jaundice was getting worse. The nurse told me it would wear off but she isn't feeding as well as she was to start with and her face is a vivid yellow colour. I knew her immune system was weak and that she might be susceptible to problems with her gut. The doctor told me I had to be prepared for a lot more health problems than other children suffer but I don't want her to face a lifetime of illness, always wondering what will go wrong next. When Branimir went to work yesterday I heard a knock at the back door. Castevan and Anousk were there and I'd been dreading them reappearing as it meant making a decision. I was distracted by how unwell Zora seemed and Anousk saw it straight away. She told me not to worry and picked her up, cradling her to her chest then wrapped both arms around her tiny body, one hand covering her head. She stayed like that, just rocking the baby, covering so much of her that I could barely see her. Part of me wanted to grab Zora and shout at them to leave but I knew she wasn't going to hurt her, not when I'd seen how she held her own baby, so I made myself wait until she was ready to hand her to me.

'When Anousk put her back in my arms, the yellow in her eyes was already fading. Over the next few minutes her skin got back the healthy peachiness it should have had and shortly after that she took a whole bottle of milk in one go, with a hunger she hasn't shown for days. I knew then that it was the right thing to do. Anousk would keep the baby healthy in a way I never could. I told them they could take her and I saw a look in Anousk's eyes when I did; she had wanted me to say no. I realised I'd sealed the fate of her baby, not just my own. It made me feel better, that look, knowing this was something she didn't really want but had to do. I told them I wouldn't be able to bear handing Zora over, that they would have to organise it themselves. They said they would exchange them two nights from now, when everyone was asleep. There was nothing else to say. Anousk left without speaking and I waited until they'd gone before I cried. I'll have to give Branimir more wine than usual with his dinner to make sure he sleeps soundly. I have a pain constantly in my chest and I find myself looking at the clock every other minute. I don't know how to bear the agony of my decision. I hope that when she's grown up, she can find a way to forgive me for what I'm about to do. How do you put your baby to bed knowing it will be the last time you see her?'

The entry ended there, I couldn't have read another line anyway. Tears blurred my vision. Adela had made an extraordinary sacrifice and now poor, precious Zora lay sick if not dying, with Anousk unable to save her.

The next morning I was up at sunrise and packing my bag. I'd had so little decent sleep that it was a relief to be getting out of the room. The journey back was uneventful and the queasiness of the previous day was finally wearing off. I knew I'd spend six hours worrying about what Anousk had told me if I didn't distract myself, so I selected The Proclaimers on my MP3 player, diverted it through to the headphones in my helmet, put the volume up as loud as I could and concentrated on the road. By the time I pulled into the ranch I knew every word of the songs I'd had on loop and could barely remember the drive. As I walked past the stables I wondered where James was now. It would have been good if he'd called to see if Naomi and I were safe. He must have found it easier to come to terms with losing me than I had him. By the time I got into my house, I hadn't seen anyone except ranch hands out exercising the horses. There was no sign of Sabina but I found a note from Naomi on the kitchen table.

'Gone to the theatre with Sabina as she's working on next production with set designers. Daniel went back to San Francisco today. We'll be home for dinner - I'm cooking for us all tonight so don't fill up on toast. Text me to let me know you're back safely, okay? N xxx.'

I was grateful for the opportunity to log on to my computer with no-one else around. Naomi knew me too well. The toast was half made before I'd finished reading her note and I spread on butter and marmalade, then sat down to trawl the internet for anything to do with cambions. As expected, there wasn't much information available. What little there was, confirmed that in ancient mythology a cambion was the offspring of an incubus or succubus with a human and that, whilst they looked human, they had no breath or pulse for the first few years of life. The thought gave me the creeps. Twelfth century writings implied that King Arthur's advisor, Merlin, was believed to have been a cambion, supposedly often visiting some "other world" and possessing special powers inherited from his demonic father. It seemed absurd when it was written in black and white like that, yet the story had endured for hundreds of years. I guessed that at the same time religion started to lose its powerful hold on the populace, monsters and angels also began to fade into fairytales.

All the same, it was reassuring that part of my bloodline was just plain human; it made me feel as if I still belonged here. The fact that Adela was a distant relative made her diaries all the more meaningful and I was glad we were linked through more than mere coincidence. It also meant that Sabina really was the closest thing I had to family here. No wonder Adela had been so keen to move to California, knowing she'd be that much closer to Zora.

Naomi came in late that afternoon and it was a joy to hear her chatting about what was happening at the theatre and Sabina's latest plans. She managed to get through a good half hour of arranging flowers and pulling washing out of the dryer before asking about my trip. I told her it was fine, that nothing had happened, not seeing the point of telling her how my room was invaded; she'd been made to feel scared enough already. Incubi demons can fly, so following people is easy and Perun had always been able to find me whenever he wanted. The need to be covert about my movements just hadn't occurred to me. I had to make my excuses for dinner as I'd arranged to see Aedan but I promised we'd spend a few days together without me being distracted by anything else after that. Naomi tentatively asked if we could go and see a bit of the city.

'That's a great idea. Let's disappear for a few days next week,' I said impulsively. 'We'll get a hotel in San Francisco, go sight-seeing, and spend some proper time together. We can invite Xander to join us if you like, no-one shops like him. We could both do with some time out, as long as you're feeling up to it?' Naomi said she was and looked pleased at the prospect. If the Perelesnyk were watching me then we'd be safer in the city anyway. I gasped as I looked at my watch. I still had to make myself look presentable and get to Monterey where Aedan moored his boat. I threw on some clean clothes and walked Naomi over to the main house. This time, I'd borrowed Sabina's driver for the night. It was a luxury I rarely felt comfortable about, but I'd spent enough hours on my bike to last me a month. I settled down and watched the world go by as we cruised the seventeen miles up the coast to the harbour.

Twelve

The sun was just setting as we reached the edge of Monterey. The driver dropped me at the marina gate and I phoned Aedan so that he could meet me. I'd never been to his yacht before and was pretty sure I wouldn't find it without help amidst the rows of boats rocking gently on the water. A figure jogged slowly out of the dusk and Aedan looked relaxed as he greeted me.

'Ready to meet my other girlfriend?' he asked.

'You'd better be talking about your yacht,' I said, digging him gently in the ribs. He laughed and took my hand as we walked down a jetty to a gleaming white boat. I could just make out the name "Lady Luck" along the side and then Aedan was on deck, holding a hand out as I jumped aboard.

'This is yours? You called it a dinghy, for goodness' sake. This is more spacious than my old apartment!'

He ran his hand along the spotless woodwork. 'I may have done her a bit of a disservice. She's fifty foot of the best therapy imaginable. I work very hard, after all.' He slipped one hand round my waist and the other into my hair. 'Surely I deserve a bit of pleasure after all those hours in the operating theatre, don't you think?' He bent his head down and kissed me, pulling me towards him with a possessiveness that left me in no doubt what type of pleasure he was thinking about. For half a second I wondered just how many women had been invited to enjoy Aedan's very personal brand of rest and relaxation on the boat, then decided to stop worrying about it. I had no one else around to spoil me with this sort of attention so there was no point ruining it now. 'Fancy taking her out for a tour round the harbour?'

'Isn't it kind of dark to be going out now?' I wondered out loud.

'Very observant, MacKenzie, but the wonder of modern technology has given us,' he flicked a switch behind him 'lights.'

'Fine, if you promise to cut out the sarcasm, I'll try not to make any more stupid comments this evening. How would that be?' I didn't wait for his comeback, choosing instead to reach up and return his earlier kiss. He brushed away the hair that was blowing across my face in the breeze.

'You seem different. Everything okay? That wasn't a complaint, by the way.'

'I've been reassessing my priorities lately,' I shrugged, thinking again that James could have checked on me if he'd really wanted to. That small act surely wouldn't have made things any more dangerous for either of us. He'd obviously moved on with his life and it was about time I did the same. 'Now teach me how to drive this thing.'

For the next half hour I sat on the top deck huddled under a huge coat of Aedan's while he got ready to take Lady Luck out of the harbour. By the time we were away, the water was black. It was spectacular being on the sea at night. You could see the lights from the houses and bars along the shore and it was clear enough to make out the stars above. Once we were further out in the bay there was nothing but peace and the rocking motion of the waves. Aedan put some music on quietly in the background and suggested we go below deck. Inside, the yacht was a masterpiece of design ingenuity and elegance. Everything was cream leather, wood or polished steel. There was an internal cockpit overlooking the galley and up a few steps was a dining area with luxurious seating around a mahogany table. Aedan told me to make myself at home so I opened a variety of cupboard doors to reveal a music system, an enormous television screen, a computer and a well stocked bar. By the time I'd finished pressing buttons to see what they did, Aedan coughed politely to get my attention. The table was covered in a white linen cloth on which was a platter of crab, lobster, smoked salmon, tiger prawns, iceberg lettuce, cold pasta and cherry tomatoes. A soft granary baguette had been ripped into pieces and buttered. I stared at the mountain of food while Aedan opened a bottle of champagne and poured it into chilled glasses.

'Aedan,' I said. 'I forgot to tell you, I'm allergic to sea food.'

'You're not serious,' he rolled his eyes to the ceiling and I saw his jaw clench.

'Yeah, gotcha!' I grabbed a plate, feeling as if I hadn't eaten for a month. Aedan had obviously spent hours, not to mention a small fortune, preparing this and I wasn't going to waste a morsel.

'I can't believe you did that to me. You little...' This time I was ready for him. I shoved a tomato in his mouth before he could carry on and it was some time before either of us could talk for laughing. A glass of champagne later and I felt as if I didn't have a care in the world. I was in the middle of nowhere with a charming, gorgeous man who thought I was worth quite a lot of effort and I was damned if I'd ruin it with brooding and introspection. We chatted our way through the next hour, finishing off the meal (as if we needed any more) with cherries dipped in melted chocolate.

'You do realise I'm trying to seduce you,' Aedan said, taking advantage of the fact that my mouth was crammed full.

I suppose I could have been a little more coy, but the combination of alcohol and high spirits made me more blunt than usual.

'Well, I didn't think you brought me out here to test my rope knotting skills.'

'I like the new you. Does this version come with a sudden overwhelming desire to wash dishes and mop the deck?'

'No,' I reached out to pick up another cherry but Aedan took my outstretched hand and put it round his neck instead.

'Good,' he whispered, 'because I can think of a much better way to spend what's left of the evening.' I let him push me backwards onto the sofa and tried to move my legs so that we could get more comfortable but the furniture simply wasn't designed for two adults to lie down together. I giggled as Aedan rolled onto his side and ended up with one leg stuck under the table. 'I'm not sure I thought this through properly,' he said, sitting up, by which time I was giggling helplessly. 'Shut up, you. I think what's needed is a tour of the rest of the facilities.'

He pull me up and I followed him to a slim door at the back of the boat. He pushed it open and stood back for me to enter first and get the full effect. It was worth it.

The cabin was finished in polished, almost black, wood with inset lighting and a double bed that fit neatly at the aft, with a window above providing a stunning view of the night sky. The bed was covered with a bronze silk duvet and throw pillows. I felt as if I'd accidentally wandered into somebody else's life.

'Wow. I'm impressed,' I murmured, aware that Aedan was right behind me and watching my reaction.

'Impressed enough to throw all your clothes on the floor and tell me you're willing to fulfill my every fantasy?'

'Sorry, not quite although it was worth a try.'

'I'm so pleased you said that. It wouldn't be any fun if you didn't put up a bit of a fight.' With that, he picked me up and dropped me in the middle of the bed then sat on top of me, already half way through unbuttoning his own shirt.

'You don't waste any time, do you?'

'You're not wrong. It's taken me long enough to get you here; if you think I'm giving you the opportunity to change your mind, you're seriously deluded.' His torso was lean from the gym and weathered from days on the yacht. I ran my hand across his chest and he stopped joking around for a moment, staring at my face.

Slowly he moved to one side of me and lay propped up on one elbow. He undid the wrap top I was wearing and I sat up enough for him to slide it down my shoulders.

'Turn over,' he said softly. I shifted onto my stomach and lay my head on a pillow. Aedan began to push his thumbs into the base of my neck and then rubbed down into my shoulders. Just as it was all going so well, he'd reminded me of James and the night we spent together. He must have felt the muscles in my neck tense up. As I was about to ask him to stop, he ran his fingers up the sides of my neck and into my hair. Starting with his thumb and forefinger pinched together, a couple of inches above my hair line, he ran his nails apart towards the sides of my head. The result was electrifying. Whatever nerve he'd hit pulsated down my spine and straight into my crotch. Any thoughts I had of calling a halt were gone. He pulled his nails back together along the same path and the sensation was like sinking. When he moved over the top of me and ran his tongue down my back I was shuddering with the effort of trying to disguise how turned on I was.

He slid one hand under my stomach, popped the button on my jeans then unzipped them and began to pull them off. For one awful moment I thought this was going to turn into one of those embarrassing stuck clothing moments, but Aedan was more practised at removing difficult clothes than I'd appreciated. In just seconds they were lying in a crumpled heap on the floor next to his and when I tried to turn over he whispered a husky 'no' in my ear and lay on top of me completely, just taking enough of his own weight that I could breathe easily.

My bra was gone without me even feeling it and one of Aedan's hands was underneath my torso, rubbing one nipple whilst he ran the other beneath my hips to slide in between my legs. I could feel how hard he was through his jeans, pressing into me. It was dangerously erotic, the sensation of being unable to move, having no choice but to wait and see what would happen. In any other circumstances it would be terrifying. Here, with this incredibly sexy man, it was like a masterclass in sensualism.

He trailed his lips down to the base of my spine and started to draw tiny circles with his tongue, hooking a finger under the side of my knickers and pulling them off in one move. He pushed a knee between my legs and moved to kneel at the end of the bed, licking the inside of one thigh and moving slowly, unstoppably upwards. I gasped at where this was going and pushed up on my elbows to call a time out.

Instead of stopping, Aedan was up on his knees before I could speak. Where I'd raised my body, he met my hips with his own and pushed himself into me in a breathtaking maneouvre that he couldn't have orchestrated better. I cried out, put one hand on the head board and closed my eyes. Aedan was thrusting into me, grinding with a steady rhythm and then he ran his nails hard down my spine so that I arched my back fully and he pushed harder and faster.

Finally he pulled me upright again and then matched his plunging with the movement of his fingers on my clitoris. Suddenly I exploded into an orgasm so powerful it felt like every muscle was seizing. My body spasmed against his hard enough that he had to brace us both from flying backwards and then he was with me, lost in his own world until we fell together in a crumpled heap across the bed.

After a few minutes getting our breath back, Aedan sat up and leaned over to kiss me.

'Well, that wasn't a bad start to the evening. Would you like coffee or shall we skip the refreshments and just do that again?'

'Milk, no sugar, please. I'd like to get the use of my legs back before morning, as tempting as the offer of a repeat performance is.' Aedan disappeared off to the galley while I recovered in the bathroom. I looked in the mirror and wondered how I'd ended up here. Aedan wasn't really my type, truth be told; I'd be constantly trying to keep up with him. I gave myself a mental slap and splashed water on my face. Aedan was intelligent, funny and here. Wishing for someone long gone was futile. I went to find my coffee and educate the lovely doctor about the benefits of sleep.

When I awoke the next morning we were already approaching the harbour. Aedan evidently needed fewer hours sleep than I and had showered, dressed and cleared up the chaos we'd left in the dining area. I tried to make myself look less dishevelled and went to the top deck for some fresh air. He grinned as I appeared and kissed me good morning, the sight of him driving the boat in the sunshine a great way to start the day. Once we were safely moored, I packed my bag and got ready to leave. It had been twelve hours I wouldn't forget in a hurry. As I put away my hair brush and perfume, my hand touched the bottle of Zora's blood. I'd forgotten all about it last night. Now I had to find a way to explain it to Aedan. He came in with coffee just as I was contemplating how much to tell him.

'What's that?' he asked. He took the vial from my hand and I figured the best thing would be to keep it brief.

'It's the blood sample I told you about.'

'Alright. What am I checking for?'

'Anything. Viruses, bacterial infections, organ failure I suppose.'

'Tell me what her symptoms are.' He was being remarkably easy on me. In his position I'd have had a lot more questions. 'By the way, I'll have to put your name on this, I can't just send it in marked Jane Doe.'

'I understand. She started off with chronic headaches, fever, then she developed diarrhoea and vomiting. Now she's very weak, sleeping a lot, her pulse is irregular. She's barely eating and is even bringing plain water back up. Her nails have got whitish spots under them and her eyes look dark and sunken. That's all I saw.'

'No other tests have been done yet?' I shook my head. 'And she won't get medical help?'

'No,' I answered, not meeting his eyes. If only Zora had the opportunity to see a doctor.

'Fine, but you need to think about what you'll do with the results. If she needs hospital treatment, and from what you've told me that seems likely, then sooner or later you're going to have to persuade your friend to accept help.' He pulled out his mobile, punched a couple of buttons and spoke into it without pausing. 'Cat, I'm bringing in a sample for you to send off, please, labelled Eve MacKenzie. I want a full blood count, viral serology, erythrocyte sedimentation rate, C Reactive Protein and Thyroid function tests, M, C and S as well as a toxicology screen.' He put the phone back into his pocket without missing a beat.

'And I thought lawyers were good with jargon,' I said. 'Thank you. I owe you a huge favour.' He put an arm round my waist and tilted my head back.

'I would suggest you pay it off right now but I'd better get you home before Sabina sends out the troops.' He glanced down at his watch. 'Not to mention the fact that if I'm not in surgery two hours from now Mrs. Breamore won't get her new knee.'

'Well, come on then. Can't keep Mrs. Breamore waiting!' We walked off the yacht hand in hand and I refused to be sucked into the guilt that kept nudging the back of my mind. Aedan was good for me. Time to move on, I repeated to myself. We got back to the ranch in about half the time of last night's journey, courtesy of Aedan's lack of respect for road laws and I insisted he drop me in the parking area and go straight off. I needed the few minutes walk back to my house to get my head straight before I saw Naomi. If I were lucky, I'd be able to sneak in and climb into a bath before anyone could recognise the telltale signs of too little sleep and too much action.

I was just settling into water almost hot enough to scald, with bubbles going everywhere, when Xander burst into my en suite.

'Xander, I'm in the bath!'

'Uh huh. I'm all packed. Sabina's booked us into a suite at The Clift, can you believe it? Two nights, she's paying. Boy, am I glad I made friends with you! We're leaving in precisely fifty-five minutes. And you'd best wash your hair whilst you're in there, you look like you went a few rounds with a grizzly this morning.'

'Would you get out of my bathroom, seriously, you may not be interested in looking at women's bodies but that doesn't mean it's okay from my end.'

'Oh, get over yourself. Where were you anyway? I've been trying to figure out what I should take to wear in the evenings.'

'I was with Aedan in Monterey. You need one pair of good jeans and one pair of smart trousers in case we go to a grown-up restaurant. And don't take the leather ones this time, I'm not spending another night with you cutting off your blood supply just to look cool.'

'Aedan's flat is in Carmel. What were you doing in Monterey?' I should have noticed the sudden pique of interest but I was too busy thinking about what to pack.

'He has a yacht moored there. The Lady Luck.' I said. Xander let out a squeal that a fourteen year old girl would have been proud of.

'And did the lady get lucky? You did, didn't you? I mean, seriously, a night on a yacht with the delicious doctor. Who wouldn't succumb?'

'Last chance, get out right now or I shall tell Sabina that you ended up dancing on the bar the last time I stayed at a hotel with you. I'm sure that'll get her cancelling bookings at The Clift pretty quickly.'

'Bitch.'

'Out!' I yelled.

'Love you.' I sank my head under the water. There was no point arguing with Xander, partly because he would believe what he wanted to believe, but mainly because I was too tired. He was right about the state of my hair though, so I gave it a quick wash and climbed out of the bath to dress. A couple of days away with Naomi and Xander was exactly what I needed. I wanted to catch up on how Naomi was doing and I certainly hadn't been supportive enough since we'd left England. I was worried about her. She'd stopped talking about Tim and it was if she'd pushed everything so deep inside that she could pretend it hadn't happened. I didn't blame her for that, but I was hoping the trip would give me an opportunity to get her to open up. In true Sabina style, it had all been organised so that I didn't have to think about anything except getting myself to the car. An hour later and I was packed and ready to go.

Thirteen

San Francisco manages to bustle without overwhelming, and excite without exhausting. The city prides itself on a laid back, friendly attitude that I really admired. Under any other circumstances Naomi would have fallen in love with the place straight away but on this trip I'd settle for the city just taking her mind off the sharp end of her grief. She and Xander had obviously spent time planning which shops to visit and I happily let them make all the decisions.

The Clift is a study in opulence and I thought we'd never get Xander out of the beautiful suite Sabina had so generously booked for us. The fact that it's right on Union Square helped considerably with the shopping, as at least we could pop back every now and then to drop off bags. We headed straight for Westfield, an enormous shopping centre which could keep you happy for quite a long time if a state of emergency were declared and you got stuck in there. Naomi and I had to physically remove Xander from a super trendy men's clothing store, but not before he had 'accidentally' dropped his mobile number at the feet of one of the male models adorning the place.

We had lunch on Chestnut Street where Naomi and I felt much more at home, with its smaller, more relaxed shops and fabulous deli counters. In the afternoon we did what all self-respecting tourists should and had a nap before heading out for the evening. We were walking through China Town when Xander's mobile started ringing. To his delight, the sales assistant he'd admired had decided to call and Xander was lost to us for the evening. We made him promise to be back at the hotel by midnight, although privately I suspected there was no chance of that, then waved him off to a bar on Geary Street. Naomi and I wandered around looking for a good place to eat and soon found an Italian restaurant that looked warm and welcoming. We ordered without delay and settled down to our favourite pastime of people watching.

After a while I had to break the silence and bring up the subject she'd been almost expertly avoiding.

'How you holding up?' I asked. She didn't answer straight away, thinking about the question as she sipped her wine.

'I don't know,' she said. 'Sometimes it's all so unreal that I feel as if it didn't happen. I wake up and forget he's dead, then I'll look at my watch and think that there's no point getting up because I don't have to be anywhere. Those moments are almost worse than when I think about it all the time, because for a few minutes everything's normal. I miss him and this is going to sound awful but there are still other things on my mind that seem so selfish.' She was quiet for a moment so I prompted her.

'Like what?'

'It's just that you wonder if you have a future; if you'll ever find anyone else, if life can be as good again or if you're jinxed forever. Sounds stupid, doesn't it? I just can't see how there can be another person out there who'll make me feel the way Tim did. I can't imagine getting married again, the concept of having sex with anyone else is bizarre and then I think what a waste it all is, and how I should just be grateful I'm alive.' She finished on a half sob and I reached across the table to hold her hand.

'There are no answers for those questions, not yet anyway. The important thing to remember is that you don't have to do anything, or move on or make plans for the future until you're ready. You can't bring Tim back but you also can't punish yourself for being alive.'

'Neither can you. This isn't your fault. I was too hard on you back in London and I'm sorry. I don't know what I'd do without you.' She forced a change of topic. 'So what's happening with Aedan?'

'Nothing, just dating, you know.' This wasn't the right time to start dishing the dirt on my new sex life especially as I wasn't quite sure how I felt about it yet. 'But Zora's ill and nothing they do seems to be making her any better.'

'Did you see her?' I nodded. 'And your mother?'

'Yes.' I knew what she was going to ask before she spoke, not because of some super sixth sense, but because it's exactly what I would have asked.

'Did you find out what those things were that killed Tim?'

'They provide mercenary services to the Perelesnyk. In return, the incubi let them feed off the bodies of their human victims once they've finished with them. You don't need to hear this.'

'Yes, I do,' she said. 'I need to know exactly what we're dealing with because you're still in danger, which means that Sabina is too.'

'So maybe it would be best if you went back to London.' It pained me to say it, but I couldn't bear the thought of Naomi being hurt any further.

'You need me and the truth is I need you. Here, I can worry about you and Sabina and that gives me a reason to keep going. If there's a fight then I'd rather be with you, in the middle of it, whatever the cost. Don't worry about me. It's oddly liberating when you feel you've lost everything that matters to you.'

I picked up my glass and thought of Bryn. 'To those we've loved and lost,' I said.

'Tim and James,' said Naomi and we drained our glasses.

I was right about Xander. He didn't reappear until four in the morning, not that I'd have known it if he hadn't woken me up to tell me all about his new friend, Lincoln, and the amazing adventures of their first date. I sent him to bed, still talking, and knew we wouldn't be spending much of the next day in his company.

With Xander out of the picture, Naomi and I did the Golden Gate Bridge in the morning and a chilling trip to Alcatraz Island in the afternoon. As I listened to the audio guide describing the most notorious prisoners and the horrific things that happened there, I found I was practically seeing the long-dead inmates appearing around me. It made me think of Naomi on the phone describing Tim's murder and how the whole scene had played out in my head with full colour and sound. I made my excuses to skip the remainder of the tour and, after a few minutes, Naomi came to check what was wrong. I reassured her, but we both felt the afternoon had taken a downturn. With hindsight, Alcatraz probably wasn't the best place to have gone. Naomi suggested we go and find ourselves new evening dresses. It wasn't something I'd planned to buy but I wasn't going to say no to Naomi when she was making such an effort to be upbeat and as I was supposed to be attending a formal dinner with Aedan next month, I had enough of an excuse to go a bit crazy. We spent two hours going around the monumental stores in Union Square before Naomi found a strapless silver dress with a sweeping skirt. I fell in love with a deep sea green satin dress, with a beaded halter neck and a split up to mid thigh on one side. I wasn't sure I'd ever have the nerve to wear it, but I wasn't going to leave it in the store for someone else, even if all I did was stare at it in my wardrobe occasionally.

We lost Xander to Lincoln again that evening so Naomi and I went to the cinema, ate popcorn and got an early night. The next morning we all went to one of San Francisco's fabulous spas for facials, waxing, and anything else we could have done in four hours. After that, Naomi surprised me with a hair appointment in the sort of celebrity salon I'd never have had the courage to enter alone. She and Xander watched as I was snipped and curled into a very nineteen-fifties style.

'I thought it would be a nice treat for your birthday,' she said. 'Do you like it?'

I gasped, feeling like an idiot. 'I didn't even know what today's date was, I've lost track of everything so badly,' I said. 'And yes, I adore it. It's a shame we're going back to the ranch instead of having another night here. Thank you honey, what a lovely thing to have organised.' I kissed her and she hugged me for a long time.

'Come along you two, our car is waiting!' Xander called us back to reality. Sabina's driver had already picked up our bags from The Clift. After escaping the city traffic, we moved fairly quickly down the coast and before I knew it we were on our way into Carmel. My mobile rang when we were a few miles outside town. It was Sabina.

'Darling, are you nearly back? Only a few of my old friends have popped round and I was telling them all about you. Anyway, they have deep pockets and a love of drama and I was hoping to persuade them to invest. Could you put something glamorous on and come straight to mine for a black tie dinner, sorry to ruin the end of your weekend away. Do bring Naomi and Xander, naturally.' I couldn't refuse Sabina's request after she'd just funded our fantastic weekend away but the only thing I had that even vaguely fitted the bill was my new green dress.

'Well, you needed an excuse to wear it,' said Xander. 'And I already look amazing so I don't need to change.' He made the driver pull the car over and Naomi and I looked at each other as if he were mad. 'Oh, get your clothes off, for goodness' sake.' We grabbed our bags and, in the confined space, did our best to climb into our new outfits to impress Sabina's guests. I have to admit, when I looked in the mirror and saw the combination with my new hair style, I was pleased. Even Xander was forced into a whistle when Naomi and I finally gave him permission to turn round.

With that, we arrived at the ranch. I could see an impressive array of cars and wondered just how much funding Sabina was trying to secure. Naomi and Xander went ahead as I negotiated the driveway without breaking my ankle or ripping my dress. We went straight in through Sabina's front door but I couldn't hear anything at all. The lights were off and there was no sign of life. My heart rose in my throat and immediately my palms were slick with sweat. I knew it couldn't last; there was no way Perun was going to leave me or the people I loved alone until he had punished me properly for what I'd done to him. I pushed between Naomi and Xander, moving as fast as I could given what I was wearing. In the lounge, at the back of the house there was still nothing, everyone had simply vanished.

I shoved the doors to the back porch open and strode out into the open air and as I did so flood lights came on, streaming directly into my eyes.

'Surprise!' When my vision recovered, I saw a sea of people on the grassland at the back of the house, backlit from a huge marquee. Naomi was right behind me with an arm round my waist and Xander was jumping up and down on my other side. A band I couldn't even see started to play Happy Birthday and I had to stop myself from sinking to the floor, my legs were shaking so badly. Sabina walked up the porch steps to kiss me.

'Happy Birthday, my darling Eve,' she said. 'Did you suspect?'

'No, not this, anyway.' I hugged her and accepted the cocktail a passing waiter was offering me, swallowing the glassful in one gulp.

Sabina took my arm to walk me down into the crowd and at once I was surrounded by people wishing me well. I saw Aedan from the corner of my eye. He didn't come straight over, just stood where he was and raised his glass, looking me up and down appreciatively. I guess it was a bit of a change from my regular jeans and shirt. I winked at him and did an impromptu twirl to show off my new look. That made him come over, and the kiss he gave me couldn't have left anyone in any doubt that we were very much together.

'Now you're pleased I made you buy the dress, aren't you?' whispered Naomi as she walked past. Feeling more relaxed with Aedan there to hold on to, I had a proper look around. All the staff from the Pacific Repertory company were there, as were my fellow actors and the regular benefactors. Everyone from the ranch was dressed in their finest, as were numerous friends of Sabina's and a variety of people I was getting to know who lived in and around Carmel. Inside the marquee was a large seating area where people could eat, drink and socialise and in a separate section the band were encouraging people to dance. I couldn't believe Sabina had managed to organise all this without me knowing a thing and I was even more impressed by the fact that Xander had managed not to let anything slip for the whole time we were away. A gentle cough behind me announced a new person waiting to say hello. When I turned, I couldn't believe my eyes. Bryn stood, obviously uncomfortable in his dinner jacket but beaming from ear to ear.

'Bryn!' I threw my arms around his neck, overwhelmed that he had come so far for me. 'It's so good to see you.'

'Miss Sabina suggested it when we spoke after you left London. She'd been planning this for months, apparently. Now I understand why you haven't come back to live in England.'

'It's not normally like this, in fact it's never like this. Have you seen Naomi yet? Come on, let's find her.' We circled the party together and I introduced Bryn to everyone we met, then left him with Xander who was determined to get him drunk and extract any gossip about my past life he could.

It was a wonderful party. By the time I was on my third cocktail and Naomi had dragged me to the dance floor, I became quite sentimental watching Sabina in Daniel's arms, swaying gently to the music with him holding her securely and looking at her as if it were the first dance he'd ever had. I gave them both a slightly drunken hug and thanked Sabina several times for throwing me the party of a lifetime. I also told them they were made for each other and that they should make up for all the time they'd lost. Luckily, they were feeling indulgent and decided I was being sweet rather than meddling, and just packed me back off to Aedan. He asked the band to slow things down and they played something suitably smoochy, giving Aedan the perfect excuse to pull me into his arms.

'Looks like you've really settled down here. You've made a lot of friends.'

'I've been so lucky. Between Sabina, the theatre, Naomi and you, Carmel now has everything I need.'

'I'm very glad to hear that,' he said. 'I'm getting used to having you around.' Whilst I wasn't drunk, I certainly wasn't in a fit state to have a conversation about our relationship right then so I opted for putting my head on his shoulder and swaying to the music. By the time the song had ended, the dance floor was crowded and the marquee was heating up. Aedan went to find me a drink and I chatted with a couple of the ranch hands as I waited for him to return. The tent seemed to be getting fuller and the atmosphere was definitely becoming more charged. For a second I wondered if I'd had more alcohol than I'd realised, then noticed some of the people on the dance floor becoming increasingly salacious. The sound of my glass dropping to the floor didn't disturb anyone, the impact softened by the grass beneath the matting and I didn't even flinch as a wave of fruit juice and spirits splashed my beautiful new dress.

I turned three hundred and sixty degrees, counting as I went, seeing more and more of the flawless, unlined and unnaturally beautiful faces of the Perelesnyk entrancing my guests. In this part of the marquee alone, I identified at least thirty of them. The incubi and succubi were working the room and it wouldn't take long for their presence to have its customary hypnotic effect. None of them came towards me and I froze, completely lost as to what to do. I knew that there was more to come; only Perun could have orchestrated an assault on this scale. On the dance floor Xander was the only person looking confused, staring around as if everything had switched into slow motion. He caught my eye and I motioned for him to come over.

'Friends of yours?' he asked, instinctively soft voiced.

'No,' I said, taking him by the arm and putting my mouth next to his ear so that no-one could hear us talking. 'Listen, because I need you to do something really important. Find Naomi and Sabina. Get them to the main house, away from these people and lock all the doors and windows. Better still, if Sabina's driver is still here then get everyone into a car and as far away as possible.'

'Who are they?' he asked.

'You just need to know that they're dangerous and we're out of time,' I said. Of course, the succubi held no thrall over Xander, and the incubi were only interested in the women. 'I promise I'll explain everything later, now for my sake, please, just get yourself and the others safe.' Xander nodded without speaking and I could see how scared he was. He may not have known what they were but he could feel just how wrong everything was. I saw him walk behind the band who were playing unnaturally slowly, watching some of the succubi dance before them. Xander pulled some pegs out of the ground and ducked under the canvas. I made my way through the crowd to the other part of the tent and although a few of the Perelesnyk raised their eyes to watch, none spoke to me or tried to stop me. My heart was thumping in my chest and I felt nauseous with fear. If they had come here in such numbers, in the open, then they meant to do harm. Fighting them was not an option, I knew. I had to find out exactly what they wanted. If it was me, then they could have me, no-one else was going to get hurt because of what I'd done.

In the other room the scene was much more shocking; they'd obviously been here for longer. They were everywhere, some already pushing people down onto tables, and seduction was much too romantic a word for what they were doing. It was as if everyone had been drugged, inhibitions were long since lost and I didn't think it would be many minutes before it turned into a debauched orgy. As I walked past an incubus who had an actress I vaguely recognised sitting on his lap, he slid his hand up my thigh. I grabbed his wrist, snarling instinctively and when he raised his eyes to see who I was, he pulled his hand out of mine as if he'd been burned. They weren't going to touch me and that was all the confirmation I needed that they were waiting for Perun to arrive. He enjoyed making an entrance and I knew he'd want the carnage to be at its height before he stepped in. As much as I wanted to go and check on my friends, it occurred to me that going to them would only increase their vulnerability. Aedan was nowhere in sight and that was exactly how I wanted it. There was nothing to be gained by waiting for Perun to have the advantage so I decided to take the fight to him. I buried my fear as deep as I could and grabbed an empty wine bottle, winding a napkin round my hand and smashing the glass on the edge of table. I found the nearest succubus, kicked away the man on the floor between her knees, tightened my left arm round her neck and pressed the broken end of the bottle into her throat hard enough to let everyone know I meant business.

Blood trickled down her smooth, white skin and, although she was startled, I knew the puncture would heal without so much as a scar.

'Where's Perun?' I hissed into her ear. She said nothing but smiled lasciviously at the man I'd shoved away from her. With one hand she pulled her tunic up to her waist to display her nakedness in all its glory, parting her legs wide and leaving no one in any doubt what was on offer. Instantly at least four men barged past me, pushing me away from her. I had no choice but to release both the succubus and the bottle before someone innocent ended up badly hurt. I could hear her laughing as they carried her off to finish what she'd started.

Bodies were writhing, naked, fighting each other to be next with the demons and I was powerless to control the situation. All I could do was find the people I needed to protect and get them away from the ranch. I changed tactics, determined to get to Naomi before they did and ran into a hard, tall body whose vice-like arms wrapped themselves around me as if greeting a long-lost lover.

'Beautiful, isn't it? Humans are just animals after all, controlled by their most base desires. And yet they call *us* demons. How are you, my beautiful Eve?'

I wanted to be unafraid; I wanted to say something clever, to make him feel insignificant. But he wasn't. 'Tell me what you want Perun, you don't need to hurt these people. You win, now make it stop.'

'Say please,' he mouthed, leaning down over me.

'Please,' I sobbed.

He ran a hand up my back and into my hair, grabbing a handful and whipping me round. He held me in a way designed to hurt and control me, moving my head back and forth to get a good look around the room.

'But no one is being hurt here. From what I can see, they are all enjoying themselves, except you of course. I have always loved California, it attracts the young and beautiful; they produce by far the best off-spring. You really are not entering into the spirit of this, are you?' I didn't have to answer, he shook my head left and right for me as if I were saying no but got bored with the charade quickly enough, pushed me to my knees and I stayed there, not stupid or brave enough to get up. He stood directly in front of me and put one hand across my throat, squeezing persistently but not so hard as to make me lose consciousness.

'Remember this, Eve. Understand what I can do to you and the people you love. The only reason I am not taking your life is because, unlike you, I actually want peace in Manitu. My problem is that I know you were there last week. Did you think we wouldn't be able to follow you? I thought you'd have known better after the death of your lover but apparently you need to be taught another lesson. Well, here I am, in person, so that we can talk face to face. I hope you appreciate the effort I'm making for you.' He released my throat and tossed me backwards onto the ground where I lay gasping. Even in my terror, I realised he still believed the man killed by the Moroi was James and I wasn't going to disabuse him of it.

Perun sat on the floor next to me, looking down at me as if he were considering whether to kiss me or kill me and I didn't move a muscle. 'If I kill you, it will start a war in my world that will take an age to burn out, so I've come to warn you. Your time in Manitu is over. If you try to intervene again I will come back and find these pathetic people you surround yourself with and, one by one, I will destroy them. You may be strong in the midst of your true family in Manitu, but in the human world you are nothing. You know you cannot stop me here.' He barked out an order in a language I didn't understand and the marquee doors were pulled aside as Sabina was dragged in by two Moroi. They were freakish, human in size and stance but animal in every other way. They were restraining Sabina but at the same time sniffing her, licking at her throat and clearly getting excited by the sight of the vein pulsing in her neck. When one of them extended his claws I screamed and did the only thing I could. I threw myself towards Perun, pleading to him with every ounce of humility and desperation I could find, to spare the woman I'd grown to love.

'It's over, I promise. No more, I'll stay away. Please don't hurt her; I'll do whatever you say. You're right, I can't fight you and I don't want to. I just want this to stop.'

He stroked my back as if he were soothing a young child and it made me cringe.

'That's better. It seems you are beginning to see sense.' I felt a fraction of hope return. Perhaps this could all end without bloodshed. Then a boot kicked out hard and smashed into the side of Perun's head without warning. I looked up to see Aedan's hand reaching out for me and then Perun was up on his feet, one hand raised to keep his fellow demons out of it and sizing up the man who had just dared to attack him.

'Get your filthy hands off her,' Aedan said, almost growling. Perun took his time dusting himself off.

'It didn't take you long to replace the last one, did it?' He turned his back on Aedan and then pulled me next to him. Close in, so that I was the only one who would hear, he whispered into my ear. 'He'll be the first to go.'

To the Moroi holding Sabina, he said, 'Give her something to keep her busy while we're leaving.' Before I could speak a talon shot out across Sabina's cheek leaving a bloody gash. When they released her, I marvelled at how she would not be drawn into crying out. As Perun moved, the other Perelesnyk began to extricate themselves from the humans pawing at them, and followed him. Perun paused briefly as he passed Aedan, sizing him up and I was terrified he would strike a blow but instead he reached out a hand and gently stroked Aedan's cheek. Aedan slapped the hand away and stepped forward threatening violence again so I grabbed his arm and pulled him back. Perun just laughed and walked out. When I was sure he'd gone I put an arm round Sabina's shoulders and looked at the cut on her cheek.

'Let me see,' said Aedan.

'No, I can deal with this, it just needs a cloth. You make sure no one else is hurt and tell everyone to go home. Meet me in the main house.' As I led Sabina out of the marquee, people everywhere were looking as if they were waking from dreams, startled to find themselves half naked or lying on the ground. Xander threw the door open as we got to the top of the steps.

I sat her down and looked at the wound. It was long and deep but the gash hadn't gone full depth through to the inside of her mouth. I put my hand over it and tried to calm myself. I could feel her pulse inside my head and slowly the blood flow from her cheek lessened. Naomi sat beside Sabina and held her hand while I did my best to heal her so that she would be left without a scar. It took a few minutes before I could concentrate enough to make a real difference but when I felt Sabina relax, I knew her pain had gone.

Daniel ran in from the porch, bursting through us to take Sabina in his arms. The Vilya are healers and I knew I could put right this relatively minor injury. What I wouldn't be able to mend was the emotional damage. Naomi sat staring at her hands and even Xander was silent as we considered how to start the inevitable conversation. We were saved the trouble of finding the answer.

'The stables are on fire,' shouted one of the ranch hands from outside. I looked to the far end of the paddocks and could see a deep orange glow, the smoke a distant haze rising in the night sky. I kicked off my shoes and started to run as fast as I could through the meadows towards the stable block where all Sabina's beloved horses had been secured for the night. There were others ahead of me and Daniel was on the phone to call the fire fighters but there was no way they could get here quickly enough to make a difference. By the time I reached the outside of the block, someone had unbolted the first of the stalls and as the frenzied animals were freed, they stampeded out towards the fresh air. Smoke filled my lungs and my eyes were streaming. The sickening stench of burning meat filled the air and I could hear the unmistakable sound of an animal crazed with pain and panic. I tried to run towards it, unable to leave any animal to burn alive but within seconds I couldn't see or hear anything. Suddenly someone had hold of my arm, hauling me out before the roof collapsed. We moved away a safe distance. The horses had scattered, but those we could see were unharmed. It was impossible to do a head count in the dark so we concentrated on getting them together into a paddock for the rest of the night. By the time the fire trucks arrived, all anyone cared about was preventing the spread of the fire and no-one questioned the state the guests were in. There was a flurry of checking that people were accounted for and reclaiming coats and keys. After that, they all drifted away, cabs arrived to take people home and lifts were offered by those in a fit state to drive.

The fire had filled two functions perfectly; it distracted everyone from the events of the evening, and I knew that most of the guests would have little memory of the evening, but for me it served as a final warning. It wouldn't take Perun an assault with a legion of demons to destroy me. All he needed was one match. I went to gather the people I loved around me and do the one thing that would put them out of harm's way forever.

Fourteen

I reassured Aedan that we were all fine and sent him home. He didn't ask a single question about what he'd seen and whilst I anticipated some sort of aftermath, now wasn't the time to deal with it. For the next two hours I was holed up with Sabina, Naomi, Bryn and Xander answering their questions about what had happened. Naomi knew most of it already and Sabina had lived with Adela long enough not to have been surprised by very much, especially having translated the diaries for me. Xander looked like a rabbit trapped in headlights, hardly speaking or moving during the conversation. Bryn was completely silent and I recognised him assessing the situation and giving himself the time to reach a careful conclusion. I was more nervous about him than anyone else. He knew that the information we'd given him about Tim's murder was less than the whole truth, but Bryn was the single most practical man I'd ever met. I wasn't sure how he'd deal with being asked to believe in things beyond the limits of most imaginations. When they'd exhausted themselves with questions, I suggested that they go to bed and sleep on it for the night. I could feel that the danger was over for now; Perun had made his point. Bryn was staying in the main house with Sabina and Daniel; Xander would stay with Naomi and me. On the way back, Naomi asked why the guests hadn't seemed more outraged by what they'd been through.

'I think that when people are faced with things they don't understand or don't believe are possible, they just shut down. Given how many people joined in, I suspect they're happy to consider it an alcohol induced hallucination. The way the Perelesnyk hypnotise you, I should think that's easy to do.'

'And Aedan?' Naomi added, quietly. 'Will he buy that, do you think?'

'I don't know,' I replied. We walked the last few steps in silence and I gave Xander my bed, telling him I'd share with Naomi. He disappeared off without an argument and I suspected that by tomorrow morning he would bounce out of bed and disappear home as if none of this had happened. Xander was a survivor and he'd do whatever was necessary to keep his world intact. Good for him. I wished I was free to do the same. I waited until Naomi was in bed then wrote her a note. I knew what I needed to do the second I'd seen the barn on fire, but my friends had deserved an explanation and that had to come first. I picked up a pen and scribbled as fast as I could.

'Naomi, forgive me for disappearing without telling you in person but this way is safest for you. I'm going away for a couple of days. It's vital that no-one knows I've gone. You should stay indoors as much as possible, put my bedroom light on and off and behave as normally as you can. Tell everyone I've got a virus and that I'm staying in bed, whatever you can come up with. I promise to be careful but I need to put an end to this. I'll take my mobile but I won't switch it on until I'm on my way home. Look after Sabina for me. Love you, Eve.'

I put it in an envelope, laying it gently next to her on the pillow so she'd see it first thing then changed into more sensible clothes for travelling. Perun would not have been careless enough to leave without having me watched, and sneaking out of the window like a teenager on a forbidden date wasn't going to be enough to avoid detection. I'd spent the last few months refusing to acknowledge the non-human aspects of my character. Now I needed to switch them back on if I wanted any chance of getting away from the ranch unnoticed.

With my backpack full of emergency supplies, wearing dark clothes with my hair tied in a black scarf, I sat on my kitchen floor with the lights off so there was no chance my silhouette would show. In my mind I reran the events of that evening like a film. I conjured up every tiny detail I could in my imagination; the sounds, the fear, the horror of seeing that monster slash Sabina's face. This time, unlike before, I felt the storm start to grow from inside me. I let go of my repulsion of the Perelesnyk and embraced the small part of myself that I'd inherited from

103

them. I thought of the destruction they'd brought and their unremitting desire to conquer. I thought of the way they used other, lesser races, to do their killing as they had with Tim and Ellette. Fury spilled out of me and I heard the wind buffeting the sides of the house. I saw Naomi's face when she'd been so sad and brave in San Francisco, so broken that no amount of fear could make her run anymore. Rain was pelting down now, the atmosphere had turned icy and I knew the visibility outside was dropping. With one last push I shoved my memory towards Zora and how I'd felt, seeing her ashen face. It was enough to cause a tree to crash in the woods outside and there wasn't going to be a better moment than this to run. Whoever was out there watching had to be seeking shelter now. I crawled from the kitchen to the other end of the house and opened a window just wide enough to climb through, grateful that I didn't need to worry about being overheard amidst the din.

I crawled out, shutting the window behind me and pulling my backpack on as I ran. I sprinted across the open lane towards Sabina's, barely able to see my own feet splashing in the water on the path. Once there, I unlocked the kitchen door and let myself in, taking the key to the jeep Sabina was lending Naomi as I went through the house. The car was out front so I didn't have to open the garage before I could get going. I turned the engine over and started down the driveway without lights or revving. It was a painful few minutes but at last I felt able to put my foot on the gas and move faster. The headlights, though, I didn't dare switch on until I was several miles away, steering by occasionally hitting the verge and shifting back towards the centre of the road.

As I neared the outskirts of Carmel I was calmer but I couldn't stop for fuel or rest until it was absolutely vital. Three hours later I figured out that I was going to crash if I didn't sleep. I stopped at Redding, parking my car in the busiest lot I could find, dragged myself onto the back seat, pulled over a blanket and fell into oblivion. Fours hours after that I awoke to sunlight streaming through the windows, pain in my shoulders and a couple having a row outside. I had to wait without moving until they'd settled their differences and climbed into their own car. Now that it was light I had to be even more careful. I took dark glasses out of my bag, made sure my scarf was still covering my hair and set off again, the only luxury I afforded myself a drive thru breakfast and coffee. I had about another two hours to go and I was running out of energy fast.

It was already ten o'clock when I arrived at Tulelake. The plan was to get back to my mother but I couldn't risk retracing my steps from Little Medicine Lake, the way I'd gone with Serenta. This time, the town I'd chosen was further north and I'd have to travel south to the lava tubes. I hired a mountain bike then drove with it as far into the preservation area as I could go. I parked the jeep, left everything but the essentials and set off with my compass and a map of the parklands. The bike wasn't my preferred means of travelling but it was all I could find to get across country faster than on foot. My muscles were unused to cycling and it wasn't long before I was sore and tired. As I rode, I thought about Serenta and Anton, my half brother who I hadn't yet had the chance to get to know. I pictured Anousk in my mind and tried to call out to her but felt nothing. I rode south as far as I could until the bike was useless on the woody trails. By the time I ditched it, I'd lost my bearings on the map and was wandering blind. I stopped to fill my canteen with water from a stream, then found a high peak and stopped.

Alone, for the first time, I had to find a way into Manitu that wouldn't call too much attention to my presence. The fact that Perun knew I'd been here before meant that they were roughly aware of where the Vilya were living, although I doubted they'd be bold enough to attack the lava tunnels. Once I had rested enough I tried sprinting, as I had with Serenta, but I was too down trodden to spark enough adrenaline. I stopped running around, hoping suddenly that no other hikers had wandered along and seen me or they'd be making some fairly nervous calls to the authorities by now. I lay on the ground on my back and watched the light fading from the sky. I thought of Adela's diary and pictured my mother stroking my face as she held me, Adela watching on, knowing what it was for a mother to stare at her baby as if the rest of the world did not exist. I felt myself falling asleep and didn't fight it. Either the Vilya would find me or nature would resolve the situation another way.

I thought I was still dreaming, feeling a soft hand stroking my cheek and saying my name as I struggled to open my eyes. When I was fully conscious, I saw Serenta next to me and others with her were lighting a fire. I was shivering and so stiff it was an effort to move at all. They'd put a cover over me but even so, I could barely feel my legs. When the fire got going Serenta helped me sit up and move closer to it. I huddled into her while they fed more wood to the flames and heated water over the top to make a fruit tea. By the time I'd sipped a cup of it, I felt strong enough to speak.

'I have to see Anousk,' I said.

'She's on her way already,' answered Serenta, feeling my hands to see if I was warming up.

'Aren't we going to the lava tubes?' I couldn't get rid of the chill that had invaded my body and moved even closer to the fire.

'It's too dangerous. We know the Perelesnyk are watching this area. Every time we enter or leave there is more chance they will find us. It's better not to take you there.' I felt Anousk getting nearer even before I heard her horse approaching. I tried to stand and greet her but I wasn't up to that yet. She smiled at me and seated herself at the opposite side of the fire.

'Eve, you have taken a terrible risk. You would have died out here if Serenta had not found you when she did. I was not expecting to see you again so soon, daughter.' I told her through chattering teeth about the party and the invasion by Perun and the Moroi. When I finished speaking she waited, knowing I had come to say something more.

'I am glad you are unharmed. Zora is no better, fading we think. Perhaps when Manitu takes her to the last sleep, the Perelesnyk will feel they have won a victory that can stop this madness.'

'I won't wait for that to happen,' I said. 'I came here to tell you to cede the rulership. I only accepted it because I thought it would stop Zora from being cast out. Now she is ill, the Vilya are hiding underground and the lives of everyone I love are under threat. I want you to call the Council together and announce that the Perelesnyk can ascend to the throne for the remainder of the

Vilya's time and their own after that, if that's what must happen. The price everyone has paid is too high. I can't let it continue.'

'Then they will win, through murdering and threatening and bullying. Isn't that what you stood against when you came here?' Anousk asked gently.

'I cannot let anyone else get hurt, mother. It sickens me to give in but I don't see how we can fight them anymore, not here and not in my world.'

'I do not seek to dissuade you, child, only to make you understand that the Vilya are warriors. We will do all we can to keep Perun's evil at bay.'

'It's too late. Whether we admit it or not, he has won,' I said, unable to keep the bitterness out of my voice.

'Then so be it. I shall send messages out to the Council members to convene. It will take some time for them all to assemble. It is harder to travel in Manitu, as dangerous as it is at the moment.'

'How long?' I asked, having thought stupidly that it would be simple, that I could just turn up and instantly put things right.

'Perhaps ten days,' she said. 'I will need to send an envoy on behalf of the Vilya. I cannot leave Zora in her present state. Does this mean I shall not be seeing the daughter I have only just found again?'

'It does,' I answered. This time I was dry eyed. I had finally met my mother and had the chance to speak with her, to get to know her a little. It had to be enough. If I tried to come back, to have more than just this, then everyone I cared about would suffer. Anousk stood.

'I am so proud of you,' she said. We didn't say goodbye. She mounted her horse, nodded at me one last time and rode away. Serenta doused the fire and covered its trace with leaves and twigs. We didn't talk as we had done before. I didn't want to know any more, to have any other memories to obsess over. She helped me onto her horse and I showed her the point on my map where I'd left the car. We rode for an hour until she told me to close my eyes and hold on tight.

'Just concentrate on the movement of the horse,' she said. It was easy, this time, going back through, perhaps because all I wanted was to go home, curl up with Naomi and be safe. The difficult part was done. I'd said my goodbyes and set in train the way to a lasting peace.

'Can I come, as agreed, in case you have news of Zora's illness?' I had forgotten about that. There were still things I could do to help.

'Of course,' I said. 'It won't be me though, I'm not sure I can bear to see you knowing I can't come back again. I'm sorry.'

'I understand,' she said. I described Naomi to her and promised to do all I could to find out what was wrong with Zora. By the time she was galloping off into the distance and I was back in my car, I had been gone from the ranch for a day and a half. I wanted to find a hotel and sleep but there was a limit to how long Naomi would be able to keep everyone from figuring out I was gone. I switched on my mobile but had no signal, so I started the long drive back.

I'd done what Perun wanted. Perhaps now he would leave me alone for good. I was certain he'd be delighted with the price I'd had to pay for it. When the Council met, I hoped Perun meant what he'd said about wanting a resolution in Manitu and that my family could return to the way their lives were before.

Fifteen

I began trying to phone Naomi at the ranch when I hit the outskirts of Carmel. There was no reply and by the time I'd dialled on four occasions the first sparks of concern were starting to fly. I put my foot down, as exhausted as I was and raced home. Once there, I was out of the car in seconds and running into Sabina's lounge. There was no sign of anyone until I bumped into her housekeeper making up the beds. She told me that Sabina had taken Bryn on a sight-seeing tour and suggested I call her mobile. I wasn't going to wait any longer to find Naomi, so I put that idea on hold and went to see why my friend wasn't picking up the phone. The house was locked and there was no answer. Inside I found no sign of a struggle, in fact the place was perfect with fresh flowers arranged as only Naomi can. I relaxed, thinking she must have gone for a ride or walk and made myself some food. I hadn't eaten properly for days and lunch just couldn't wait. Afterwards, I showered and then picked up the phone to check in with Sabina and Bryn. I caught them walking along the beach.

'Sabina, it's Eve.'

'Hello, my darling, are you feeling better? Naomi asked us not to disturb you but we've been worried.'

'I'm fine now, just wondering if you knew where Naomi had gone. I woke up late and she wasn't here.'

'She didn't leave a note? Silly thing. Anyway, you don't need to worry, she went off with Aedan. He called in early this morning to see you, then he and Naomi disappeared off together. I assumed they were running errands.'

That was good news. If Naomi was with Aedan they were probably shopping or lunching. I just wondered what she'd told him about where I was. I rang off and told Sabina and Bryn I'd meet them for supper. It would give me a chance to get everyone together and tell them what I'd done, to reassure them that they were out of danger now. I allowed myself the luxury of a rest for about an hour while I waited for Naomi and Aedan to reappear but all I could see was James' face and, as hard as I tried to push the image away, it just wouldn't go. It was guilt, of course. I'd moved on with Aedan and my emotions were a mess because of the last forty-eight hours. Still, every time I closed my eyes, there he was, calm and quiet as ever. James had a way of making everyone else look like they were rushing around in circles. He had an amazing inner stillness that I was never going to achieve, although when he wrapped his arms around me a tiny bit of it rubbed off for a while. I missed it.

I gave myself a mental shake, determined not to slip into self-pity and reinvent the past. I had to appreciate the here and now or life would pass me by so I reached for the phone again. Speaking to Aedan was a sure fire cure for what I was feeling. His mobile rang several times and I was about to give up when he finally answered. I was babbling before he could get a word in.

'Aedan, it's me. Where on earth are you two? I've been waiting all day. Anyway, I just spoke to Sabina, so if you're free it would be great if we could all eat together tonight. What do you think?' There was an almost imperceptible pause and then I heard a soft squeal in the background. 'Aedan?'

'I think the real question is; where have you been, Eve?' Aedan's voice was different. He sounded cold and strained. Naomi must have told him I'd gone away without leaving the details of where I was going. Fair enough, I'd have been cross, too.

'Look, I'm sorry, I had some things to sort out and I didn't want anyone else involved. I should've told you. I'll make it up to you, okay?'

'I think it's Naomi who's owed the apology, after all, she's the one paying for it, not you.' I hadn't a clue what he was talking about and I definitely wasn't enjoying the way he was speaking to me.

'Fine. You know what, could I just speak to her please? You're obviously not in the mood for this,' I said.

'Of course,' Aedan replied. 'I'm sure she has plenty she wants to say to you.' There was some rustling in the background and I was planning what to say, when my ear piece exploded with the most piercing scream I'd ever heard. I was shouting and shouting for Naomi, clutching the phone hard against my head in spite of the pain it was causing my ears. Even then, I was convinced there was some mistake, a crossed line or an accident, then there was the unmistakable sound of a hard blow against a cheek and the screams became muffled sobbing. The next moment, Aedan was back on the line, cool and entirely in control.

'This is what happens when you lie. You said you wouldn't go back there and what do I find not two whole days after you've made such promises to Perun? That you're gone and Naomi doesn't know where you are, only that you've asked her to make sure no-one finds out. Well, if that's the way you want to play the game it's not a problem, as long as you understand that the stakes have changed. Are you ready for that, Eve? I think you need to see in person what you've done. Why don't you join us for lunch on my yacht? Naomi's thoroughly enjoying her visit, aren't you, sweetheart?'

'If you lay a finger on her, I'll fucking kill you,' I said.

'Really? You think that's going to help at this stage? I thought you were more intelligent than that.'

'Aedan, wait,' I screeched but he'd already cut the connection.

'No!' I screamed. 'No, no, no.' The phone rang again. I grabbed it.

'Aedan, I'm sorry about what I said. Please don't hurt Naomi. I'm coming right now, I can be in Monterey in twenty minutes. Just wait, okay? Wait for me, please,' I was crying and pleading into the phone before I registered that it was Xander's voice yelling at me.

'Eve? What the hell is going on? Eve? Talk to me!'

I couldn't speak, I just held onto the phone, crying and trying to pull myself together. I was running out of time and couldn't afford any detailed explanations.

'Xander, I've got to go. Naomi's in trouble. I'm sorry, don't call anyone else okay? It's too dangerous. Stay away from the ranch while I'm gone.' I dropped the phone, picked up my bike keys and sprinted to the garages. Seconds later, the engine was roaring into life and I was out on the road. I drove faster than I ever have in my life, only slowing for bends and junctions and then not taking enough care. The miles flew by and still it felt like the slowest journey imaginable. I parked the bike as close as I could to the edge of the jetties, hearing it crash to the floor where I hadn't put the stand down properly, but I left it where it fell and ran to the Lady Luck's mooring.

I slowed down as I climbed on board, not wanting to call out as I went in. The galley and dining areas were untouched and everything was completely silent. I walked to the bow cabin first but it was empty. I felt lightheaded and realised I'd been holding my breath since I arrived. Suddenly the door to the aft cabin flew open and there was Aedan, grinning at me as if I'd wandered into the middle of a wonderful joke.

'Come on in,' he said. 'And well done for finally doing something right and making your way here alone. I saw you ditch the bike, very dramatic. Say hello to Naomi, she's missed you.' I started towards the bed at the end of the cabin but Aedan clamped an arm around me. 'Not too close, I don't think she wants you to make me nervous, do you my love?' Naomi was on her back with a gag in her mouth, hands tied above her head and secured to a cup holder on the wall that usually held nothing more sinister than a mug of coffee.

'Aedan, this isn't your fault. Something's happened to you. I know you can hear me, please fight this.' I turned my attention back to him. If I carried on seeing the terror on Naomi's face, I'd be paralysed by fear myself.

'Eve, you're right, please help me,' Aedan pleaded with me and then began to laugh. 'That was pathetic even given the circumstances. I tell you what, I might just go easy on her if you give me a repeat performance of where we left off last time you were here. How about it?' He leaned down to kiss me and I turned my face away in repulsion.

'You didn't bring me here for this, so why don't you tell me what you want and let Naomi go?' Aedan sat down on the end of the bed.

'Never one to relax and take your time were you? Fine, we'll do it your way. I want you to sit down in this chair and stay still while I make sure I have your undivided attention. Then we'll talk.' He pulled a chair out which he positioned at the end of the bed facing towards Naomi and in his hands he held a length of nylon rope.

'I'm not doing anything until she's free. Untie her right now or that's the end of the conversation.' I was bluffing and he knew it. I wasn't going to walk out and leave her there. Aedan sat down next to Naomi so that he could look her right in the eyes. From under the side of the bed he pulled a medical kit and Naomi began trying uselessly to wriggle away from him.

'I love my work, I really do and I have no problem bringing it home with me. Would you like to see what I've got in here?' I let him talk as I looked around the room to see how I could get Naomi out of there. It was really confined at the bed end and I'd have to get through Aedan to free her. Even then, the knots restraining her had been made by someone who knew a lot about handling ropes. I'd need a knife to get through them and it wouldn't be quick. Aedan was taking a horrific looking array of instruments out of his bag.

'I came prepared!' he announced, loving the reaction from Naomi. 'These are artery forceps, Mcindoe scissors, toothed forceps, a cat-paw retractor and a gigi saw. Some of the most beautiful and simple pieces of equipment I use.' He ran his fingers along the lengths of stainless steel and then picked up the saw. It had a t-bar handle on each end, attached to a length of lethally sharp wire. He wrapped it around Naomi's ankle and started to pull it tight.

Naomi's eyes bulged visibly with the sensation and I immediately threw myself in the chair.
I wasn't going to let her get hurt through some prideful stand off. Aedan knew I cared about her way too much to try it.

'Do it,' I said. He sighed, as if disappointed that I'd complied so soon, but he had me exactly where he wanted me. He dropped the ends of the saw and picked up the nylon rope. It didn't take him more than a few seconds to have me tied firmly to the chair by my ankles and waist but he only bothered securing my left arm.

'I'm going to need your help with something shortly, but don't get any ideas. There's no way you can untie yourself with one hand faster than I can slash Naomi's jugular, so be a good girl and sit still.' He went back to Naomi on the bed where he picked up the saw again.

'Naomi, you need to do exactly as I tell you. If you don't, I will use that saw to slice through the bone in your leg. Do you understand what I'm telling you?' She nodded, tears leaking from her eyes. I didn't dare speak. The Aedan I knew was long since gone. I didn't know who this monster was and, until I had a better idea of what he wanted, watching and listening was the best course of action.

'And Eve,' he picked up an implement resembling tweezers, but longer with inward pointing teeth on the ends. 'These are toothed forceps.' He walked over, knelt in front of me and held my jaw with one hand. 'You're going to answer all my questions, without being deceitful or evasive, and if I suspect you of lying then I will punish you like this.' He shoved a finger between my lips to force my mouth open and then gripped the end of my tongue hard with the forceps. He wrenched it out of my mouth and waggled it around. It brought tears to my eyes and I felt as if my tongue would never fit back into my mouth. I was gagging repeatedly by the time he let go. Back on the bed next to Naomi, he tightened the ends of the saw around her ankle and settled back to the business of why I was here.

'Perun would like to know where you were yesterday and last night. He sent me round to check on you when his scouts got caught in a freak storm. Did you think they wouldn't be suspicious?'

'I went back to Manitu,' I said, not even sure it would make any sense to him. 'But I went to see my mother and tell her it was over. I abdicated whatever authority I had. My family will pass power to Perun. He's got what he wants. Why are you doing this?'

114

'You went straight there, just hours after he told you to stay away? It seems likely that he will interpret that as disobeying his wishes.'

'I had to tell the Vilya that it was time to end the battle. He said he wanted peace, I was trying to help.'

'You never do what you're told, do you?' He was getting angry and I could see the vicious serrated metal cutting into Naomi's leg. She was doing her best not to scream. 'Are you sure that's what you were doing there?' he asked and pulled the ends of the saw sharply.

'Yes! It's over, he's won! I had to tell them myself and make them convene the Council. How else could I have let them know?'

'Why not go there with Perun, talk to your family together?' He was pulling the ends of the wire backwards and forwards and I could see droplets of blood appearing around her ankle.

'Stop that! I'm doing what you asked, it's the truth. I wanted to see my mother on my own and I didn't trust the Perelesnyk not to slaughter them where they're hiding, that's why. Please, please stop hurting her.' I didn't know whether to scream or cry and I wasn't sure he wanted to stop, or would even be capable of it, once he got going.

'So it's over,' he said. 'That's the end of your little coming of age fantasy about reuniting with your mother, is it?'

'It's over,' I agreed and breathed out hard when he dropped the saw handles.

'I believe you,' he said. 'Mainly because I just don't think you have the strength to be able to sacrifice your friend's foot. But I do believe you.'

'Then let her go now,' I begged. 'She can't hurt Perun, he's beyond anyone's reach. And we know this isn't your fault. We won't come after you. It can all end right here, Aedan, you have to listen to me.'

'As much as I'd like to oblige, I need Naomi's help with one last task, then of course she'll be free to go.' I felt as if someone were pouring ice water through my veins. It was as if Perun were in the room. I could hear his sneering mockery when

Aedan spoke and I knew there was no chance of escape for either of us. Pleading was not going to work, Aedan was too far gone. I just couldn't figure out what more they could possibly want.

'Now that you've come to your senses and done the right thing with your family, it's only fitting that you should pay the price for your humiliation of the Perelesnyk. They can't assassinate you or they'd have done it before now. Apparently, it's something to do with forfeiting their right to rule in Manitu if they kill a ruler and they seem to think that your family will know if there's been foul play. They don't want the war to continue but the Vilya and their sympathisers will always suspect them if you suddenly end up in a river with a concrete block tied to your feet. So they asked me to help persuade you to commit suicide. Here's how I'm going to do it.' Naomi was thrashing backwards and forwards, trying with all her might to get free and protect me. It was futile, of course; no-one ties knots like a sailor. All she did was tighten the cords around her own hands. My last hope was that Aedan would spare her if I did what he wanted. It was the least I could do.

'Naomi, honey, stay still. It's alright. Aedan, swear to me that you'll let her live if I do what you want. Swear it and I'll do what you want, right here, right now.'

'You're absolutely right about that last part, you certainly will do what I want. As for sparing Naomi, I'll see. What might help persuade me is if we stop talking and start doing.' He selected what he'd called the cat paw retractor which had a blunt miniature garden fork end with its teeth curled under. From his bag, he took a long needle and held the two things up so that we could both get a good look at them. 'Did you know that as long as the needle is thin enough and perfectly clean, you can stick it right through the white of a person's eye. Provided I don't damage the lens, if she stays nice and still for me then it might heal completely, as if it never happened. If she struggles or you make a fuss I'm likely to lose my concentration and that wouldn't have such a happy ending. Do you want to watch me do that, Eve?'

'No,' I whispered. Naomi was shaking and I was hoping desperately that she would just pass out and not have to hear any more.

'Then you need to take hold of this in your free hand,' he passed me a razor sharp scalpel, 'and slice through your wrist. Not across it, like in all those awful movies. I want you to slice downwards, making a cut several inches long from just below your elbow towards your wrist. My advice is be brave. The deeper the cut, the quicker you'll bleed out and the sooner it'll be over.' I tried to hold the knife still and imagine myself doing it. I didn't see how I could. It was already slippery in my grasp where my hand was sweating so badly. Aedan didn't seem at all surprised by my inaction. 'Now you understand why I need Naomi's help. It's not an easy thing to do, to harm yourself like that. I'm sure we can persuade you though.' He picked up the retractor, held Naomi's face still with one hand and scooped the implement effortlessly under her right eyelid. 'Hold still or you'll damage the eye,' he told her and moved aside so that I could get a better view of what he was doing. Naomi couldn't close the eye and her eyeball, exposed and reddening by the second, was rolling around like a grotesque marble. My hands were shaking but I managed to manoeuvre the knife so that the tip was pointing downwards into my flesh. I pushed it in but the pain stopped me in my tracks.

'It is going to hurt,' he said. 'You need to prepare yourself for that.' I tried again but I just couldn't bring myself to pull the knife along my arm. The tears that were streaming down my face and blurring my vision didn't help. I pressed the knife into my arm and this time I managed to move the blade along but my instinct was to stop and I just couldn't force my hand to do what my brain was telling it not to.

Aedan shrugged each shoulder in turn as if he were entering a boxing ring and then climbed on top of Naomi so he could bend right over her eye, leaving just enough space that I could see what he was doing. He picked up the needle and put one knee to the side of Naomi's head to prevent her from twisting away. She was fighting her instinct to move so that she didn't rip her own eyelid. With his left arm pushing down hard on her

117

forehead, he began to press the pinprick of the needle into the white of her eye and Naomi shouted the one thing that ended my brain's resistance completely.

'Tim! Help me!' In her terror, she had forgotten that he wasn't there, would never be there again. I vomited bile down myself, choking on it as I tried to shout out.

'I'll do it, wait, I can do this,' I yelled. I took a deep breath and shoved the scalpel in hard, biting back the pain that it brought and willing myself to stay conscious. Bright red blotches were appearing before my eyes and even then I wasn't sure I could rip my arm open all the way to my wrist but I could see Aedan continuing to push the needle in and I didn't believe he wanted to stop. I was shouting over and over again that I was doing it, that I was cutting, but he didn't let up.

Then the cabin door flew open and suddenly Xander was charging towards Aedan with a baseball bat, not knowing that Aedan held Naomi's life in his hands.

'No!' If he hit Aedan now, the needle would go straight through the back of Naomi's eye and, I guessed, into her brain. My shout was all it took to give Aedan the advantage and duck to one side of Naomi avoiding the full force of the blow, but it left Xander vulnerable to an attack from a crazed and much stronger opponent. The two of them fell to the floor, Aedan throwing punches that Xander couldn't avoid or hope to return. I hacked at the rope around my left arm with the scalpel, slicing wildly at it until it snapped. There was no time to free my legs or waist.

'Naomi, the bat, kick your left leg,' I shouted and as she did so, I launched myself, still in the chair, at the baseball bat which had landed on the bed out of my reach until Naomi pushed it towards me. I didn't have much leverage and I was on my knees with the chair strapped over the top of me. I had one shot and I knew it.

'Xander, move!' I screeched. He did as I said and I brought the bat down heavy and hard, contacting Aedan's skull with a dull thud. Xander rolled away, panting, one side of his face already starting to swell from the fight and his nose bloodied. 'How the hell did you find us?' I asked.

'There aren't that many marinas in Monterey,' he said. 'The motorbike on its side was helpful and you'd already told me the name of the yacht, although it seems more ironic than amusing right now.' He sliced through the rest of the ropes holding me to the chair and then together we carefully freed Naomi, pulling the needle from her eye and taking out the retractor as gently as we could. Remarkably, as Aedan had said, apart from the pain there was little other damage.

'Is he alive?' I asked. Xander checked for a pulse while I wrapped up my bleeding arm in a makeshift bandage using one of Aedan's shirts. I helped Xander tie him to the bed using the rope from Naomi and put cold flannels over her eye and ankle.

'Can you tell me what happened when he came to the house?' I asked her. She nodded, and I was more concerned about her emotional state than the injuries Aedan had inflicted.

'He knocked on the door, quite early in the morning. I wasn't expecting him and he'd taken me by surprise so he was through the door before I could stop him. I was tired and not paying much attention but, looking back, he was stressed and snappy. I told him you were under the weather and sleeping in, said I'd get you to phone him later. He wouldn't have it, insisted that as your boyfriend and a doctor it was ridiculous to suggest you wouldn't want to see him. He stormed through, opened your door and that was it. I realised straight away that he knew you weren't there. That's when he grabbed me by the hair and dragged me from room to room until he found your note. He made me call Sabina to say we were going off together but she was still in her house and he said that if I wasn't convincing he'd go over and snap her neck. I couldn't let him hurt her so we got in his car and came here. I can't remember much of the journey and I must have passed out for a while because I woke up already tied to the bed.' I sat down next to her and hugged her while she got the worst of the immediate shock out of her system.

'He was Perun's insurance policy,' I said. 'He was marked from the second he kicked him in the head at the party, that's why Perun didn't retaliate at the time. I'm such an idiot. They must have followed him home that night.'

Xander had fetched ice from the galley and was trying to reduce the purple swelling threatening to take over his face. 'I still don't understand what they've done to him. Is this like at the party, when they put all those people into a trance?'

'I don't think so but, honestly, I'm not sure. I've only ever seen the Perelesnyk have this much power over a human when they are actually in their presence. And he knew so much, used names as if he understood everything that had happened. This is something I've never seen before. What the hell are we going to do with him?' I asked.

'Is there a laptop on board?' Xander said. I pointed him toward one of the cupboards in the seating area where I'd been nosing around the week before. 'What am I looking for?'

'Incubi, demonic possession, spirits taking control of humans, that sort of thing.' Xander was staring as if I were the one who should be tied up rather than Aedan. 'I know what you're thinking, but I'm not crazy and I don't have time to explain. Indulge me, okay?'

Xander shook his head in disbelief but disappeared to investigate while I checked Aedan's ropes were secure and made Naomi a cup of hot, sweet tea. Ten minutes later Aedan was starting to stir and I still had no idea how to handle a man captive on his own boat and dangerous if he got loose.

'Xander, come on, he's waking up. Whatever you're doing, do it faster.'

'I think I've got it. It's not easy wading through centuries old mythology. Most of it's about bloody vampires.'

'What have you got?' I asked, amazed that he'd found anything at all.

'Well, honestly, there's loads about incubi so if we're assuming this is Perun's work...'

'Oh, it is,' I said. 'Go on.'

'There was only one mention of an incubus possessing a human but it's something called a liderc, I'm not sure how you're supposed to pronounce that, but supposedly they lay a sort of egg in the human's mouth and once it's in their stomach, the incubus can control them. That's seriously twisted.' I sat down next to him at the computer.

'Does it say how you get rid of it?' I asked. 'Only we can't take him to a hospital or the police whilst he's still possessed. They won't know what to do and he'll come straight after us again.'

'Here you go. The possession ends when either the liderc is removed or upon death. Eve, are you going to kill him? Only I'm not sure saying we thought he was possessed by a demon will stand up in court as a defence.'

'I'm not going to kill him deliberately,' I said. 'In fact, I'm going to do my best not to. That said, if my plan goes wrong, we're going to have some explaining to do.'

Sixteen

I knew exactly what we had to do, the problem was that I needed Aedan to help us do it. I got Xander to lock every exit and Naomi recovered enough to boil water and sterilise Aedan's surgical instruments. We stripped the bed so that Aedan was lying just on the under sheet and went through his medical kit to find anything that might prove useful. I had plenty of experience healing wounds and alleviating sickness, both Xander and Naomi had seen me do that before, but what I needed to do this time was bring enough of the human Aedan back to tell us how to remove the liderc. I had no idea if it would work, but it was the only chance we had without chaining him up for the next two weeks until Perun had been given the power he so desperately craved. Even if we did simply restrain him until it was over, there was always going to be the question of what to do with him afterwards. One way or another, we had to get the liderc out of his body.

Once Xander was through his denial phase, we tied Aedan by both arms and legs to make doubly sure he couldn't move and I splashed cold water in his face to bring him round. While he was still groggy and confused, I took his head in my hands and did my best to visualise the man he'd been before the party. I thought of how bright and funny he was and how protective he'd been of me. It took a while, mainly because of what I'd seen him do in the last few hours, but after several minutes he returned to a fuller consciousness. If I thought it was going to be that easy, I was wrong. As soon as I took my hands off his head he became verbally abusive, threatening us in ways graphic enough to have Xander stuffing a gag in his mouth.

'If he's going to make any sense, I've got to stay here holding him. Xander, I need you to do exactly what he tells you.' Xander blanched but didn't disagree. He cut Aedan's shirt off and washed his torso with hot water and soap. When we were ready to start, I brought the real Aedan back again and tried to communicate with him.

'Aedan, we think there's something in your stomach that's making you behave like this. Do you remember anything at all? Something being forced into your mouth?'

It took a while for him to be lucid and I could tell he was having to work hard just to talk to me. 'I had a dream,' he said. 'I couldn't breathe or speak and it was difficult to move but when I woke up I was fine. What are you doing to me?'

'It wasn't a dream, Aedan. There's something inside your stomach, controlling you, and I need you to tell us how to get it out. We can't leave you or help you until we know it's done, so there's no choice. The more you fight whatever this is and give us good instructions, the easier it'll be.' To my surprise, he didn't even argue. For me, it was a sign that part of him was aware of the possession and wanted the alien monstrosity out as quickly as possible. The alternative was that the controlling force was aware of what was going on, thought that we'd kill him for sure and didn't care at all about the life of its host. Either way, there was no time to lose.

'You're sure we can't just call a Catholic priest and have it exorcised or something? I don't think I can do this,' Xander was looking paler by the minute and the hand holding Aedan's scalpel was visibly trembling.

'I'm not convinced the church does that sort of thing any more and I'm positive it wouldn't work anyway. Xander, you have to get your head round this, we're running out of options. Aedan, how do we start?'

'There are some vials of local anaesthetic in my bag. You'll need to inject a small amount with each layer you cut or I'll pass out,' he said. Xander found the vials and held them up for Aedan to nod at. 'Before you start, get my soldering iron from the boat's tool kit. The best way to make sure I don't bleed out is to cauterize the blood vessels as you go.' I nodded at Naomi and she went off to find it. It took a few minutes but she was back soon enough to hear Aedan's continued instructions.

'You'll need to make a cut, about twenty centimetres, from the bottom of my rib cage towards my belly button.' Xander managed to inject anaesthetic in the right area and it worked in seconds.

'Right, let's get going before that wears off,' I said. Xander held the scalpel in place and started to slip it along the skin but then stopped.

'It's no good, I can't do this.' He looked as if he might pass out and I was swearing under my breath when Naomi stepped in.

'Give me the bloody knife,' she snapped, holding her hand out to Xander.

'Honey, you've been tied up for hours and you must be traumatised. There's no way you're up to it,' I said.

'Are you kidding? This might be the only thing that'll make me feel better. I may not give the bastard quite as much anaesthetic as he'd like, though.' She took the scalpel, steadied herself and cut neatly down Aedan's body. Xander rallied enough to hold towels either side of the wound and mop up the blood that was seeping out. Even I could only watch through half closed eyes, grimacing at the rawness of the inside of a human body.

'Once you're through the skin you'll see the anterior abdominal wall, cut through that in the same way, and then you'll get to the peritoneum. It's really sensitive. Put in plenty of anaesthetic or I'll be no use after that.' Naomi did it with only minimal muttering to herself. She seemed completely at home with the knife in her hand, not squeamish at all and I hoped her nerve would hold. In spite of the injection, Aedan still screamed when the knife went in. I held him as still as I could, terrified he'd break free and we'd end up chasing a man with his stomach cut open around the boat.

'Naomi, you've got to give him more anaesthetic, right now,' I said.

'I don't see why I shouldn't be able to hurt him just a bit,' she growled through clenched teeth.

'As much as I sympathise, I just need him under control,' I whispered, but she was already slipping the end of the needle in and he relaxed under my hands as the pain reduced.

Under Aedan's instruction Naomi cut on through to the linea alba, which Aedan described as the part of the abdomen that makes the vertical line down a six pack. He was fading in and out of consciousness by then and it took all my concentration to bring him round long enough to talk in short bursts. 'The alba is really strong fibrous tissue and sort of greyish white. You'll need the artery forceps to grab it and lift it up like a tent.' Xander took some persuasion to do that but once he had it, Naomi cut without hesitation. 'Soldering iron,' said Aedan as he slipped away again. This time it took all three of us to mop up the bodily fluids, figure out what was what and use the soldering iron to burn the cut ends of the blood vessels.

By now Aedan was an awful colour and his breathing was erratic. 'You sure we shouldn't just call the paramedics?' Xander said. I thought about trying to explain what we'd been doing and knew that the opportunity to involve outside help had long since passed. I told Xander it wasn't an option and urged them to hurry. 'Would have been easier to just kill him,' he muttered.

I couldn't get Aedan conscious again for several minutes but when he did he was in dreadful pain and not making much sense. 'Xylocaine and adrenaline,' he murmured. Xander took another look at the bottles in his bag. Aedan needed more anaesthetic but with adrenaline to keep him lucid. Even with us cauterizing every vessel we could find, the sheets and our clothing were a bloody mess. How we'd get out of the marina without being arrested I just couldn't conceive. Once Naomi opened up the last cut, Xander mopped up with more towels and pulled the sides back to look in. I heard him retch and turn his head away.

'I think we've found it,' he said through the gagging. 'There something disgusting in there. It's yellow and glistening, like it's alive.' I peeked over his shoulder. Inside Aedan's abdomen was what resembled an organic carpet and we all stood staring until I realised Aedan was trying to speak.

'Omentum,' he whispered.

'Speak English, you bastard' said Naomi.

'Move it to one side, the stomach is underneath.' Naomi did as she was told, not the least bit fazed, pulling the freakish yellow layer across, then slipping her other hand deeper inside the cavity.

'This is the stomach, like a C-shape, right?' she asked. Aedan didn't answer and this time when he lost consciousness, groaning occasionally, instinct told me that I nothing I did was going to bring him round.

Naomi lifted the stomach and put her hand around it. I could see her feeling tentatively along its curve. She moved her fingers slowly and carefully up and down a few times, then looked at me.

'I've found something,' she said. 'I don't know if it's what we're looking for, but it's spherical, a couple of inches from top to bottom.'

'That has to be it,' I said. There were blood vessels running across the surface of the stomach so Naomi cut centrally downwards, avoiding the vessels where she could and getting Xander to cauterize those she nicked. Inside, Aedan's stomach was filled with what looked like rumpled pink silk and when Naomi put her hand in to draw out the object, a fluorescent green liquid oozed out. It was the first time Naomi had so much as flinched but by the time she'd cleaned her hands off we could see the small, shining black egg, still perfectly whole in her palm.

As Aedan seemed lost to us, I released his head and went to look at the liderc. For a few moments we all just stood around, staring at it until Naomi asked us how we were going to close Aedan's wounds up again. I finally saw him from a different angle and the pain in my chest was so sharp I thought I was having a heart attack. Laid on the bed was the beautiful, healthy, strong man with whom I was just starting a new life and he'd been gutted like an animal in an abattoir, his abdomen a gaping mess, head lolling to one side, more dead than alive. This was what Perun had reduced me to, someone who was willing to butcher her own friends to survive.

'Eve?' Naomi prompted me.

'We've got to finish this. There's the needle he put in your eye,' I said. 'Xander, check his bag to see if there's any sort of thread.' We rummaged around as fast as we could but there was nothing. In spite of their best efforts to cauterize the ends of the vessels, he was still losing blood and other unidentified fluids. I felt nauseous and Xander was looking like he might bolt at any moment. 'That's it, search the yacht, there must be something here we can put him back together with.' It seemed to take forever and I had a sense that we were losing Aedan when Naomi shouted.

'I've got it! It was in the tool kit,' she yelled, running back into the cabin holding a staple gun.

'You're bloody kidding,' said Xander.

'Naomi, I don't think that's a good idea,' my hands were shaking at the thought of what she was about to do.

'Oh, get a grip would you? It's not like we've got other options. Anyway, I've read about this being done in emergencies. I'll need a flat knife, not serrated.' Xander disappeared into the galley, shaking his head but to my relief he returned almost immediately with a butter knife.

'Will this do?'

'Perfect,' she said. As long as I'd known Naomi I'd never seen her like this, completely in charge in a situation that would have floored anyone else. I kept quiet and let her get on with it.

I held the knife inside the wound to give Naomi something to press the staple gun against. She put six staples down the stomach, as Xander pushed the edges of the organ together and I gently retracted the knife, pulling it further out as each staple closed. Although it wasn't an aesthetically impressive job, we made sure there was no bleeding as we put each section back together, repeating the process backwards through each layer we'd sliced. The second Naomi had closed the top layer of skin, I got my senses back sufficiently to know what we had to do.

'Grab the egg,' I said to Xander. 'Get all your stuff together, we've got to get out of here.' I knew where the harbour master's details were so I took Aedan's mobile and used it to send a text, asking for paramedics and saying that the owner of the

Lady Luck had undergone emergency surgery. We threw on some clothes to cover the worst of the gore and were on our way out of the parking area, Naomi in Xander's car and me on the bike, when the ambulance went past. As far as Aedan was concerned, we'd done all we could for now.

We travelled in convoy back to the ranch, slowly enough to ensure we weren't stopped for a traffic violation. We made it into the house with minimal fuss then bundled all our clothes into a cold wash, diving into showers as quickly as we could. I scrubbed at my skin under burning hot water for as long as I could bear and, even then, I still felt unclean. By the time the three of us were in the kitchen, the adrenaline had worn off and the shock of what we'd been through, and done, was just kicking in.

The liderc sat ominously in the middle of the kitchen table. There was complete silence, and I knew we were all thinking the same thing. What the hell were we going to do with it now? A couple of times I could have sworn it moved, very slightly, making the light reflecting off its surface waver. It was mesmerising, like looking into the depths of the sea. I had the oddest feeling that if I stared at it long enough I'd be able to see inside. When the phone rang, we'd been entranced for so long that we all shrieked and jumped.

'Don't answer it,' said Xander. As tempting as that was, if we failed to act normally we'd only attract more attention and after what we'd done on the boat that didn't seem like a good idea. It turned out to be Sabina's housekeeper asking if we were on our way over to supper. None of us had noticed the sun going down outside. I'd shed my watch before getting in the shower and had lost track of time.

'I don't think I can eat,' said Naomi. Now that things were calmer I was more worried about her. The extraordinary strength she'd shown earlier could only last so long, after all.

'I can't leave you here,' I said. 'Will you just come over to Sabina's? We're going to have to give them some sort explanation. At the moment I'm too scared to leave any one of you alone. I had no idea they could possess people like that and the more I find out about the Perelesnyk, the more impossible it seems to fight them.'

'And what about that?' Xander asked, pointing at the egg. 'Do we just leave it here? What if it hatches or something. We don't even know what might come out of it.' I took a mug from the cupboard and put the liderc in it, pleased that the tight fit meant it couldn't move.

'Come on. I'll have figured out what to do with it by the end of the evening. If I don't show my face soon, Bryn will be over here demanding to know what's going on.' We picked up torches and walked briskly over to Sabina's, starting to feel the long term effects of fear. The world looked skewed; every shadow made me jump and I didn't want to be more than an arm's length from my friends. Naomi and Xander had that same skittish look and it was going to be pointless making any pretence with Sabina and Bryn; the story of the day was best told briefly and straight away, and that's exactly what we did.

When Sabina heard what Naomi had been through, she sat with an arm clamped firmly around her shoulders for the remainder of the night and Xander sat at my feet next to the fire. We ate a little, but only to distract ourselves. Soon enough the conversation came back to the egg.

'We should just destroy it,' said Sabina. 'Throw it into the fire right now, before it can do any more harm.'

Bryn, who had said virtually nothing throughout the evening, finally got involved. 'I understand why you want to do that but in my experience you don't do anything with a weapon until you know how it works and this is just another type of weapon. If we try to destroy it, there might be repercussions we can't even conceive. It might change into something worse or it might send out a distress signal and I, for one, do not want to come face to face with those Moroi things again without being properly prepared. What we need is better intelligence. Until then, I say we watch but don't touch.'

He was right and we all knew it. We were no match for the sort of demons that the Perelesnyk had at their beck and call and I was all out of courage for the night. Whilst Bryn's theory was sound, I wasn't sure how we could get any better information about the liderc.

'I don't know where to start. We got everything we could from the internet. There's limited folklore about the liderc and most of it doesn't make sense. The only people who could tell me more are the Vilya and I'm not risking going back into Manitu again. If Perun found out, the consequences would be devastating. At the moment we don't know if he thinks I'm dead or alive.'

'So we have to find the source material, investigate where the information on the internet comes from. What do we know about the Perelesnyk and this liderc thing? Where do they come from?'

I thought about what my mother had told me when I'd shown her the Moroi claw. 'The Perelesnyk are from eastern Europe. They live in the Tatra Mountains where I first saw Perun and the train crashed. Most of the mythology we've found about the incubi is Slavic and the source materials won't be easy to get hold of.'

'At least I can translate them when we do,' interrupted Sabina. 'But I no longer know anyone there who can help. I wouldn't know where to start.' The housekeeper knocked before bringing in a tray of coffee and homemade fudge. The domesticity of the scene made me laugh; sitting around a roaring fire, sipping hot drinks and eating sweets whilst staring at a demonic egg with who knew what sort of monster inside, from a different world.

'What about the man you met after the train crash?' asked Naomi. For a moment my mind was blank.

'Patrick,' I said. 'Naomi, you're a genius. I haven't been in contact with him for a while but it's worth a try. He's posted at the British embassy in Slovakia and speaks the language.'

Sabina looked at her watch. 'It's six in the morning in Bratislava,' she said. 'You've got a couple of hours to come up with a way of explaining this whole thing to him. We need to give him something concrete to look for, after all.'

It was the only thing any of us could think to do. We locked every door and window, left the lights on and bedded

130

down together upstairs with every door open so that no-one was out of sight of others. Finally, we all fell into an uneasy rest and I drifted to sleep wondering what to tell Patrick. That night, I dreamed of Ellette as she lay dying in my arms in Manitu. She was begging me to stay away, saying that returning meant death for them all. I tried to tell her that I'd find a way to protect them but the words wouldn't come out. I just sat on the ground, sobbing uselessly as the life dripped out of her, rocking her pathetically in my arms as she went. At first light, my eyes were red from crying and I began the day mourning the loss of my sister all over again. Small wonder after the traumas of yesterday and how close I'd come to losing my darling Naomi. I made myself be grateful for the fact that I hadn't and forced some composure onto my face before I went downstairs.

Seventeen

Before I went to sleep, I sent Patrick a text to say I was trying to contact him urgently and he'd replied to let me know he'd be in his office that day I if wanted to talk. Sabina was up before me, so I joined her in the study to use her computer and send a brief email so that Patrick could get working on what we needed.

'Dear Patrick, I hope this email finds you well. I'm afraid, as ever, that I need a favour and believe only you can help. It's urgent and easier to send you written details but I'll phone you later today to speak with you about it. I need to know about something called a "Liderc". From what little I know, it's best documented in Slavic mythology. Anything you can find out - what it does, how it behaves, how you destroy one - would be greatly appreciated. I know this sounds absurd and I promise I'll explain later. Please help. Very best wishes, Eve.' I pressed send and doubled up with a text message to ask him to check his mail.

The liderc itself hadn't moved or changed overnight and I hoped that perhaps the simple of act of removing it from Aedan's body had been enough to kill it. The thought reminded me that I hadn't checked on Aedan. I'd been avoiding phoning the hospital as I had no reasonable explanation for knowing he was there. Sooner or later I'd have to make the call as I wanted to reassure myself that he was recovering. When Sabina went off to check on the others, I made myself sound as normal as possible and phoned Aedan's personal assistant, Cat.

'Hi,' I said, my voice sounding awfully high pitched. 'It's Eve, I don't suppose Aedan's there is he?' I heard Cat sigh at the other end and carry on clicking away on her keyboard as she responded.

'You mean you haven't been contacted?'

132

'Sorry?' I said. I crossed my fingers like a child and hoped he hadn't told the hospital staff that I'd been with him yesterday. I needn't have worried, Cat was just enjoying the fact that she knew something that Dr. Verne's 'girlfriend' didn't.

'He's in hospital. Apparently there was an accident on his yacht yesterday and he needed surgery. He's stable but they're not expecting to release him for some time. I'm surprised no-one thought about letting you know.' She sounded horribly smug and I maintained my air of ignorance through gritted teeth.

'No, I had no idea,' I said. 'Can you give me the details of where he is, please?' I asked and she tutted as she dictated the hospital and ward to me. 'Thank you, Cat, sorry to have bothered you. I'll go and see him this morning.'

'That's alright, I just assumed you were phoning for your test results,' she said and I could tell she was enjoying the build up to yet more unexpected news. I'd forgotten that Aedan had put the blood test in my name. 'Dr. Verne would normally give you the results himself but as he's not going to be back for so long I'm sure he'd want me to pass this on.'

'Yes, that would be really helpful,' I said. 'What's the diagnosis?'

'Well, you're going to need to refer yourself to another doctor anyway, so if you let me know who you're seeing I can send them the paperwork.' I made a non-committal noise and waited for her to carry on. 'The toxicology screen came back positive for arsenic. It's at unusually high levels so the notes say it may indicate deliberate rather than naturally occurring consumption.'

I paused while I thought about that. Cat must have taken my silence for concern although she didn't exactly sound sympathetic. 'Like I said,' she carried on 'You'll need to get seen straight away for treatment. And be careful what you eat or drink until this is sorted out, it seems you're not very popular with someone.' I thanked her and rang off before my tone of voice betrayed how much I disliked her, concentrating on Zora instead. It didn't make sense. The Vilya existed on a diet of hunted wild meat, fresh fruit and vegetables. They were tucked away under the ground so no-one could contaminate their food source unless it was one of the Vilya themselves.

I'd dealt with a range of different murder methods in court, but arsenic poisoning wasn't one of them. Luckily Bryn had a few more years experience than me and was quite knowledgeable on the subject.

'It's not always deliberate,' he said. 'Sometimes the environment becomes contaminated and a lot of arsenic pollution comes from natural sources. It would need extensive tests to confirm where it was coming from but basically there are three ways it can be transmitted: air, water or food. It would be hard to put enough in the air to have such a dramatic effect. You reckon they couldn't really get it into the food. So where's her water coming from?'

'It's natural ground water that seeps down through the rock. They've constructed a well to hold it.'

'And you said you were sick when you were there, as well?' I nodded. 'It's possible that the water's the source and if it's the same thing that made you sick so quickly, the quantities would have to be high. Unlikely to be natural contamination at that level.'

I knew the Perelesnyk hadn't found their way through the lava tubes to the Vilya but it was entirely possible that they'd identified their ground water source. I put my head in my hands and sighed. 'How would they do it?' I asked. 'It can't be that easy to get your hands on arsenic, surely?'

'I'm afraid that for years it was used in pesticides, animal feed and even some medicines. If they got their hands on enough, it would be easier than you think. They're already at war, though. I don't see why they'd go to so much trouble to get rid of Zora.'

'They can't be seen to have killed her. With arsenic poisoning, there could never be absolute proof that it was them and they know the Vilya can't accuse them without cause. It's the same reason they can't just kill me; if they do, they'll never be allowed to take power in Manitu and they'd rather have every family under their control than limit their power to those who already follow them. The Council has to be united in its approval for them to ascend to rule. And it's not just that; Perun is proud.

I think he wants to be a leader people revere, not hate. He wants the sort of authority where his subjects naturally bow down when they see him. In some deluded way, I think he actually wants to be loved.' Even I couldn't be sure that the water was being poisoned by the Perelesnyk but whatever the source, the most important thing was to make sure I got word back to my mother about the cause of Zora's illness.

Naomi came in, pale and tearful, stopping our conversation instantly. She poured herself coffee and sat staring out of the window. I went and gave her a hug.

'You were incredible yesterday. I couldn't have done what you did. It was bound to make for a bad night's sleep, though. Can I get you anything?' She laid her head on my shoulder.

'I'm not hungry and it's not yesterday. I dreamed about Tim. He was telling me to come back to England. He kept saying he was there waiting for me, in our flat. It was so real that when I woke up, for one minute, I honestly thought...' She couldn't speak any more and the image of her waking up thinking Tim was at home, safe and well, brought tears to my eyes as well.

'We've all been under too much pressure,' I said. 'My dreams were messed up as well. We need to get a little distance from all this. I could do with some fresh air. Let's get breakfast and then I'm going to walk down to the paddocks if anyone wants to join me.' Xander hadn't appeared yet and we decided to leave him to sleep. No one had much of an appetite but after some toast, cereal and fruit everyone scattered to find fresh clothes.

I was in my bedroom trying to do something with my unruly hair when I heard screaming from the room next door. Naomi and I ran to see what was going on and found Xander still asleep but howling and curled up in a foetal position. When we tried to wake him he lashed out at us, shouting incomprehensibly. Eventually Bryn pinned him down hard enough to make sure he couldn't do any damage while I stroked his head and tried to bring him round. He babbled a while longer then his eyes flew open, looking straight at me. In spite of Bryn's weight he managed to sit bolt upright and scream into my face.

'Get off!' he shouted. I was taken completely off guard and flew backwards, knocking my head painfully on an open drawer as I went. With that, Xander fell into a crumpled heap. I'd never seen him cry before and my friend was suddenly unrecognisable, shaking and rocking. I scrambled back to him, ignoring the blood seeping from my scalp.

'Xander, it's okay, I've got you. You're safe.' I put my arms round him and carried on whispering until he gradually stilled himself. 'Do you know where you are?' I asked. He nodded. I could see that he was himself again and my terror, that he too had been possessed, subsided. 'Can you tell us what happened?'

'I saw my parents,' he said. 'My mother was hugging me, reading to me like she did every night and then my father came in. He said I didn't belong there, that I'd betrayed them. He was trying to pick me up, he wanted me out of the house. My mother got between us and he hit her. I couldn't stop him. I just sat on the corner on my bed and he kept on punching her in the face and the stomach and when she was finally on the floor he kept kicking until it was like listening to someone flogging a sack of sticks. I could hear her bones snapping, all the air coming out of her. I didn't do anything at all.'

'Xander, it's not real. You were dreaming. Don't be upset, none of this is anything to do with you.' I was powerless to take away the horror of what he'd seen and eventually I left Sabina and Naomi persuading him to sip sweet tea and putting blankets round his shoulders. I pulled on my jacket and some boots, slipping out of the back door to walk through the morning mist.

I climbed the fence of the furthest paddock and watched as a few rays of sunshine tried to break through the cloud. The distant hills were purple in the haze and I felt my pulse slow as I breathed in and out, my breath swirling in the chill. One of the horses trotted over and stood completely still for a moment, waiting to see what I was doing there. He whinnied softly at me but when I held out my hand, he galloped away. His companion, Tempest, had been killed in the fire. I thought how upset James would have been by the slaughter of such a beautiful animal and was glad he hadn't been here to see it. I imagined his big, rough hand sliding over the top of mine, keeping me warm and letting me know he was there.

He'd have told me that none of it was my fault; that blaming myself was, at best, a waste of time and, at worst, self-pity. I looked down at my hand as if he were really there and caught my breath as I saw his face, tanned, laughter lines spreading out from the corners of his eyes. Just as I tried to capture the image, to hold on to him a bit longer, he turned away. His walk was unmistakable, straight backed, deliberate and slow. I wanted him so badly. I needed someone to tell me what to do, how to fix things. It wasn't just about giving Perun what he wanted any more; he was out for vengeance and in my heart I knew there was no stopping him. Whatever I'd tried to do, it had made things worse and I'd set the stage for a bloody massacre that was gathering momentum. I'd never felt so helpless, so utterly lost. I wanted to get on my bike and run away and it made me cry with shame. The responsibility, the guilt, the hopelessness were too much.

I don't know how long I sat there but when Bryn called me from the porch I was too stiff to move quickly. I shouted that I was on my way and trod back up the path to the house. By the time I could see Bryn clearly, I realised he was waving my mobile at me. A text had come through from Patrick to say he'd emailed some information; to check it was what I needed and call him back. He'd done it much faster than I'd expected, thinking that at the very least it would take a day of searching through the library at Bratislava not to mention some tricky translation from old, possibly even handwritten, texts. I logged into my emails expecting to be disappointed and was amazed at the amount of information Patrick had sent for me to download. The email was classic Patrick, ever polite and with his usual sweetness.

'My Dear Eve, It is lovely to hear from you and please don't trouble yourself at all with such a small request for help. I hope that what I've attached is sufficient to assist. As it is obviously an urgent matter I shall give you some time to read before calling to check if there is any more I can do. Warmest regards, Patrick.' As the attachments started to open up on the screen, everyone gathered to see what information Patrick had found. I scanned through, reading the relevant parts out loud as I went.

'Apparently the mythology is originally Hungarian. The liderc is a demonic animal form of an incubus, which can disguise itself as a man or woman. This text says, "Born of fire, with wings of flame, the Liderc appears as a light in darkened skies to attract those watching from their windows. It chooses one who appears alone, entering through window or chimney to sit abreast them as they sleep. An egg is laid in the victim's mouth; sometimes called the kiss of the incubus. The Liderc cares only for riches and power, seducing his victims to control them. It cannot enter a house protected by branches of the silver birch or walls wrapped with vines. It cannot possess a child who has not yet learned to desire gold or riches. In their animal form they have no defence against wild dogs, foxes or wolves and will by choice avoid any home where a dog is kept." Well, it wasn't after gold this time,' I muttered to myself. As interesting as it was, there was nothing very useful there, so I flicked on to the next document.

'The Liderc, sometimes referred to as the Demon Chicken, lays a tiny egg into the mouth of the victim to be swallowed as they sleep. When the egg has made its way to the stomach it will grow so that it cannot be passed and, when the egg is at full maturity, the spirit of the possessed is under the influence of the demon. Inside the egg is the demon itself, diminutive in body but sucking the life from its victim as long as it remains within. Eventually, when the host body has been of all the use it can be, the egg will grow to such a size that it kills the host whereon the demon is born from the egg to slash its way out of the body with its claws. Under cover of night, it flies away again to find a new host and lay an egg of its own. The incubi can send it to their enemies to possess them, marking the target with a single touch so that the liderc can find them.'

I was grateful beyond measure that Aedan hadn't housed the liderc any longer. I turned to the last document from Patrick.

'The liderc is sent out from the incubi and succubi to fulfill their earthly requirements. Those who touch the shell of the liderc may see projections of loved ones in dreams or hallucinations, to distract them from harming the liderc until it can be reclaimed by its sender.' I looked down at my hands and realized that my vision of Ellette was nothing more than a trick. As I raised my eyes to see if Naomi had realised the relevance of her dream, Xander lurched out of his chair towards the liderc on the table.

'Don't!' I shouted, but before I could move Bryn had intercepted and tackled him to the floor.

'You don't know what that thing made me see,' Xander was yelling. 'We have to destroy it; let me go, just fucking well let me go.' Sabina rose unnoticed to her feet as the men fought on the floor and I saw her lift the cup in which the liderc sat. I watched her, waiting for a sign that she was acting rashly, but she put one finger to her lips as she passed me and I knew she was taking the alien object somewhere it could not be found until we'd decided what to do with it. Xander was starting to calm down as Sabina reappeared and Naomi waited a few moments before going to comfort him. I finished reading.

'The Liderc is vulnerable only at times of transition; when the egg is being laid, when it transforms into flame or when the demon is exiting the human body. At such times the demon emerging can be killed by splashing it with molten silver, such is the purifying effect of the element. The longer the victim is under control of the demon, the harder it is to shed its corrupting influence and for the host to return to its original untainted nature. Destruction of a liderc egg will alert the incubus that sent it out.'

'But it hasn't transformed in front of us. We interrupted its normal process,' said Naomi. 'So we really don't know what it's going to do next. Can we just pour silver over the egg and kill it while it's still in there?'

'There's no guarantee that will work,' said Sabina. 'We should try to induce one of the transformations that we know will make it vulnerable enough to kill it.'

'We also have to be able to find enough silver and a way of smelting it, when we figure out how to do that,' Bryn cut in. That silenced everyone for long enough for me to hear my mobile ringing in the kitchen. I left them to work out a way of dealing with the liderc, grateful to think about something else for a moment. Caller display showed me that Patrick was on the line and I picked up the phone, looking forward to hearing a friendly voice.

'Patrick, hello. How are you?' I said.

'All the better for speaking to you after so long. How is sunny California?' he asked. His stereotypically English accent was heart warming and reminded me of simpler times.

'Oh, you know, sun, surf and endless other clichés. Truthfully, I'm very settled here. Sabina has taken me under her wing and I couldn't have been luckier in many respects.'

'If I'm not much mistaken, I'm sensing a substantial "but" on the end of that sentence. Is there anything else I can help you with?' Ever the diplomat, I knew Patrick wouldn't just come out and ask why I needed such strange information.

'You've done more than enough already and I'm sorry to have made you rush around for me like that. I know how busy you are.'

'Not at all. The first time I looked for this stuff it took me days of searching around dusty book shelves at the national library. It was lucky that your friend asked for similar subject matter so recently, some of it was from exactly the same volumes so I was able to find it immediately.' If I'd been half distracted with pleasantries a second ago, Patrick certainly had my full attention now.

'My friend?' I asked. I swallowed hard, nails cutting into the palms of my hands. Surely Perun couldn't have found Patrick as well. There was no way he could have linked him to me so far away.

'Yes,' he said. 'Sorry, I assumed you knew he'd been here. He asked specifically for me, said that you'd told him all about how we'd met and asked for a bit of help with the language and some travel plans. He wasn't terribly well prepared when he arrived in Slovakia.'

'He wasn't?' I asked, not knowing how to tell Patrick that this so called friend was nothing of the sort.

'Of course, after what he'd been through in London, having his passport and money stolen, that's quite understandable.

Lovely chap, though, James.' I felt light headed for a second before recovering enough to stop Patrick from worrying that anything was wrong.

'Yes, I met him at Sabina's ranch. I'm so pleased you two made contact. We haven't heard from him for a while and were wondering what he was up to. When was he was with you?'

'A week ago. He said he was doing some research about mythical creatures originating in the Carpathian Mountains and wanted to go to the primary sources. He hired a cabin up in the foothills, I took him there myself.'

'But in Slovakia, that's not the Carpathians, they're the Tatras aren't they?' I was holding my breath and feeling dizzy, waiting for Patrick to answer.

'The Tatras are part of the Carpathians, some of the very highest peaks are in northern Slovakia, not far from the region you and I visited. The Carpathians stretch all the way from Romania.' I couldn't get my breathing into a rhythm. 'Eve, are you still there?'

'Patrick, I'm going to have to call you back.' I said as everything went black.

Eighteen

I heard Sabina's voice before her face came into focus. I was trying to talk but they just kept pacifying me. I knew they couldn't understand what I was saying and felt a cold flannel being wiped across my face. I shook it off but Sabina was telling me to relax, that I was over tired.

'You don't understand,' I whispered. 'It's James.'

'I'm sure he's fine, my darling. If he needed anything, he would have let me know.'

'No, he's not fine.' I took hold of whoever's hand was wiping my forehead and gently but firmly pushed it away, sitting up as I did so. 'He's gone to find Perun and I don't think he's planning on coming back.'

'How do you know that?' Naomi asked as she helped me to my feet.

'He contacted Patrick, that's why we got the information we needed so fast. James has been researching the history of the Perelesnyk and has already found out that their homeland is the Carpathian Mountains, in Slovakia.'

'Why would he do that?' asked Xander. It was the one story I hadn't told anyone but Naomi and, until I did, none of them would understand what James had been through.

I explained that James had been cursed when he rejected a succubus intent on seducing him on his wedding night. 'When James ran from the succubus he burst back out of Manitu, surprising his wife who was searching for him. She slipped and fell over a cliff edge to her death. When the succubus finally caught up with them and saw what had happened, she cursed him to lose every woman he loved in an equally tragic way. I suspected that when Tim was killed, he couldn't bear the guilt of thinking it should have been him and decided to avenge both deaths. He must know that even if he finds Perun, he won't make it out alive.' There was a breathless silence around the room when I finished speaking.

'You poor child. So that's why you two parted. I wish you had told me before now, I could have been more...' Sabina was struggling to find the right words so I finished for her.

'You couldn't have been more anything. You got me through losing him and helped me start a new life. And there's nothing any of us could have done for James. The curse can't be lifted, as far as I know, but right now his life is sand in an hourglass and I won't sit here knowing what he's facing without going to help. He'll be slaughtered before he gets anywhere near the Perelesnyk whilst they're guarded by the Moroi.'

Bryn was on his feet and unusually angry when he spoke. 'You can't go back into Manitu. If you follow him, all you'll do is throw away two lives when the first is already beyond hope.'

'Then so be it,' I replied. 'You don't know him, Bryn. He'd do the same for me.'

'The man you've described would want me to stop you. Eve, if you're right, then he's made up his mind to end his pain and wants to make the world a better place at the same time. You have no right to take that from him.'

'I have every right. He went there with me when I needed him and that's why Perun went looking for him.' I was shouting and, although I knew in my heart that Bryn was trying to protect me, I had to vent my feelings. 'I have as much right to go after him as he had to choose to go. You can help me or take the much more sensible decision to stay out of it. What you can't do is persuade me not to go after him.'

'And what then?' said Naomi. 'I'm not saying you shouldn't go, if I'd had the opportunity to save Tim no-one could have stood in my way, but if you and James by some miracle survive and manage to get back here then you'll either have to separate again or be forever looking over your shoulder, waiting for death. You can lie to us and say you've moved on, but you can't lie to yourself.'

'I'm going to Bratislava,' I said. 'Patrick can take me to the cabin where he last saw James. We'll keep working on a way to deal with the liderc. I'm going home to pack and book myself on the first flight out.' I made my way back to my own house. It didn't matter now if it were crawling with Moroi; I was past the point of caution. I still had to keep everyone safe but all I could see was James' face. I needed to phone Patrick to let him know what was happening.

There was one flight leaving tonight with seats available but as I was about to book, I realised that this was the evening Serenta would visit for news of Zora. I still had to ask Naomi to meet her and pass on what we'd found out so I picked up my keys, locked up and dashed back to the ranch house.

Judging by the red faces, there had been a heated discussion going on but silence descended as I entered the room. The rational part of me finally found her voice again. If they were going to let me go, I need to convince everyone that I knew what I was doing. I fiddled with my silver key fob as they all sat down and with that tiny action, the fate of the liderc was sealed.

'Listen, you all have my best interests at heart, I know that and I couldn't ask for more love and concern than you've shown but I'm not going on a suicide mission; I want to come back and I believe James does too, or I wouldn't go. I can get a plane to Bratislava tonight if I book it now. That means I'll be there by mid-afternoon tomorrow, Californian time. What I need to do is take the liderc with me. If Perun sent it, and I'm sure he did, then he'll know when it's smashed. Once he sends his soldiers to find it, I can follow them back into Manitu and look for James.'

'How are you going to get the egg through airport security?' asked Xander.

'The same way I'm going to make sure it doesn't transform before I want it to,' I said. 'We need to cover the outside of the egg with silver. I just need an old jewellery case and some wrapping to make it look like a gift in case I'm stopped.'

'If you're intent on doing this, then let me handle that part,' said Sabina. She phoned over to the ranch hands and asked them to light up the gas forge they kept for shoeing the horses. From a cabinet she took out a silver jug which she handed to Xander. 'If you don't mind, my darling, take this over to John and ask him to start melting it down. Tell him, when he's ready, to call me and we can take the egg over. You'll have to make up some story about what's going on but I spent enough time teaching you how to improvise that it shouldn't be too difficult.' For the first time that day Xander seemed happier at the prospect of having something positive to do.

'I'd better go and book my flight,' I said.

'Book two,' said Bryn, pulling out a backpack from behind his chair. 'You've known me long enough, Miss MacKenzie, to know when not to argue. It's either both of us or you'll have to fight me to get out of this house.' I didn't know whether to laugh or cry. I settled for hugging the gruff, lovely man who was so intent on protecting me. He was a former soldier with an utterly simple idea of how the world should be. With the possible exception of James, I couldn't imagine anyone else I'd rather have at my side. Head strong I might be, but I'm not stupid to the point of self-sacrifice. I set about booking seats on the night flight whilst Sabina arranged for her driver to take us to the airport. Naomi, Sabina and Xander would stay here and I'd already sent Daniel an email asking him to come over as well. I didn't bother explaining why; he was fond enough of Sabina to come for no other reason than to entertain her.

Naomi came to help me pack. It was only when I was alone with her, throwing a few essentials into a case that I felt the enormity of what I'd decided to do.

'When you find James, tell him I said it wasn't his fault. I can't bear the thought of him there. Remind him that he saved my life already, would you?'

'I will,' I said, concentrating on all the things I might need. If I stopped and spoke to her for too long I might never go.

'You are coming back, right?' Naomi put a hand on my arm and I patted it twice, as reassuringly as I could. She had already agreed to act as go-between for me tonight but I still needed to go through the details.

'When you see Serenta, take this with you so that she knows you can be trusted.' I gave her my locket, within which was a length of my mother's hair. 'You'll know her when you see her. All the Vilya have the same colouring. She looks a bit like me, only healthier and slimmer.' Naomi managed a smile at that, then wiped a tear from her cheek. 'Don't.' I told her gently. 'You must tell them to get drinking water from a different source. It won't cure Zora at this stage but it will stop any more damage from being done. Much of the harm from the arsenic will be irreversible by now. Don't tell Serenta what I'm doing. They won't be able to reach me in time to help and I don't want my mother worried about me as well as Zora. They need to go ahead and convene the Council of Families, try to resolve the situation as we discussed. Are you sure you don't mind doing this?' I was asking too much of her after everything she'd been through but I couldn't see an alternative.

'This is nothing,' she said. 'What happens if you don't come back?'

'I will,' I said. 'And when I do, we'll take that road trip we talked about. See the deep south, drive down to Florida and party in Key West. How does that sound?'

'Sounds great,' she whispered.

'Come on,' I said. 'I've got one other visit to make before the airport.' At the main house, Sabina was frantically looking through an old chest for a jewellery case to house the cooling, silver-encrusted egg. I phoned Patrick who agreed to meet us at the airport. When everything was packed, I gathered everyone on the porch to say a very obvious goodbye in clear view of the woodland at the back. If we were being watched, and I was sure we were, then I wanted Perun's spies to be in no doubt that I had left. I said my farewells and there was nothing left to do except memorise their faces and wish them all well.

'I hope you don't mind if we make a stop on the way, but there's someone I need to see.' I said to Bryn.

'Where are we going?'

'To the hospital,' I replied. Bryn looked at me but said nothing. As we moved down the long drive way, small creatures fluttered around the windows of the car. I remembered the bat-like things at the flat in London and my suspicion of spies was confirmed.

At the hospital Bryn waited in the car. It was one the busiest medical centres in California and I was in no danger but I needed to see with my own eyes that Aedan was recovering. More than that, I needed to say sorry for the nightmare I'd brought into his life. It took a while to negotiate the corridors and stairs but I finally found him in a room which wouldn't have been out of place in a five star hotel, save for the medical equipment, fitted discretely into the walls. He was sleeping when I arrived and appeared much better recovered than I'd anticipated. I sat by his head and watched him. He was so peaceful that I hadn't the heart to disturb him. The clock was telling me I had to go but I couldn't resist taking a look at the wound just to make sure he was healing. Carefully, I lifted the sheet just enough to peer in and look at the area below his rib cage where Naomi had cut. There was a long pink scar but it was flat and much paler than we'd left it. There was obviously no infection and the surgeons had done a good job of repairing what damage we'd done. I breathed a sigh of relief and lifted my head. As I did so a hand with a vice-like grip grabbed at my wrist and pulled me back down towards his face.

'Seen everything you wanted?' Aedan said. I laughed with relief. He'd terrified me for a second. I was so pleased he was conscious and that I could say goodbye in person.

'Aedan, I'm so glad you're getting better. Do you remember much?'

'I remember enough. Come here sweetheart,' he smiled. I leaned across to kiss him on the cheek and as I did so his free hand came across and smashed into my temple hard enough to leave me seeing flashing lights. His other hand was still around my wrist and I felt the effect of whiplash as the blow flung my head one way and his hand wrenched me back towards him. He wound the hand with which he'd hit me into my hair and pulled my face so close to his that spittle struck my lips as he spoke.

'I remember you tying me up and cutting me while I was awake. I know you didn't call for help because keeping your dirty secrets was more important than saving my life. I remember how good it felt seeing you cry when I hurt your friend. Now get out of here before I finish what I started.'

'Aedan, I came to apologise,' I was shaking from the shock of the violence and the hatred in his voice. 'I didn't mean for anyone to get dragged into this, least of all you. I had no idea what Perun had planned or what he was capable of.'

'And I had no idea what you were capable of,' he said.

'Please, let me explain?'

A female voice behind me, rich with enjoyment, butted in. 'I'm fairly sure I heard him ask you to leave,' said Cat. 'You have precisely three seconds before I call security.' She beamed at me, waving her mobile phone in the air, gloating. I choked back the urge to tell his assistant where she could shove her phone, knowing I didn't have time to deal with another incident.

'This isn't the way I wanted it to be' I said to Aedan. He stared at me hard, his eyes cold and emotionless. This was one apology that would have to wait until I got back. The lump in my throat prevented me from saying anything more and that was probably just as well; there was really nothing I could add that would make it better. I left quietly, stepping around Cat in the doorway. She waited until I'd was an inch through the door and slammed it behind me.

Back at the car, I told the driver to get us to the airport as fast as he could. California was rapidly becoming the last place in the world I wanted to be.

Nineteen

Bryn and I boarded the plane without fuss and settled in for the long flight. There would be one stop to refuel but other than that sixteen hours of cramp and boredom stretched out ahead of us. I watched a movie, sipped as much tea as I could bear and waited for Bryn to fall asleep. When he did, I slipped Adela's diary out of my hand luggage, wanting to find out more about my adoption.

I skipped forward a few weeks from the last entry, found the day she came home to find Branimir holding my feet over a fire and I just couldn't read it. I thought it would have no effect on me, after all, I'd survived relatively unharmed but the images were too powerful and Adela translated her pain onto the page with more skill than she could possibly have known. I'd decided to put the book away when at the bottom of the opposite page I glimpsed Castevan's name. Curious as to my father's reappearance in the story when I thought he'd disappeared, I settled down to read more.

'5 May. The baby's feet will heal, I'm sure, although they will be scarred. Branimir is staying with his parents; he won't see me or speak to me at the moment and, really, I'm glad. I don't think I can stand to be in the same room with him again. He's still ranting about Eve being the devil's child and his parents think he's lost his senses. I feel guilty but all I can do now is protect the baby in the same way I hope Anousk is protecting Zora. I received a terse note from Castevan this morning. I hadn't expected to hear from him so soon. He's coming tonight after dark and I can only guess he found out what happened.' The air steward interrupted with the offer of another drink but I waved him away, eager to find out what happened next.

'6 May. Castevan was very late and I didn't hear him knocking at the back door until after two in the morning. When he came in he looked terrible. He usually appears so robust but last night he was pale and drawn, with huge circles under his eyes. He's lost so much weight in such a short time I was worried he was seriously ill. He said not, but that he's been hiding out. He and Anousk had to keep Eve's parentage a secret; she returned to Manitu with Zora saying only that she had let her baby go to settle a debt and she and Castevan have agreed not to contact one another again. He was worried that someone had found out about Eve and would try to take her, so he's been watching my house for several days. Apparently he's seen things that don't belong here flying around and he cannot leave Eve where she might be in danger. He says I must send the child elsewhere for safety, as far away as possible. He was so agitated I didn't have the heart to tell him about Branimir burning her and I had no choice but to agree to his request. I cannot keep her if it means she'll be at risk and Castevan spent so much time looking out of the window that I ended up quite shaken, too. I told him I would do whatever he wanted although I did ask why anyone would want to hurt a helpless baby.

'Castevan didn't answer straight away so I pushed him on it. All he would say is that the baby has mixed cambion, Vilya and Polevoi blood and that there was no way of knowing how she would turn out. Sometimes, as with him, there is no effect from having a cambion father as all his traits are from Reema, his mother. Occasionally, the cambion personality skips a generation and if Eve turns out to inherit her grandfather's genes then Castevan says she might be more powerful than any of us could control. Castevan wouldn't be drawn much further but he said that she could be as evil as the incubi or as ordinary as a human and never be any the wiser. What's certain is that she should be sent away in case the Perelesnyk have figured out that I'm related to Castevan. He is planning to remain in the human world from now on, but when he said goodbye it felt terribly final. I don't believe I will ever see him again and this poor child will face a lifetime without any of her blood relatives around her. I pray that she never finds out what lies in her past. I've telephoned an adoption agency. Branimir will agree the adoption without hesitation, I know. As for me, I don't think I can remain here with all the memories of my own child and this little one I failed to protect. I cannot explain to what few family I have left that I've given my only child away. My patient, Sabina, is talking about moving to America to pursue her acting career. The thought of it terrifies me but perhaps a fresh start is the best I can hope for.'

Poor Adela. She gave up her baby for its own good, believing she would have another to love and then had to part with that one also. I felt desperate for her. I'd always assumed that what caused her to have me adopted was my immolation. Now I knew it was to keep me safe from the Perelesnyk and I wasn't sure if that made me feel better or worse. I was still staring at the page when I realised that Bryn was awake. I tried to close the notebook casually so that I didn't alert him to how upset I was.

'Do you remember the first case we did together?' he said. I thought back but honestly, there were so many over the years that I couldn't recall that particular one. 'Well, we were defending a girl, just fifteen years old, who'd robbed a shop at knife point for money to buy drugs for her mother. She was a skinny thing, only looked about ten to me, she was so underweight and no-one could get through to her. She wouldn't say a word about why she did it; just wanted some cash was all she'd tell us. You kept Judge Bodrill waiting for two hours while you sat in a cell with her, not even talking most of the time, just giving her tea and cigarettes until she told you what was going on at home. Her bloody mother wasn't even at Court to watch her go down. That kid should've got a year of prison time. By the time you'd finished telling her life-story, the Judge was barely able to speak.'

'I remember now. Her name was Nicky Stock. But you're telling the story as if it were me that made a difference. It wasn't me, Bryn, it was just the truth. She'd been used her whole life. She'd been threatened and beaten and who knows what else that she couldn't bring herself to say out loud. The judge knew no-one could have come up with a story like that. If memory serves me, she got a stretch of probation which she breached a week later and ended up in prison anyway.' I smiled ruefully. 'So what's your point?'

'My point is that you know who you are on the inside and no amount of finding your parents or grandparents, or wondering what lies in your past, has any bearing on it. The woman I saw in court that day was someone who knew how to shut her mouth and listen, a much underrated skill I might add. It's the sign of a person who gives before taking. Never forget that you control your own destiny.'

'What about nature versus nurture? We can't change what we're handed genetically.'

'And yet mankind has evolved, learned to comply with rules and laws even when our baser instincts tell us to do otherwise. Being unable to change what you start with is not the same as being incapable of controlling yourself.'

I kissed him on the cheek. Bryn was a cure for all the evils of the world. I put the translation of Adela's diary back into my hand luggage feeling as if there might be light at the end of the tunnel. After that, Bryn asked me all I knew about the Perelesnyk and the Moroi. I told him about Patrick and what I knew of the mountain region where James had gone. We whispered to one another, aware how bizarre our conversation would sound to anyone else. Bryn had bought a map of the area and had a good idea of travelling time and the challenges of the terrain but not what was waiting for us at the other end. He'd also drawn up a list of items he would need to get hold of in Slovakia, including some weaponry. When I dared to ask how he was going to manage that, he simply patted me on the hand and told me there were some things a lady ought not be troubled with. I put my head on his shoulder and slept. I must have been more tired than I imagined, because I stayed that way until we were preparing to land in Bratislava.

When we'd disembarked we had one of those rare runs of luck which meant we got straight through immigration before the queues built up and immediately found our cases on the luggage belts. I pulled my roller case through the 'Nothing to Declare' section only to find a dog sniffing at me and getting increasingly agitated as he did so. I instinctively stopped and looked completely confused, not appearing in any rush to move on and was taken aside by a polite but formal customs officer who spoke to me in English when I asked what the problem was. Bryn walked on and away from the scene. I didn't call ahead to him, not at all sure what he had in his case but suspecting there were some things in there that might raise unwanted questions. My case was put up on a desk and I opened it freely.

'Do you have anything in here that is forbidden, Miss?'

'Not as far as I know,' I said, hoping this was only a random spot check and that the liderc hadn't given off some strange odour alerting the dog to the presence of a living thing. 'Certainly there are no drugs, no alcohol, no cash in there.'

'And you packed the bag yourself?' he continued. I nodded and then he put his hand on the jewellery box. It was beautifully wrapped with red paper and a white bow and I mentally apologised to Sabina who I'd teased for being over-zealous in her preparations for just such a disaster. How wrong I was. 'Can you tell me what is in here?' he asked.

'A present for a friend,' I said. 'It's a silver trinket in the shape of an egg, only plated not solid as you can feel from the weight.'

'I will have to open it, you understand, so I can check what you say.' I told him that was fine and he undid the wrapping, doing as little damage as he could. When he opened the lid I was relieved to see the egg was still in one piece although it had shifted in the box quite substantially. I crossed my fingers in my pocket and hoped that the movement was the result of turbulence rather than an attempt to break through the shell.

'Do you have a receipt for this?' the officer asked.

'No, it's an old family piece, I've never seen a receipt but I don't think it has any substantial value.' I saw the egg shift in his hand and he obviously felt it. He focussed all his attention on it, watching carefully and I knew he was trying to decide if he'd imagined it or not. I couldn't lose the liderc; I was going to need it when we got into the mountains or I might never find James.

'I'm afraid I will have to confiscate this item. You can apply to have it returned to you and I will give you the correct forms before you leave.'

'Oh, officer, please. That thing means an awful lot to me. I wouldn't feel safe just leaving it here.'

'I can assure you madam that it will be kept safe until it can be investigated and then returned to you if satisfactory. Until then, I will require the address where you will be staying and you must sign for it, of course.'

'You don't understand. If that item doesn't go with me then my trip here was for no purpose.' I must have been raising my voice although I was trying hard not to. All I could think was that the liderc was my last hope of saving James and that I would fight for it if I had to.

'If you do not calm yourself, Miss, I will have no choice but to place you under arrest until this is processed.'

'That will not be necessary, thank you officer.' Another man with significantly more stripes on his shoulder appeared and began repacking my bag. I didn't dare speak as he put it on the floor. The officer I'd been talking to looked irritated but not argumentative. 'Please, follow me.'

We went through double doors to one side and I was taken along a brightly lit corridor adjacent to arrivals. I held my breath as he opened another door in front of me, hoping that I wasn't simply being put on a plane home but when the door opened fully I saw Patrick leaning against the desk.

'Eve, my darling,' he said and stepped forward to kiss me on each cheek, and take the case from my hand in the same move. 'Allow me to introduce Gustav Novac, head of customs and immigration here in Bratislava airport.' The man who'd escorted me down the corridor bowed slightly as he took my hand.

'Forgive the misunderstanding, Miss MacKenzie, my officer did not realise you were here as a guest of the British Embassy. Please accept my apologies.'

'No apology necessary,' I said. 'Your officer was extremely polite. May I say how reassuring it is to be at an airport where everyone is kept so safe by the diligence of the people in your command, Mr Novac. They are a credit to you.' It was all I needed to ensure that I'd be released without further fuss although my hand was still trembling when I slipped it through

Patrick's arm to walk to his car. 'I have to find Bryn,' I said quietly as we exited.

'No need; he's in the car, that's how I knew where you were.' I slid into the limousine and relaxed into the black leather seats, glad the windows were dark and feeling like an idiot. Patrick handed my case to the driver and got in next to me.

'Patrick St. John meet Bryn Williams,' I said as the car pulled away. The men shook hands and I closed my eyes, trying to imagine for a second that I was on my way to some embassy ball.

'It's a pleasure to have you both here,' said Patrick. 'I hope you don't mind but I thought you'd be more comfortable staying at my accommodation than a hotel. We'll be better assured of privacy.' I shifted uncomfortably. I still hadn't told Patrick more than was absolutely necessary to ensure that he'd meet us and take us to James' rented cabin. Other than that, he had no clue about what was really going on.

'Patrick,' I began, my hesitation obvious.

'Eve, don't,' he said. 'I've spent enough years learning the language of diplomacy to know that when someone opens a sentence with your name, as you just did, they are about to either deliver bad news or tell you a lie. Whatever you and your friend James are doing here obviously has nothing to do with exploring the tourist highlights of this wonderful country. If you need my help, and I suspect you do, then have some faith. We will be at my home in no more than fifteen minutes. May I suggest you wait until we are settled and then tell me what I need to know to help you as best I can.' Bryn chuckled beside me and I turned to him, incredulous that he could find such a moment amusing.

'What?' I asked him.

'I like him,' Bryn replied. 'Anyone who can shut you up mid-sentence has to be alright.' I raised my eyes to the ceiling in mock frustration but inside I was thanking whatever divine forces had brought these two good men together when I needed them.

Patrick lived in a three storey town house in the centre of the city. It was old but beautifully preserved inside. A housekeeper ushered us in, showed us our rooms and gave us enough of a tour that we'd be able to find the sitting room once we'd freshened up. All I wanted right then was a hot bath and a good meal to make up for the aeroplane food. An hour and a half later I was washed, changed and fully fed. No-one said a word about our business there until Patrick dismissed the housekeeper for the night in flawless Slovakian and we were sat drinking coffee.

'So,' Patrick said. 'You don't have to tell me everything but the more I know, the more use I'll be and I'm not letting you disappear off into the mountains unless I know exactly what you're expecting to find there.' I would have held back more but when Bryn trusted someone he didn't let caution stand in his way. Evidently, he and Patrick had recognised kindred spirits so I let him take over and recount all he could before bedding down for the night to recover from the journey. Patrick said little, looking briefly at Bryn's map and marking the last place he'd seen James. At last, exhausted, I made my excuses and left them still chatting. This might be the last decent night's sleep I'd get for while and I wasn't going to pass on a comfortable mattress and warm duvet.

Twenty

By morning, the sitting room resembled a war room more than the comfortable lounge I'd been in the night before. There were empty coffee cups strewn on tables where maps, photos and indecipherable reference books covered every spare inch.

'Good morning,' said Patrick. 'Did you sleep well?'

'I suspect I should be asking if you two slept at all,' I replied although, in fact, he and Bryn looked more invigorated and energetic than me, even after I'd crashed out for a solid ten hours. 'Sorry I'm up so late, you should have woken me.'

'Nonsense, you're better off getting all the rest you can. Anyway, Bryn and I are just off out for a while. There's breakfast keeping warm in the oven, plenty of hot coffee and no-one should disturb you. I'll lock up behind me. If anyone rings the bell may I suggest you ignore it, likewise the phone.'

'Okay, but where exactly are you going?' They were both wearing scruffy old clothes with large jackets and when I hugged Bryn goodbye I felt a solid bulk under one arm that scared me.

'Bryn, is that a gun?' I asked.

'Everything'll be fine, don't you worry. There a few things I need and the place we're going you sometimes have to prove you mean business.' I was about to argue then thought better of it. I'd brought them to this and I had to get over the fact that I wanted the world to be a soft, gentle place where nobody got hurt. Bryn could handle himself. It was only when I hugged Patrick that I really got worried.

'You as well? What the hell are you guys up to? I know Bryn knows how to handle a gun but you Patrick? I thought this was going to be the easy bit.'

Patrick kissed me on the cheek and looked genuinely pleased that I cared. 'The thing is, I know you a lot better than you know me. I only got accepted into the diplomatic service because I did my officer training at Sandhurst with a man whose father was an ambassador. When I left the army he offered me the place he'd always hoped his son Joss would take.'

'Joss?' I asked.

'Was fatally wounded in a bombing in Iraq. He was a good friend. A lot of people in my profession are from military backgrounds. I should have told you,' he said.

'I knew as soon as I saw him,' Bryn said. 'Of course, I expect you young ladies don't get past looking at that pretty face.' He winked at me and I threw a nearby book at him.

'Oh, she's not interested in me,' Patrick chipped in. 'I'm guessing she only has eyes for the cowboy we're off to help rescue. I never understood why women always fall for that strong, silent stereotype.'

'That's it, get out. I take it all back. You are both more than capable of handling yourselves,' but I was laughing with them as they left and this time I noticed they drove away in a small unrecognisable car rather than the stand-out-in-the-crowd limo. I locked the door and went to get breakfast out of the oven. When I'd eaten, I decided to phone the ranch and check on everyone.

Xander picked up sounding much brighter than when I'd left and I was glad I'd put some distance between him and the liderc. He quickly confirmed that everyone was fine and called Naomi to the phone.

'Eve, did you and Bryn arrive safely?' she asked. I told her about the incident at the airport more to entertain than anything else, while I gauged how she was feeling. 'I met Serenta' she said, her voice low as if no-one else knew what she had done. 'You didn't tell me.'

I was confused. 'Tell you what, Naomi?'

'How wonderful they are. It was like talking to someone filled with sunshine. She was so natural and, oh, I can't really describe it. Just being around her made me feel better, stronger. And she looked so much like you. Is it weird being there with all of them having your hair and skin colour? I had to reach out and touch her, I couldn't believe she was real. She must have thought I was crazy.'

'I'm sure she didn't think that at all,' I said. 'She knows how important you are to me and unlike incubi, the Vilya rarely mix with humans. She was probably just as delighted to meet you.'

'I told her what you'd found out about the arsenic poisoning. She seemed saddened but she knew the Perelesnyk had been in the area and I got the impression she thought they must have been poisoning the well. They've been drinking the water from that source for years. If the arsenic came naturally from that environment Zora would have become ill long ago.'

'I suspected as much,' I said. 'Still, at least now they can stop doing any more damage.'

'Zora isn't doing well at all. They don't know how much longer she'll live. I'm sorry, I know you care about her.' I forced back tears; this wasn't the right time to allow myself to become blinded by emotion.

'What about you. How are you doing?'

'We're holding up. It's nice having Daniel here, he really lifts the mood and Xander's getting back to his usual self. Sabina is worried sick about you but trying not to show it and I feel better since meeting Serenta. She hugged me before she left and it was like she mended something inside me.'

'Did she ask where I was?' I asked. Naomi was quiet for a few seconds before responding.

'No,' she replied softly. That was a good thing, I thought. They had to believe I was sticking to my original plan and staying away from Manitu.

'Patrick and Bryn have gone off on some secret mission. Apparently it's too covert even for me to know what they're up to.'

'They've gone for take out food then, knowing Bryn.' Naomi giggled and I wished she were with me.

'I'd better go; I need to have a good rummage through their papers whilst they're out. No harm me knowing what they've got planned.' We rang off after the usual goodbyes and I tried to decipher some of their notes. Most of the books were in Slovakian but I could see where Patrick had marked up the route map to the cabin. It was in the foothills of Gerlach Peak, the highest mountain in the Tatras. The cabin itself was incredibly remote, used mainly as a lower camp for serious climbers and equipped with everything you might need for a fairly lengthy stay if you got snowed in. Once the weather made the roads impassable you had to grit your teeth and wait it out. The cabin backed into a steep cliff and had a clearing to the front with woodland a hundred yards away. The chances of finding it unless you knew it was there were negligible. The cabin had its own generator and a massive underground oil tank a short distance from the house, so at least we'd be warm and able to cook.

A tourist guide had pictures of the natural flora and fauna in the high forests which included brown bears, lynx, wild boar and even wolves. I hoped James had gone properly prepared but he was no stranger to outdoor survival. From the map I could see that the cabin was north west of Brezno, where Zora was born and where Adela and Branimir had lived happily enough for many years. I switched on my laptop to do some of my own research about the Carpathian Mountains but the only legends that the search engine presented related to Transylvania and vampires. The reality of the Moroi was something vastly less romantic. Bram Stoker wouldn't have wanted to join me on this adventure, even given his passion for the occult. Two hours later, Bryn and Patrick reappeared. They didn't carry anything in with them, but when I looked outside I saw that the earlier car had been exchanged for a large four-by-four and that the trunk looked full already.

'Get everything you needed?' I asked. They both confirmed that they had. 'Don't suppose you stopped to buy any food though, did you?' They glanced at one another, slightly embarrassed. 'Don't worry, we can stop on the way but if nothing in the back of that vehicle is consumable then I really don't want to know what it is.' We packed up soon afterwards and crammed ourselves into the car. Patrick made sure he had his diplomatic papers with him and I took one last look at the liderc to make sure nothing had changed before we set off. Either all movement had ceased or I'd imagined it in the first place and there was no sign of anything sinister happening. Given that my whole plan rested on the liderc still being alive, I hoped that what little information we'd found was accurate or this would be the best organised waste of time on record.

Bryn took first shift with the driving and Patrick navigated our way through the streets of Bratislava. Beyond the grandiose city centre, where much of the architecture had a Bavarian feel, we passed through a sea of high rise blocks, testament to the harsh economic climate many still endured here. On the outskirts of the city we pulled into a petrol station next to a supermarket where we went to buy supplies. We picked up a selection of smoked cheeses and meats, traditional in Slovakia but also perfect for a long journey without a fridge. We took as much fruit as we could, some dried mushrooms, potatoes, oil, eggs, milk and bread. I knew that Bryn had already packed all the tea and coffee he could carry, the two staples he couldn't bear to be without. None of us were really sure how long we might end up in the mountains, so we erred on the side of caution. At least there would be no shortage of fresh water.

It only took us about three hours to get to Brezno where we made our next stop for coffee and to stretch our legs. The final part of the journey into the mountains was easy in terms of distance but would take a lot longer because of the increasingly windy roads. Hopefully, no trees had fallen since Patrick came up here with James. I wanted to be inside that cabin with the doors firmly bolted before nightfall. Bryn went for a walk around the town centre whilst Patrick and I huddled in a coffee shop, warming ourselves up. I wrapped my hands around a steaming mug of hot chocolate as Patrick took a double hit of espresso.

'How was James when you left him?' I asked.

'Quiet,' he said. 'If I'd had any idea what was going on, you know I'd have called you. He covered it well, seemed completely self-assured, at peace with himself.'

'That sounds like James. It's not your fault. If you hadn't been here I don't know what I'd have done.'

'If I hadn't been here, giving him the translations and maps, maybe he wouldn't have ended up here at all.'

'He would. One way or another he'd have figured it out and made his own way. That's who he is. Once he's made up his mind, there's no stopping him.' I put my hand on Patrick's so he would understand this wasn't his responsibility and he held my fingers in his for a moment.

'You're in love with him?' he asked.

That wasn't an easy question. I stared out of the window at a young couple walking hand in hand across the market square. 'Trying not to be,' I said. Patrick just nodded.

'And what about you? You're full of surprises: The army, your ability to be completely unsurprised by anything you've been told since I arrived. Aren't you struggling with this even a little bit?' He settled down in his chair with the air of one about to tell a story and I wasn't disappointed.

'When we came to Brezno before, I told you that these people were superstitious. Slavic culture is built on folk tale and myth. Even my own mother, growing up in Czechoslovakia in a very strict and proper family, would never dare to say that the myths were just stories made up to scare children. There were always fresh flowers in my grandparents' house, with twigs and different foliage mixed in. I didn't notice for years until I asked about it one day and my mother explained that different types of wood and herbs warded off evil spirits. Back then I thought it was just sweet, a tradition, nothing more.'

'So what changed your mind?'

He finished his espresso. 'The war in Iraq,' he said. 'You develop your own rituals, you find a talisman where before you only saw an unusual stone, but if you picked up that stone just before you walked away from a car bomb that should've blown you to pieces, then it stayed in your pocket for the rest of your tour of duty. And who's to say what's real and what's not? Seeing action makes you aware of every twist of fate, chance, coincidence or otherwise. I defy any person not to believe in something whilst they're in a war zone, whether it's the position of the stars or the faith they were taught in infancy. There has to be something that will stop you from being captured or maimed or killed.'

'How long were you there?' I asked.

'Two years, couple of trips home but that always just made it worse going back again. Honestly, I'd rather have stayed there the whole time. Every time I came back there was another

162

memorial service for men and women I'd served with and seeing their partners, children...'

'I'm sorry,' I whispered, but it sounded hollow and pathetic. I had no idea what he'd been through. I began to realise why he and Bryn were so immediately comfortable in one another's company. It must be reassuring to be with other people who know, really understand, what war is like without having to paint a picture.

'I'd been posted there eighteen months and we'd lost plenty of men but death was always fast, everyone racing to get medics to the scene or just picking up the pieces after a bomb blast. I was in charge of a company of about one hundred men. I knew each of them by their name, nickname, the cigarettes they smoked, the photos of their children but we never talked religion, not once. It was the closest thing to a taboo subject my boys had. It starts arguments, makes some of the men uncomfortable. For most of us, it was a step too close to acknowledging the chances of dying. Anyway, one afternoon, I was leading a small troop on a reconnaissance mission, just checking the lay of the land for a night raid planned later that week, should've been quick and simple except we walked into a trap. Nothing sophisticated, just a handful of unoccupied buildings that had been confirmed empty the day before, then suddenly we were surrounded. They didn't even want to kill us, I think they were just trying to get their hands on our weapons. By this stage in the conflict we had the enemy retreating and were effectively cutting off their supply chain. It made them desperate and even more dangerous. We fought back straight away and ended up trying to hold out in an old bath house. We managed to get an SOS signal out at the start of the fighting but we were in enemy territory and they had gunmen on the roofs so there was no way of getting a helicopter in. We had to stay hidden and hold them off until ground troops could reach us.' As Patrick talked I could hear background noise, bursts of machine gun fire, the distant rumble of larger guns, and the awful silence in between trying to figure out which direction the enemy would come from. I could smell the explosives and the dusty rubble clogging the air. At the back of my throat I could taste something metallic, coppery. I closed my eyes and saw the pale yellow walls and the sand blowing across the floor where the building had been abandoned too long. Patrick's voice cut through my vision.

'My second in command was trying to access the roof to see if we could shelter up there whilst firing back. He stuck his head up too far, not knowing they had a sniper in an adjacent building. The only thing that stopped him being killed outright was that he slipped at the precise moment when the bullet made contact. Instead of a clean headshot, it went through the back of his neck, damaging his spinal cord. We gave up trying to move him and I posted what men I had left at the windows to provide some cover and hope the enemy didn't have grenades. Benson hit the floor hard. I thought he was dead but he lay there trying to talk. I told him not to, that the medics were on their way but he wouldn't stop. He was whispering something over and over. I eventually figured out what it was. "Confession" he kept saying. When he pulled his shirt open I saw a cross. As much as I knew about him, I didn't know he was Catholic. I told him he had nothing to confess, he was going to live but he grabbed my shirt and pulled me close so that I could hear. He was crying and I listened just to take his mind off the fact that it was taking so long for help to arrive.

'He had to repeat most sentences a few times before I could understand him and even now I look back and wonder if my memory wasn't playing tricks on me, but as he lay dying he told me he'd killed a boy. He was just eleven years old. He lived by the coast in Dorset and he went sea fishing one Saturday with his best friend. It was October, cold and stormy and there was no-one else around. His friend had cast a long line and spent ages pulling in something heavy. Turns out it was a leather pouch, obviously very old, with a crest burned into it. Inside they found gold coins. The area was rocky and famous for ship wrecks. They both thought they'd found ancient treasure. Anyway, an argument started about whose it was and they got into a fight. Eventually his friend just picked up the bag of coins, refusing to share and Benson saw red. He grabbed the nearest rock and threw it, as hard as he could, at the boy's back. His aim was good but a little high and the rock smashed into the back of his friend's head. He was dead before he hit the pebbles. Benson said he didn't even think about it. He threw the body into the sea, waited for the tide to go out then ran for home saying a freak wave had hit them and that his friend had been taken out to sea. They never found the body and Benson kept those coins forever, never showing another living person.

'When he finished his story he said he was going to hell. Said he'd seen it in his dreams, he knew they were coming for him. He believed he'd sold his soul for the gold. He was rambling and mostly incoherent by then but he was genuinely terrified. In all the action I saw, I'd never seen a man so petrified in my life. I told him he could rest easy since he'd confessed; that he'd repaid his debt by serving in the army. I said anything I could to release him from that awful terror. He reached into his pocket and pullet out something dark and soft, almost wilting. He shoved it in my hand and I could smell leather and something else, salty and rotten, like seaweed that's sat too long in the sun. When I pulled the drawstring open I saw the gold shining inside. He'd carried it with him all that time. He asked me to put it back, throw it into the sea for his friend to keep. I promised him I would, he was on his way out by then and you don't pretend any more when death's that close. He told me he was ready to go and that's when I saw the shadows around me. The temperature in the room dropped off the scale, I could see my breath. I wanted to make it easy for him, hold him while he passed, but I was too scared. The room grew darker. It was the middle of the day in one of the hottest countries imaginable and whatever those things were that came for him leeched every ounce of light and warmth from the air. I froze like a child, thinking that if I didn't speak or move they wouldn't notice me. They did though, they swirled around me like black mist and I could see faces in the darkness, disfigured, snarling, almost daring me to step up. I let him go and at the last moment he screamed as if he were being swallowed whole. When it was over and the room was back to normal, he was just lying there, eyes wide open, a shell. I stayed like that, didn't touch him or issue a single command to my other men, until backup arrived about thirty minutes later. They had enough firepower to take out the Iraqi fighters quickly and easily. When the medics reached us they said he was already well into rigor mortis. They put time of death at two hours earlier. I didn't say a word about what I'd seen; I'd have been discharged with post-traumatic stress disorder. It wasn't until I was back in my bunk that I checked my pocket and found the leather pouch. I closed it straight away, didn't touch one single coin. I kept it hidden until my next leave and then went to the stretch of coast he'd described. I threw the whole thing as far and as hard into the water as I could, feeling like a fool but knowing I was doing what he wanted. When the coins hit the waves a mist rose up from the sea, rolling in towards the beach and as much as I wanted to run away, I waited and watched. As the fog cleared I could see a young boy stood in the shallows of the water, as if paddling, but he was staring at me. His clothes were ragged and dripping wet. He was deathly pale, almost green and as he looked at me he grinned. He'd won, he was telling me. He got his gold in the end, all to himself. He took a single step forwards, towards me and that was all it took. I didn't just run, I fled, stumbling up the cliffs behind me, crying like a baby and wanting to be safe at home where the monsters were far, far away.' Tears were streaming down Patrick's face and I was sure he couldn't feel a single one of them. I felt the fear running off him from the memory and it made me shudder.

'Patrick?' I said. 'It's all right now. It's done.' He shook himself and seemed to wake from the remembrance.

'War is a bloody thing,' he continued. 'But I still believe that sometimes it's unavoidable. Dictators have no place in this world and we have no right to leave innocent people suffering when we can intervene. I don't regret a single thing I did when I was in the army but I regret not stepping up and trying to fight those creatures. That's why I have no trouble believing in the demons you describe.'

'You don't have to do this with me, Patrick. It's not your war.'

'Actually, it's a bit of a relief, the thought of doing something active again. I've been stagnating. You're warned it'll be like this when you leave the army. I guess you think the void will naturally be filled by other things. As much as I love life at the Embassy, I miss the adrenaline. This may not be my war, but it's one worth fighting.'

Bryn came in armed with fire lighters and flares. 'Just a few things I missed earlier. You two ready for the last leg?' We were. I got coffee for Bryn to take out and asked them to pack up a huge fruitcake that would be a welcome treat by the time we arrived at the cabin. Back in the car, Patrick had to concentrate harder on navigation and all other conversation ceased. The High Tatras were still snow covered and the roads were treacherous even with the warmer weather starting to break through. It wasn't long until we'd left all signs of civilisation behind. Patrick translated various signs about ensuring you had suitable bad weather equipment with you and that other people were aware of your whereabouts. Soon enough, our route was tree lined on both sides and the forest became more dense with each mile. The road became steeper and after two more hours of slow going, we pulled off the asphalt and followed a dwindling gravel track. After stopping to clear one sapling from the path we finally made it to the cabin.

The light was all but gone from the sky but I could just make out the outline of the structure. Its back was set against the rock face which gave it protection from the rear but meant there was only access to the front and sides, all of which were fairly visible to anyone approaching. The rocks above stretched up higher than I could see in the dark. The cabin was a combination of rock and wood construction, with sturdy walls to keep out the cold. The windows were small and leaded and I could see a brick chimney in the centre of the roof. I knew from Patrick that it had just one large bedroom, a living and dining area combined with the kitchen and one small bathroom. Bryn quickly made sure the gas was switched on and then we carted in our supplies, bedding and endless heavy crates from the back of the vehicle.

An hour later, the kettle was whistling on the stove and a fire was roaring in the grate. The windows were shuttered and we secured most of them, only leaving a couple open so we could see outside. The night was bright, and with no cloud cover the moonlight made the small clearing at the front almost floodlit. I huddled at the fire, coat still on whilst the place warmed up and Patrick brought me a tin mug full of hot, sweet tea and a white envelope with my name handwritten on the front. James had allowed for every eventuality.

Twenty-one

Both men made an excuse to leave the room; Bryn to explore the small cellar and Patrick to unpack in the bedroom. I ran my hand over the front of the envelope imagining James sitting here, in front of the fire, writing it before he left. I almost didn't want to read it. If I couldn't catch up with him then these would be the last of his words that would reach me. Finally, my desire to know what he was going through overtook my reticence, so I slid my finger under the seal and pulled out a single sheet of paper.

'Eve, I hope that if you're reading this it's because Patrick found it and forwarded it to you in California. If you are in Slovakia, then I know that pleading with you to turn around and go home will be pointless. I couldn't stand to watch Tim die and do nothing about it, but you've already figured that out, haven't you? That's why I know you'll agree that Naomi deserves better. They take away too many loved ones not to face some small retribution. Losing you made everything seem so pointless and I don't want to carry on alone any more. At least this way I can put my time to good use. If you're angry and I know you are, then find a way to forgive me and move on. I am long gone. Go home and protect the others. Sorry I missed your birthday but know that I was thinking of you. I have left a small token in the bedroom on the chest. Daniel Fortune has my final instructions about the few things I've left behind. Don't worry too much about Sabina; she'll be safe in his care. If there were any other way, you know I wouldn't have left you. I hope to see you again in a more forgiving place, James.'

It was typically him; brief, straight forward, unpretentious. With the letter in one hand, I went into the bedroom. Patrick was studying an old book and on the top of a large chest of drawers was a neat parcel, wrapped in brown paper. I took it down and perched on the edge of the bed. Patrick looked up but didn't speak as I opened it. Inside I found the most beautiful pair of riding gloves I'd ever seen. The leather was light tan and as soft as silk. They fitted me perfectly and I thought of the lesson I'd had with James just before my first journey into Manitu. The gloves smelled of sunshine and grass and the barns where the horse feed was kept. Patrick swung his legs over to sit next to me, put a companionable arm round my shoulders and we sat there, like that, until Bryn called us into action. I wondered what I was doing here, risking more lives when James had made such an extraordinary sacrifice to try to save some. Patrick pulled me lightly to my feet.

'Best not think about it too much,' he said. 'Some things defy reason.' I gave him a grateful hug and we went to see what Bryn wanted.

We found him with a large scale map of the few square miles around the cabin with details about the geology of the area.

'Look at this,' he said, tracing his finger over a semicircular line around the cabin.

'What is it?' I asked.

'A stream,' he said. 'Very narrow, only about a metre across in most parts. I can't get a good look at it until morning but it looks like it runs off a small waterfall from the cliff face about fifty yards west of the property, just an offshoot of a large river on the mountains behind us that acts as an overflow when the water rises too high. Because of that it almost surrounds the cabin, meaning we can use it as a first line of defence. I'll drain some of the oil from the tank and run it in, dam up the far end and hope enough of the oil stays there to ignite the length of the ditch.

'But won't it just get diluted with the water, dirt and debris?'

'If I'm right, the rivulet flow is so light that it'll have frozen over. The oil should stay around for long enough to provide a good flame, and if not then at least it'll provide an impressive distraction while you get away.' Bryn looked pleased with himself and it made me think that we might just have a chance. He thought it could work and that was good enough for me.

'Patrick?' I said. 'What do you think?'

'From what I've learned about the Moroi, fire is our best shot at holding them off or injuring them. That's if it's the Moroi who come. If it's the incubi themselves then it'll have been a fool's errand. The Perelesnyk aren't afraid of fire, quite the opposite. We'll need other layers of defence but it's a great start.'

'How long can you hold them off, do you think?' I asked.

'No way of knowing,' said Bryn. 'Depends how many of them there are and how good our intelligence is. The cabin's well built and secure. We got hold of some more traditional weaponry but whether or not it'll work on them remains to be seen. It'll take half a day to get this in place tomorrow, with an early kick off and then we've got the afternoon to fix up some further defences. I say we get some kip while it's dark and start fresh.' Patrick and I agreed. We cooked up a hasty meal of omelettes and smoked meats then bedded down for the night. Patrick and Bryn put their sleeping bags head to toe on the double bed and I took the sofa, more than happy not to be far from the warmth of the fire. I fell asleep wearing the gloves James had left me and holding his letter, hoping he was wrong and that I wasn't too late.

Next morning, the fire had long since burned out and the place was freezing. It took all my energy to drag myself from under the covers and light the kettle. When I called Bryn and Patrick, I was ashamed to find that they were already up and out, dressed for the harsh elements and digging in the front clearing. I made up for my late start with bacon sandwiches and coffee, which they ate and drank in seconds before getting back to work. The stream, as Bryn predicted, was frozen and they'd begun damming one end to keep the oil in. Patrick was placing a fuse to light the oil and Bryn was chopping down some of the older nearby trees, using the larger branches as a barrier between the cabin and the ditch, and the smaller ones he was cutting into lethal points to create stakes which he was securing deep into the ground. The frozen earth was making it a slow task and I knew I couldn't be much help so I followed Patrick and bombarded him with questions about his research on the Moroi and the Perelesnyk, hoping to come up with something else that might help keep them away.

The books revealed a mixture of ridiculous fairytale (I was ignoring the suggestion that you could defeat a Moroi by drawing a cross on your chest in cow dung as the Moroi would apparently be put off by both the religious connotations and the smell) and concentrating more on purported sightings of them by those who'd lived to tell the tale. People who'd evaded them had hidden in barns, among livestock or in pantries and it occurred to me that these were all places where human scent would be overpowered by other odours. I could hear Patrick and Bryn on the cabin roof and, when a power tool roared into life over my head, I decided it was time to take a walk through the forest and get a feel for the geography and pitfalls before attempting to pass through it at night.

It was densely wooded, with a carpet of fallen branches and foliage. That was both good and bad. I would need the thick tree cover to avoid being seen by the demons coming towards the cabin, as the plan was to follow their trail in reverse back through into Manitu and to their settlement. I already knew that finding the Moroi meant finding the Perelesnyk. The problem was that I couldn't risk having a torch with me and I'd have to negotiate the forest in darkness, making as little sound as possible and without injuring myself. I practised creeping first then running through the undergrowth, feeling like an idiot in the light of day. Several times I fell, once painfully twisting my ankle. I decided to leave injuring myself until later before I completely undermined my own plan. Hopefully, there would be enough moonlight to navigate a path without running head on into a group of enraged monsters. I tied my compass around my watch strap, checked my heading and turned back for the cabin. I jumped the ditch which in a couple of hours would be flooded with oil and jogged into the clearing to see what the men were up to now. As I entered the space at the front of the tree line, I heard Patrick shout but it was too late. A weighted net dropped from the last tree across me, knocking me about the shoulders and I hit the ground hard. I struggled to get up but just got increasingly wrapped in the nylon netting. Bryn yelled at me to stay still and I fought my instinct to help free myself as they slowly unwound the net. When I looked closely, I saw that what had hit me were rocks attached to the edges of the net to give it some weight and make it drop faster. Once free, I went inside to put warm salt water on my wounds.

'How many nets have you put up?' I asked.

'Twelve,' said Bryn. 'We've used every two trees at the front of the clearing to string them between. Should take down a fair number of any type of creature, as long as they come in groups.'

'Well, I'm sure it'll floor them for a while but these things have razor-sharp talons. It won't take them more than a few seconds to cut through that and get back up.'

'We only need a few seconds to get piles of them on the floor, hopefully with some others climbing over them. We got hold of some grenades, old and probably not one hundred per cent reliable, but if we lob enough of them at mounds of creatures fighting each other to get up, we're going to kill or disable large numbers at a time.' I stared at them both open-mouthed.

'You know what, I almost feel sorry for them,' I said. 'I'm going to stick to preparing food and leave you to do the soldiering. Just don't blow up the kitchen while I'm making dinner.' The two of them shared an amused look.

'We'll wait for later to do that,' replied Bryn and disappeared off outside again. 'Back in time for supper!'

'Where's he going?' I asked Patrick.

'He's moving the car. Don't want that in the way when we light the oil in the ditch,' he said. With that he stood on a chair and pushed open the cubby hole in the ceiling to poke his head up in the attic. I put a big pan of water on to boil up some vegetables and seasoned the meat with the little salt we'd brought. We'd all need a good meal this evening and whilst cooking wasn't my most well-developed skill, I could do a casserole that would keep everyone going for a good twenty-four hours. I set to work peeling vegetables and laying the table, then spent the remainder of the time getting everything together for my journey. I didn't want to be burdened with a backpack but needed a basic survival kit which meant a penknife, compass, watch and lighter, piling the few items on top of James' gloves. It was going to be well below freezing out there at night so the gloves were coming with me. I wondered if somehow he'd known and left them for just that reason. Patrick dropped back out of the ceiling with a thump, dusted himself off and brushed cobwebs from his hair.

'Anything interesting up there?' I asked.

'We've made an access onto the roof. It'll provide a much better angle for throwing the grenades accurately and for seeing the enemy coming from a distance. Means we can bolt all the doors and windows from the inside.'

'But if the Perelesnyk come as well, that'll be much more dangerous. Incubi can fly at night.'

'Are they flesh?' Patrick asked. I told him that as far as I was aware, they had the same types of bodies as humans which was why they used the Moroi to do their fighting. 'Then flying or not, they won't enjoy machine gun bullets. Fingers crossed there aren't too many of them. Now stop worrying about what we're up to, stay well clear of the cellar and the roof space and get my dinner, woman.'

'Yes, Sir!' I laughed. An hour later we were sitting down to plates piled high with smoked meat, vegetables and a passable gravy. After dinner, the men went back to tinkering with various gadgets then we all settled down to rest. It was pointless starting a battle while we were all this tired so we agreed to sleep for six hours and break the liderc at three in the morning. It would give me the cover of darkness I needed to move out and the element of surprise they needed for their traps to work. Assuming some delay before the demons got here, Patrick and Bryn should have only a couple of hours fighting in the dark until daylight naturally made the demons retreat. It wasn't perfect, night-time was naturally much more their territory than ours, but without any real alternative this was our best option.

I wasn't going to be saying any goodbyes, determined as I was to return with James at my side. We bedded down without any sentimental speeches and, in spite of the blood rushing through my veins anticipating the night to come, I fell exhausted onto the sofa and slept peacefully until Bryn shook me awake with a cup of tea just before three in the morning. I was up and dressed in a couple of minutes, loading extra sugar into my mug for energy and munching through an enormous slice of fruit cake. I couldn't believe I was hungry again after what I'd eaten just hours before, but by then my mind and body were working overtime and it was all I could do to keep from jumping up and down with nerves and what felt oddly like excitement.

Bryn and Patrick were much quieter and I could tell by the way Bryn kept looking at me that he wanted me to change my mind, say I wasn't going. It was too late for that, not that it wouldn't have been easy to run right then, but I couldn't live with myself if I didn't try to find James and backing away would only lead to a lifetime of regret.

We shuttered and bolted all the windows at the front bar one, leaving the door until last so I could get out once the liderc egg had been smashed. I was in my coat with everything I needed zipped into the pockets. Both men were in combat gear and for a few seconds I felt like giggling when I saw them. None of it seemed real. I hugged them each in turn, long and hard but there was not much I could say. Thank you was far too small a concept to apply to what they were doing for me.

I broached the one subject I hadn't been sure about until now.

'If I'm not back three nights from now, then get out of here,' I said. 'You can't wait forever and by then it'll be too late for me. I won't have you risking your lives any longer than that. Understand?' Neither of them answered. They knew what they were doing and a lot more about survival than I did, but they needed me to order them to leave. 'If I have to get out of Manitu quickly, I may end up in a completely different place so there'll be no point you staying here anyway.'

Patrick motioned to one side of the cabin. 'There's a backpack in the wood store outside,' he said. 'In it, there are flares and some dried food. If you get back and we're not here, make your way down the mountain side to the nearest road, find a peak with good visibility and let the flares off.' I nodded. 'Now how do we do this?' he asked, pointing at the liderc.

'I have absolutely no idea,' I replied. 'I don't suppose anyone else has ever done it and lived.' Bryn handed me the egg still in the jewellery case and we sat on the floor in a circle around it, captivated by the oddly beautiful thing. I put my gloves on, unwilling to touch even the silver coating with my bare hands after the effect it had before on myself, Naomi and Xander. I lifted it gingerly out of the case and put it into a wooden crate in front of me. Bryn handed me a mallet from the wood shed and I tapped on the shell quite gently to see what would happen. For a moment there was nothing and then it spun once, rocking from side to side as it came to a standstill. I sat with the mallet poised in place above it not realising how long I'd stayed there, thinking about what I needed to do, when Patrick took it from my hands.

'Move back,' he said and I shifted a foot further away. With both hands he brought the end down in a sharp blow, hard enough to smash both the silver coating and the shell, but without completely crushing what was inside. There was silence, a pile of bloody mush in the bottom of the crate and then the embryo moved like a snake uncurling, covered in slime. As it continued to unscramble itself we all leaned forward over the top of it, completely mesmerized. It was like a reptile but with a bird's beak and bulbous, unblinking eyes. As we watched, hypnotized by the constant shifting and slithering of its body, it turned its head up towards us. Its eyes were red, practically glowing and it looked steadily at each of us, one by one. I reached out a hand to touch it and it stretched its head towards my fingers as if willing me to make contact. The tips of my nails were just centimetres away from it when Bryn came to his senses enough to grab my arm and push me away. As fast as lightning, the liderc whipped its head round to glare at him and, like an outraged child, it opened its mouth wide, threw back its neck and began to screech.

The pain from the noise was like a massive electric shock, immediate and excruciating. I recoiled, curled myself into a ball on the floor with my hands over my ears and waited for the agony to end. It was the worst pain I'd ever felt and I was incapacitated by it. If I'd had the option to end my life right then and not feel those daggers going through my ears and into my brain, I wouldn't have hesitated. From the corner of one eye, I could see Bryn kicking furiously at the screaming demon, keeping his head away from it. It took no notice, only stretching its head higher into the air and repeating its piercing cries again and again. The world was going dark around me and I couldn't fight it any longer; I longed to be unconscious.

Finally, with a battle cry that had no impact on the wailing of the liderc, Patrick got to his feet, grabbed a fire iron and took the thing by its throat. I could see blood trailing from Patrick's ears down his face and neck as he got closer to the beast, but he carried on regardless and with a monumental effort he shoved the struggling monstrosity into the pan of water still hot on the stove. Bryn was right behind him, slammed a lid over the pot and weighted it down. Even then, the screaming was reduced but by no means silenced. The water had no effect on its struggling but dimmed the noise sufficiently for us to function again. Once I'd torn up tiny bits of rag and pushed them gently into Patrick's bleeding ears, I slid to the ground next to Bryn.

'You hurt?' I whispered. He shook his head but his hands were still over his ears as if he were too scared to release them. 'It's too hard,' I said. 'We can't do this. We have no idea what we're facing. This is suicide.'

Patrick was shaking painkillers out of a bottle, swallowed a few himself without water then passed the rest over to Bryn. I was still shaking from the physical effort of holding my ears shut and I couldn't take the bottle of pills without dropping it. I scooped a couple off the floor and got myself a mug of water. I looked at the state of the two men who were willing to risk their lives for me and knew I'd been completely deluded. They may both be experienced soldiers but this was no normal enemy and I felt with deadly certainty that we'd underrated their capabilities.

'Bryn, get up.' I said. 'Patrick, grab whatever weapons you can carry. How far's the car?'

'Two miles down the track,' Bryn muttered trying to get his balance, the damage to his ears throwing him off.

'We've got to get out of here,' I said. I went for the door before remembering the car keys on the table. I heard the door open then slam immediately shut again.

'Too late,' Bryn said.

Twenty-two

'Lock the door,' yelled Patrick. Bryn threw the bolts across and shifted the large chest we'd had ready in front of the door as backup. I ran to the window and peered out. I could see a mass of movement outside but all of it high up and small.

'It's the bats,' I said. 'They were at the flat in London. I think they use them as their eyes and ears. They'll have been able to get ahead much faster and it would've been easy for them to follow the call of the liderc.'

Patrick stared at me. 'What do you want to do?' he asked. I thought about it and my fear morphed into resignation. 'I think the decision's been made for us. It's too late to run, the Moroi will be here in minutes. Can you get me out?'

Bryn looked over my shoulder at the flying albino rodents with their repulsive, fleshy heads. 'If they're navigating on sonar we might be able to put them off long enough for you to make a break for it. Grab that radio, those flashlights and some pans.' I did as he asked and watched as he and Patrick climbed into the loft space to get onto the roof, donning the helmets they'd stored up there.

'We're going to make as much noise as we can and flash the lights around to disorient them. You'll need to get out of the side window and it'll be a tight fit, just try to push the shutters together again once you're out to stop them getting back in,' Patrick said.

'Sure, but don't let them get near you. I've held one of those things and they have two nasty sets of teeth. I only need a couple of minutes, then get back down, whatever happens to me.'

'Get going, MacKenzie. Make me proud.' I didn't answer Bryn, just grabbed my black scarf from the sofa and wrapped it over my head as makeshift camouflage and ran for the window, terrified that if I took too long I would cost them their lives before the Moroi even arrived. I shoved a chair up against the window ledge and pushed the pane open as quietly as I could. From within the pot, the liderc began shrieking all the louder and I wondered just how much he could sense from inside. Then, from the roof, I heard rock music, as loud as the radio would go, even more alien in that environment than the bats. The noise was exacerbated by the sound of pans being banged together and I could hear Bryn and Patrick shouting and screaming over the top. The torches flicked here and there, blinding the bats temporarily when they flew in the light and I could see them flying wildly into one another, disturbed and confused. I lowered my body out of the window, pushed it shut as well as I could behind me then hunkered on the ground for a few seconds and I was off, up on my feet and sprinting for the tree line. It was fifteen seconds, maybe twenty, from the side of the house but it felt like forever. One or two of the bats hit me but they were knocked down by the combined force of my movement and theirs, and both times I crushed them as I ran, before they could signal to the others. I was several metres into the trees before I crashed down behind a log to recover my breath. Seconds later, a battle cry echoed through the forest and suddenly the noise of the radio and the pans was silenced. Patrick and Bryn must have retreated back into the house and not a second too soon. In the distance the sounds of heavy feet came closer, trampling the undergrowth and there was a howling sound like wild dogs as they approached. The Moroi were on their way and not just the handful I'd prayed there would be. The noise and movement of animals running from their path told me Perun had left nothing to chance. A legion of demons was on its way towards us and even if I could avoid them, Bryn and Patrick were about to face an enemy that nightmares are made of.

I began to move again, conscious of the twigs snapping under my feet and of keeping a safe distance between myself and the approaching freaks. I stuck to the cliff face, erring on the side of caution and knowing that I'd be able to figure out where they were coming from just by the racket they were producing. I put my left hand out onto the rock to steady myself and moved away from the cabin, knowing that I would be near the ditch soon and that Patrick would be lighting the fuse any minute now. The Moroi sounded as if they were approaching the cabin almost face on. I could follow the cliff for some distance and then cut across towards them. It was slow going and I lost my footing every few metres, either slipping on scree fallen from the cliff or sliding on rotten branches.

Behind me and back towards the cabin I heard a sudden burst of shouting and angry protests. I guessed that the first of the nets had been triggered and after a few seconds I heard the explosion of a grenade, instinctively ducking down even though there was enough wood between me and the cabin to block any amount of shrapnel. What followed was a mass yawling, when the incoming Moroi saw what I could only imagine was a blood bath of slimly white flesh and whatever liquid pulsed through their veins. The noise only brought reinforcements even faster and after the briefest pause I heard another net go. I took the opportunity to move more quickly through the trees, knowing I wouldn't be heard over the commotion in the clearing. The Moroi hadn't expected to be met with such a show of force and I felt invigorated that some justice had been dealt in Tim's memory. I could see the banks of the ditch in outline ahead of me and wondered why it hadn't lit yet. It was supposed to be the first line of defence when we heard the Moroi coming in. I walked towards it slowly and could see the layer of oil swirling in the moonlight. There wasn't a problem with the hose from the oil tank so the fuse must have burnt out in the cold. I turned back towards the cabin, trying to decide if I should go back and help. It would only take a few minutes to reach the clearing again and I felt reasonably sure of avoiding the Moroi as I went. In my mind I saw Bryn's face, the way he'd have looked at me if he'd known what I was up to. The men knew what they were doing. If the fuse had failed there was a good chance I couldn't repair it. They had done all this to give me a chance to get away and taking a risk like returning to the cabin might be brave, but it was also stupid. I did what Bryn would have wanted me to do. I left them to fight their battle and made myself walk away to fight my own.

As I turned around, I ended up face to face with a young woman who had waited silently to see what I was up to. She didn't even flinch and when she spoke, she kept her voice low and her words precise.

'Don't scream,' she said. 'If you do, the Moroi will be here before you can draw breath and they will slice you to pieces before I can give the order to stop. They cannot be controlled when they are in battle. If you want to live long enough to explain to Perun what you have done with his liderc, then you will walk ahead of me and do exactly as I say.' The succubus was stunning. Her immaculate bone structure and skin made her look like a porcelain statue in the moonlight. I did as she suggested and remained quiet, nodding my consent. As I stepped forward to go in front of her, I pushed my arms out towards her hard and fast. The sudden assault took her unawares and she tumbled back into the ditch. I'd seen the firelight making its way towards us from the cliff face, the whoosh and stench of burning fuel on us in seconds. I jumped as far and high as I could over the ditch, hearing the succubus shriek, enraged behind me. She rose up out of the flames unhurt and I knew she'd be flying rather than running towards me. I ran on, knowing I couldn't match her pace but just buying enough time to unzip my pocket, pull out the pen knife and slip it into my glove. With a strength that knocked me off my feet, she grabbed me from behind around the neck and winded me. I couldn't breath, much less speak and I knew she wouldn't make the mistake of letting go of me again.

'I would feed you to the Moroi right now if Perun were not so insistent that he have the pleasure of watching you die. Try to escape again and I will not care what he wants any longer.' She pulled one of my arms up painfully high behind my back and gripped the front of my throat with her other hand. 'Now move.' I did as she said. It was difficult walking with her so close behind me and trying to keep the noise to a minimum. Several times I nearly tripped and she enjoyed holding me upright by either my throat or my twisted arm. Reasoning with her was going to be a lost cause so I stayed silent and kept moving as best I could. Only once did a stray Moroi stumble into our path. My heart pounded in my chest but the succubus remained calm, simply growling at him deep in her throat. Seeing me like that, in the arms of one of his masters, he thought better of whatever instincts he may have had to draw his talons, and ran off to rejoin the increasing numbers running towards the cabin. I couldn't even estimate how many there were and at times I heard orders being shouted by other incubi. We had grossly underestimated the number of soldiers he would send to retrieve the liderc and I wondered how long the defences at the cabin would hold.

We walked for another half hour although it was slow going and I guessed we hadn't come very far. The passage of demons past us had almost stopped and the succubus pushed me to the ground in a crouch in front of her.

'We need to go through now. There may be a large group of Moroi on the other side and you will have to do as I say.'

'How will you get me through?' I asked.

'The same way I take all other humans through. Look at me,' she said. I had no choice but to do as she said, scared that if I didn't do it her way she would simply knock me unconscious and drag me with her. She ran one hand into my hair, yanking my head back so that I was looking directly into her eyes. I could see how that incredible beauty would bewitch others, and felt the pull of her gaze, staring back into her eyes as if I were drunk. She started to smirk, feeling my body going limp in her arms and I let my arms fall heavily to my sides.

'There,' she snarled at me. 'Such is the weakness of humans and the reason why you were never fit to rule in our world. You have no strength of mind.' I let my body fall backwards slightly and she had to loosen her grip on my hair to lower me to the floor. Whilst she had my full weight in her arms I shot my right hand up with as much force as I could muster and shoved the blade of my pen knife full into her eye. She lashed out hard with the back of her hand, bloodying my nose, and I fell backwards waiting for the onslaught to continue but she collapsed to the floor before me, writhing in agony and crying out. I knew her wailing would attract attention in seconds and scrambled forward, standing up and putting my whole body weight onto her throat with my walking boots. She was clawing at the knife stuck deep into her face and the pressure on her wind pipe reduced her screams to a bubbling noise. I looked away until her grotesque struggling had stopped. I had taken a life in a cold and calculated way. There was no going back from it and for a moment I wondered if I were really any better than these parasites. Perhaps this was the destiny that my cambion blood held in store; an ability to kill for my own purposes without remorse.

I gave myself a mental slap. Introspection wouldn't help me now. I grabbed her body by the arms and dragged it deeper into the undergrowth, rolling it down a small gully where I jumped in and did my best to cover her with leaves, rocks and soil. Eventually, the scent of rotting flesh and blood would attract either wolves, bears or creatures far more terrifying. For now, it was the best I could do but there was one last task to complete before I could leave. I braced myself and pulled the pen knife from her eye socket, grimacing at the wet noise it made and the spurting fluid that came with it. I willed myself not to vomit, wiped the blade off on some moss and stuck it back in my glove, noticing the mess on my clothes from the bloody nose and realising the Moroi would be on me in seconds if I went through in this state. It would cause another delay and one I could barely afford but it was necessary if I didn't want to become easy prey. On my hands and knees I uncovered her body again, cursing myself for being so thorough with the dirt the first time and then stripped off her clothes. She was wearing a long shirt over trousers and a warm wrap on top. At least they weren't bloody. With my hair wrapped in the black scarf and her clothes I might just avoid detection a little longer. She was taller than me by several inches but, other than that, it wasn't a bad fit. I had to keep my own boots on and there was no way I was prepared to take off the gloves, but from a distance I could pass for one of them. Fifteen minutes later I'd hidden her body once more, marvelling at how quickly one ceased to see a dead person as anything other than an object.

She may have been able to hypnotize men into submission but I didn't have enough human blood in me to make it so easy. For once, I was glad that my veins carried something different. When I was ready to move, I knew I had to go through into Manitu. There were still a few Moroi in the area and soon enough someone would uncover the succubus' body. Originally I'd planned to run through, the way I did with Serenta, and let the adrenaline carry me across but the succubus' concern about meeting Moroi on the other side stopped me in my tracks. If I went through like that, I'd be crashing into unknown territory, virtually waving a red flag and shouting 'Here I am, dinner time!' I began to walk slowly through the undergrowth.

I had been to Manitu enough times and with each transition I had a little more control. I could do this now. I should be able just to focus on the place and take myself there. I found a large tree and stilled myself, back against the trunk, the low branches giving me cover if needed. I focussed on slowing my breathing and feeling the steady rhythm of my heart, listening only to the wind and rustling leaves. I drew a picture of Manitu in my mind, the emerald green of the leaves and grass, the sky such a bright blue in the sun that it hurt your eyes to stare at it, every outline and detail in sharp focus. I was nearly there; I could feel the lightness of the air and the world shifted around me, it was like zero gravity for a split second and then in the distance a blast erupted with such force that it echoed on and on through the woods. Seconds later, another massive explosion rocked the forest and this time I could smell the unmistakable acridity of burning fuel and the shock wave brought a cloud of dust towards me like a sand blaster. There was no doubt at all. First the cabin, then the oil tank, had exploded with such magnitude that there could be nothing left but a charred black patch. So that's what Bryn and Patrick had been planting in the cellar and on the roof. All that explosive, there as the very last resort when all hope was lost. I could hear the dim crackling of fire although the cold and damp of the forest should put that out soon enough. There was neither anyone, nor anything, left to go back to. My legs gave out and it was lucky I'd had my back against the tree. I'd tried so hard to be strong, to carry on and do what I thought was right and I had just sacrificed the lives of my friends. Was this the cost of trying to save the man I loved? The loss of two others? It was too much, freely given or not. I gave in to the tears, unconcerned that the Moroi might hear.

All those hours I'd spent on the phone to Bryn discussing cases, both of us finding comfort from each other without anyone else to talk to in the evenings. So many nights after we'd won or lost a case, sharing a beer and a laugh at the nearest bar. All the things I'd never told him; how he was like the father I'd always wished I'd had, how much I treasured his friendship, how I wished he would find someone to love and settle down with. And Patrick who, it seemed, I hardly knew but who'd stepped up for me just the same. Quiet, well-mannered, the perfect English gentleman. How could it be that he'd survived years of warfare in Iraq, only to have lost his life in a deserted forest in the middle of the mountains. I wished more than anything I could turn back time, make a different decision, let James go. My head fell onto my knees and I sobbed out all the stupid, pointless regrets that wouldn't change a damned thing now. I cried until no more tears would come and the morning sun was streaming through the trees. I didn't want to see a new dawn, not alone. I closed my eyes, huddled my body into a ball and slept.

I awoke at about noon, the day flooded with orange light and much warmer than before. I opened my eyes slowly, head still on the ground and breathed in the fragrant earth. In the trees above me were the first signs of spring blossoms that hadn't been there the day before. I sat up and gazed at the bright colours of flowers poking through the grass, a rainbow across the woodland floor. I was in Manitu. Bryn and Patrick's final gift to me, I thought, getting me here without even knowing it, in my grief last night. I hadn't been discovered and the forest was silent. Whatever horrors had happened in my world, here there was nothing around me but peace and calm. At least the decision about what to do had been made for me. I had no real choice but to go on. Although I was easily visible in the forest, I felt better travelling by day, able to see ahead and get my bearings. I brushed off the succubus' clothes to make myself less conspicuous, wrapped the scarf around my red hair and walked slowly in the direction we'd been travelling, due south from what my compass had showed when we stopped. I was surprised to find that I was hungry after all that had happened and I'd have to find supplies soon or be too weak to do anything anyway.

I'd been going about an hour when I heard footsteps approaching from behind. They were some way off but moving rapidly through the trees and I could hear the ragged breathing of someone who had been running without rest. I crouched behind the nearest bush, grateful that the thicker foliage in Manitu made for better camouflage. The runner was a lone Moroi and even at this distance I could see that his flesh was blackened and burned. For a moment I considered attacking to stop him getting word back to Perun about the events of the night. Even if I was strong enough to take down a creature like that, burned and exhausted or not, I wasn't sure I had the stomach to kill again. My shaking hands told me I didn't. I let him pass, lucky that he was too panicked to sense another being so close by. It may have been for the best to let him go. Perun would be pleased that the cabin and everyone in it had been destroyed. Maybe he would put his guard down a little after the news and perhaps even assume I'd been inside. That would help me, but I didn't like to think of the Perelesnyk announcing the news of my death to my mother. I waited a few minutes after the Moroi was gone then moved on again, more cautiously now. If one Moroi had survived there would inevitably be others.

It took two more hours of walking before the path led out of the forest to the top of a rocky slope where I sheltered in an outcrop to get a view of the landscape. Below me was a steep valley and on the other side were huddles of rough wooden structures, a collection of huts and lean-tos, resembling a shantytown. They dotted their way up the hillside opposite and spread as far as I could see. As I watched, a Moroi came out of a hut and crossed to a ditch running down between the structures. He threw something in it, then trudged back the way he'd come. This was where the Moroi lived. I looked to the upper reaches of the settlement at the horizon beyond. If these foothills were populated by the Perelesnyk's private army, then it was a safe bet that Perun could be found in the flatlands above. It would be impossible for anyone to get to the Perelesnyk without going through the Moroi settlement first. As much as I despised them, there was no doubt they had a talent for defensive strategy.

I scrabbled out of the rocks and back into the trees. There was no way I would get down the mountain side and through the valley without being visible for miles during daylight. I needed to figure out what I was going to do and that would take some time, but first I needed food and water so I went back through the bushes looking more carefully at my surroundings. I found berries here and there, the climate in Manitu so much milder that there was fruit on the bushes even this early in the year. A stream provided clear water and, as I sat to eat and drink, I could see further round the distant hill face to where another Moroi was throwing something into the ditch. Even from here, when he let go of the object the way it moved, heavy and unwieldy, left me in no doubt what they were throwing into the gullies between their huts. These were the cast-off bodies given to them by the Perelesnyk, sucked dry of blood and tossed away like trash to tumble and rot on the valley floor below. I looked at the berries, glistening red in my hands, and threw them away. What little appetite I had was well and truly gone.

Twenty-three

I knew what I had to do to get through the Moroi settlement, but the thought of it sickened me. What troubled me more was how I would find James if I actually got into the Perelesnyk stronghold. I was jumpy and ready to get on with my plan but there was still too much light in the sky to move undetected. I forced myself to rest a while longer and my quiet wanderings even rewarded me with what tasted like apricots. I thought of Zora, wondered how she was doing and wished I could have helped more. There was no way Anousk would let me bring her into the human world for hospital treatment, although by now, nothing less would help. I tried to sense them but had no impression of the Vilya here. I was glad my mother would never see this carnage, the blatant disrespect for human life and the peace accord reached by all the families so wantonly ignored.

By the time the sun disappeared below the horizon, I was calm. Sad and resigned, but not anxious. The only path was right through the middle of the Moroi camp and I would either make it or not. I took a circuitous route down the valley side and whilst I might not have been visible, starting a rockfall was a sure way to have the area crawling with hunters. I was about three quarters down when the stench hit me from below and, as I lost the contents of my stomach, I wished I hadn't bothered with the apricots. Corpses littered the base of the valley across a distance I estimated to be at least three miles along. Here and there, I noticed movement and heard the scuttling of feet and claws. Even so, there was less rotting flesh than I'd expected as many of the bodies had been heavily gnawed, whether by rodents or larger creatures I wasn't sure and I definitely wasn't going to wait around to find out. Whatever was enjoying the flesh and bones of these poor victims might be equally pleased to find a livelier meal.

There were more female bodies than male, of many different races, but all human and aged between approximately twenty and thirty. I covered my nose with the scarf but it made little difference. The only blessing was the most of organs had dried out long ago limiting the decomposition but the faces on the fresher bodies had their noses, lips and ears chewed, eyes hollowed out and mouths wide open in a terminal expression of terror and pain. The earth was stained red. As I walked, the sinking sensation I felt was evidence of the depth of the bodies piled beneath me. There was a strange textile-looking carpet, and it wasn't until curiosity made me bend down and touch it that I realised it was human hair. Of course, the carrion feeders left it and it was slow to rot. As a result there was a multi-coloured layer almost woven around the carcasses that was so powerful a reminder that these were people, not just bodies, that I swayed, perilously close to fainting. My distress made me miss my footing and tread straight on the pelvis of a newly dumped corpse. A hiss from within signalled an animal protecting its meal. I leapt away before I got my ankle bitten and ended up badly spooked, half running towards the base of a ditch. Close up, it was steeper than it had appeared from across the valley and I'd have to do more climbing than walking to get up the hill. I secured the scarf around my face as tightly as I could, put my gloves on making sure the knife was in no danger of dropping out, then took my first step up. Here and there, I saw the flickering lights of fires, deep within the settlement but none were close to the gully I was climbing and I guessed even the Moroi didn't like the smell of rotting waste too close to where they consumed their meals.

The going was difficult and the ground was littered with bones that splintered and slid under my feet. In the first ten metres, I lost my handhold twice and slipped backwards in the dirt but eventually I got into a better rhythm, bracing my legs wide against the sides of the trench and feeling in the ground for plant roots to haul myself up with. About a third of the way up, heavy footsteps above me made me freeze in place. However dark my clothes, I wouldn't stay hidden long if one of the Moroi came close enough. I had a limited sense of direction with my face pressed into the bottom of the gully but the approach was definitely from my right and near enough to pose a threat. Just as I thought I'd gone undetected a body hit me, not yet cold but limp and lifeless and I let out an involuntary scream. I only just braced myself well enough to avoid being knocked all the way down to the valley floor but the cry had alerted the Moroi to my presence. It called out and although I couldn't understand it's grunting, I knew it was investigating what it had heard. I drew in a deep breath and hissed hard and loud at him, just as the creature inside the body I'd trodden on earlier had hissed at me. Moments later my animal impression was rewarded with a heavy rock thrown in my direction. The body, which had landed on me, was still in place and the rock hit it hard enough to make a dull thud. I stayed quiet, listening until the footsteps faded away. It was a while before I dared move, having to manoeuvre the corpse off me and kick it away to tumble down the hill. My earlier calm was gone, replaced by the certain knowledge that I wasn't ready to suffer the same fate as the girl whose body I'd just released. She was young, only eighteen or nineteen and perhaps it was my imagination working overtime, but it felt as if her face was still wet with tears. I said a quiet prayer as I let her go and cursed the fact that there was nothing more I could do for her and all the others being held prisoner by the Moroi.

I continued to climb, my hands aching from the effort of pulling myself up and most of my nails broken even with the gloves on. Finally the end was in sight. I steeled my sore limbs for the last and steepest part of the ascent and moved onwards. I was only ten metres from the top of the gully when I found my way barred by a huge body that had obviously become firmly lodged in a narrow section. It had been there some time and was almost entirely skeletal but I just couldn't shift it out of my way. I was going to have to climb over it and risk showing my head above the edges of the ditch but just as I pulled my face level with the torso, I heard a repeat of the vicious hiss I'd replicated to get rid of the Moroi. This time it was only inches from my nose. I panted, refusing to panic and end up going backwards, under no illusion that a fall from this height would result in anything less than a broken spine. Another hiss joined the first, then another and another. I could see the glow of small red eyes, peeking out from the chest cavity and assumed I was face to face with a pack of highly defensive rodents. I lowered my face slowly back down. Reversing wasn't an option but trying to climb over the body whilst it was inhabited by such sharply toothed carnivores wasn't feasible either.

I felt in the folds of the succubus' clothes where I'd secreted my few precious items and finally my hand closed around the lighter. I didn't want to draw attention to my position, but fire was the only weapon I had that might have any effect on the little biters above my head. I struck a light and raised it in front of me as I rose up again. There was more and louder hissing initially, but soon enough they scuttled backwards and I wasted no time pulling myself up over the obstacle. With one hand clutching the lighter and unwilling to let the flame die until I was completely clear, I had no choice but to use the lodged body to push against and it had been so firmly stuck that it seemed strong enough to take my weight.

As I locked my knee and put most of my weight on the corpse there was a sickly crackling as it gave way beneath me. A second later I was sliding back downwards, jamming my legs painfully out at either side. Still I didn't let go of the lighter although the flame went out. The drop was short but when I came to an abrupt halt, I found myself trapped and for a moment I couldn't figure out how. I struck the light up again and a scream stuck, unvoiced in the back of my throat. I was neck deep in the middle of the corpse, having fallen straight through the torso. My mouth was millimetres away from broken sections of ribcage and I could all but taste the decaying bones. One of the rodents, not so easily scared now that I was motionless, nipped forward and ripped at my left ear with needle like incisors. I panicked and began flailing my arms around, knowing it was futile and dangerous. I pushed the flame into the rodent's mouth, singeing my hair as I did so but the creature released me and that was all it took to have me heaving myself back out. I shoved the lighter into my glove with my penknife making it hard but not impossible to grip, and sheer adrenaline gave me all I needed for a final spurt of power. Panic won over caution at the end. I climbed from the top of the ditch and lay on the ground, panting and sweating.

The sound of voices jolted me into action and I dashed for shelter between two closely built sheds. I felt the wound on my ear and found a nasty rip that I'd have to stop bleeding before I could go anywhere. I dreaded to think what sort of diseases those teeth had just transferred but that was going to be the least of my problems if I didn't figure out where I needed to go before dawn. I poked my head out and looked around. The Perelesnyk camp had to be further up the incline and the huts were close enough together to give me a fair amount of shelter. I wasn't sure if the Moroi slept at night or during the day so there was no point delaying. I stepped out as lightly as I could and made my way up the hill, my heart in my mouth, certain that at any second an alarm would ring and I'd be strung up before I could so much as scream.

Through an alley way I came to a high, smooth wall constructed of what looked like white marble. On top was an intricate lattice of beautiful but deadly wrought iron spikes and there was clearly no way over. The good news was that I'd reached the Perelesnyk's home base. The bad news was that I was inevitably going to have to walk in plain sight to get in. It was still dark although I could see the first colourful streaks of light over the easterly horizon and time was limited. I did my best to make the succubus' clothes look less tatty, having never seen them anything less then immaculate and then followed the wall round hoping to find an entrance without moving too suspiciously.

To the far side of a huge pillar in one section of wall there were gates, constantly open but manned by guards, watching the passage of people in and out. Occasionally they would stop someone, ask what they were doing, check a bundle or turn a traveller away. I could see Moroi going through, a few creatures I didn't recognise, and every few minutes an incubus or succubus took in a human prisoner. The humans weren't fighting or struggling and I guessed they weren't fully conscious of their surroundings. It was probably my only shot at getting through but I needed a man to take with me. All around the Moroi camp, there were humans discarded by the Perelesnyk and waiting to be slaughtered. I would have to find one and free them to get in but I had no idea where to start. I was desperate to get inside the walls before the full morning light made my entry more dangerous than it already was.

It took more patience than I thought I had in me but I sat and waited, watching until finally I saw a Moroi come out of the gates with a young woman, ragged, and looking half dead. He marched her down a path between huts so I followed, under cover and at a distance. Soon enough they went into a long shed and the Moroi reappeared shortly, on his own. I looked around the outside of the building but there were no windows and no door other than the one the Moroi had used. I had no way of knowing who was inside and whether the Moroi bothered to guard their food supplies so I steadied my nerve, put my head back, made sure my knife was at the ready and did my best to look as if I had every right in the world to be there.

As I did so, a feeling of dread fell over me and I was shivering as I pushed open a dirty cloth curtain to the inner part of the hut. Bodies were tied up everywhere, lying across each other and there wasn't an inch of floor space left. Many of them were quietly rocking and others were unconscious. None were making any attempt to get out and I wondered if they were so broken that they had no grasp of reality left. I had never seen human misery like this before, not first hand. I wanted to tell them I could do something, free them, rescue them but there was not one damn thing I could do to help and both they and I knew it. If they tried to flee, the Moroi would be on them in seconds. I closed my ears to the crying and my heart to their plight and did what I came here to do. I looked around the room for the healthiest male I could find, there weren't many and I guessed the Perelesnyk used the men for a lot longer than they did the women. I found a young man roped to a wall, tried to speak to him but got no response. Physically, though, he looked in a passable condition, the only problem was his clothes. New arrivals would still be decently dressed. I cut the ropes, half expecting him to come to his senses and run but he just stood there, dazed. I took clothes off other prisoners to put together what might pass as a reasonable outfit and dressed him, talking as if he could hear but knowing he couldn't. I was comforting myself more than anyone else.

'Just put this on, okay? At least if I take you back in there I can buy you a little more time. Do as I say and you won't get hurt. I just need you to walk in front of me and go where I tell you. Can you do that?' There was no response, just that fixed stare. I put the ropes I'd cut from the walls back around his wrists and pushed him in front of me. I was cautious leaving the shed, having no explanation for why a succubus might be taking back one of the reject humans but we made it out uneventfully. We had to get on to the main path as that was the way the Perelesnyk were approaching the gates and this was make or break time. I kept my body and face pressed closely into the back of the man to cover my features. Judging by the size of the town inside the walls, the population was so large that the guards couldn't conceivably know or recognize every succubus going in and out. I just needed to make my way in at the same time as others so that they'd be less focussed on me. I reassured myself with the thought that no-one in their right mind would walk into an enemy camp alone and unarmed. Just another short walk and I'd be there. The human was behaving perfectly. He had the look of trance that I'd seen the others enter with and he was giving no sign that anything was strange. I made my shoulders relax and walked as if I knew exactly where I was going. Just a few metres outside the walls, the two guards hadn't even noticed me yet and I got lucky when a group of several Moroi appeared to exit the gates, carrying a large crate. The guards immediately stepped forward to check the contents and I heaved a sigh of relief.

Behind me, a Moroi came charging up the path, roaring in its guttural language. I stepped up my pace, hoping he was directing his anger elsewhere when a huge, glutinous hand landed on my shoulder. I didn't turn my face around, just shrugged it off and kept on walking. I knew he must have realised I'd taken back one of their prisoners but getting into a confrontation now was suicide. Enraged, he came after me and tried to block my path, looking curiously at my face, half hidden by the scarf and although from a distance I might pass as a succubus in their clothes, I wouldn't pass scrutiny. I could see the guards looking over now. Running wasn't an option. I said nothing to the Moroi but smiled at him, tauntingly and carried on walking. He confronted me so that I had to release the human and I waited until he was close enough that I could shove him hard backwards. He went flying into the mud and predictably lost his temper. He was on his feet again instantaneously and the guards intervened only just in time. They forced him back to the ground, fighting and kicking, giving me the opportunity to walk through.

Inside the gates, heart pounding, I had no idea where I was going but stopping now would be the worst thing I could do. As we went forward a large square opened up ahead of us, the man simply walking onwards unless I guided him left or right. The buildings were plain but immaculately finished. There was no sign of wear, ageing or anything other than plain orderliness. Much of the architecture was simple and single level, constructed in white stone with sandy wood in doorways. Here and there were larger buildings, more ornate, but so clean that it was almost clinical. There were no trees or plants within the walls, no water features or art. It was as if life here existed in a way that it could not tarnish or diminish, much like the Perelesnyk themselves. To my surprise no-one even looked at us, moving slowly, trying to get my bearings as we went. Most of the movement was down a single, wide street and I followed the flow of pedestrians as the day became busier with the growing light. I knew now that James couldn't have come in here alone. I doubted he'd have made it through the Moroi settlement but he certainly wouldn't have got through the gates or into the town unaccompanied.

It dawned on me that he wouldn't have needed to. All he had to do was attract the attention of a succubus in the forest beyond the camp and let her take him prisoner. It wouldn't have been difficult, he just needed to watch and wait, study their movements, make her believe she'd stumbled upon a lucky find, perhaps a victim escaped from another member of their tribe. As I considered it, the whole thing made perfect sense and I could envisage him up there, close to where I'd found fruit and water, waiting patiently for just the right opportunity to get himself caught. I gently pushed the man to the floor to rest and made a show of waiting for him to recover while I spent more time studying the movements of the Perelesnyk around me. I had to find out where they took the humans.

It wasn't long before an incubus passed us with a young woman next to him, needing no encouragement to go, almost fawning over him. Their power over humans was intoxicating and even I had felt it when I first met Perun. I knew now that it was only my non-human genes that had given me enough power to resist. I got my own prisoner to his feet and we followed their progress, taking care not to lose sight of them round corners. In the centre of the city they approached a large, circular assembly, windowless and imposing. They walked straight in through double doors and I didn't see them pause to speak to any guards. The man I was leading seemed to awaken when he saw it and he walked at a faster pace, almost as if going home. I felt like a traitor, taking him back to the prison but if the choice were here or the Moroi's larder then I knew where I'd prefer to be.

Inside, there was little in the way of security and the reality was that there was no need for it. Now and then I spotted more official looking incubi wandering down corridors and I immediately branched off, soon understanding that the place was a hopeless maze. Circular corridors followed the external shape of the building with, here and there, a straight corridor leading into the heart of block. Eventually we were wandering down a line of small cells. Each room had a single woman inside but far from looking like mistreated prisoners they were well fed, obviously healthy and serene. They were all completely entranced with their incubus and would remain that way, I supposed, until they were impregnated and had provided a child to the Perelesnyk. After that, they would be tossed aside and their place vacated for a new, unused womb.

Down a further corridor were the men's cells, resembling small barracks just with bunks and toilet facilities in each room. The men, of course, could be useful to more than one succubus so presumably they were taken out to other quarters as required. As a barrister I'd defended my fair share of prostitution cases and this reminded me of the illegal brothels where young men and women, often homeless and destitute, were shamelessly sold by pimps in return for drugs, food and somewhere to sleep. I wondered why the Perelesnyk were so disdainful of humans when their worlds were so similar. At the far end I could hear voices, low and excited, all male. I moved along, silently, so as not to disturb their talk.

Through the glass in the door I could see three men, sitting on the edges of their bunks and leaning forwards as if sharing some great secret, unaware that they could be heard throughout the corridor.

'But why did he run? I don't understand where he was going.'

'Why run from here? There's good food, no work and an endless supply of beautiful women.' The men laughed together. They were obviously the most recent recruits, free of the trance that got them here but not yet drained and brain dead from the influence of the Perelesnyk. They had no idea what was coming.

'I guess it's just the lock on the door that made him panic,' replied the first. 'For some men being in a cage is the worst thing you can imagine. Guess he's never worked twelve hour shifts in a factory with a nagging wife and four kids to support. This is the closest thing to a holiday I've had for ten years.'

I opened the door and took my prisoner in, made him sit on the spare bunk and removed the ropes from his wrists.

'So who escaped?' I asked the man who had just been speaking. He looked me up and down, obviously noting the difference between me and the succubi he was used to seeing here.

'The new bloke they brought in this week. Waited behind that door for hours, not moving, 'til they brought our food in. He hit the girl on the back of the head with one of his boots, knocked her clean out and ran for it.' The increasingly familiar sensation of a vision accompanying the man's story began inside my head and suddenly James was right there in front of me, closer than he'd been for months. I saw him leaning against the wall behind the door, looking relaxed but ready to spring into action when he heard footsteps outside. I felt his brief hesitation when he knew he would have to deal such a hard blow to a female, even if it was one of them and I saw the purpose with which he moved once he'd done it, off down the hallways at a speed which the Perelesnyk could only match in flight and he was safe from that during daylight hours. The few of them he met simply stood back, surprised and let him go, believing there was nowhere for him to hide even if he could find his way out of the maze.

James was not their usual prisoner, though. I could hear him talking to himself as he ran, counting the left and right turns in reverse from when he'd been brought in. The succubus had mistakenly believed him hypnotized then, not knowing he'd fought their lure before and won, albeit at the most terrible cost. They held no power over him any more. I felt the strength of his will and was awestruck by how little fear affected him. He seemed unstoppable, driven. I lost him as he reached the doors of the prison block and returned my attention to the men with me.

'Exercise time,' I said. 'On your feet.' They looked slightly concerned. Whether that was because something new was happening or because the activity required effort, I wasn't sure. 'I need you to assist me, unlock all the doors on this corridor and make everyone follow you to the exercise area at the end on the right. Do you understand?' They nodded, firing questioning looks at each other but not daring to argue. I left the poor man I'd brought in here on his bunk, unmoving. 'Come along then,' I said. 'Hurry up.' I took the right hand side of the hallway and between the three men they did the left. I went straight on at the junction before me as they dutifully turned right to find the nonexistent exercise yard. After a couple of minutes the noise of chatting echoed through the hallways. I went out by a different route, after making a mistaken turn down another line of cells. These had much larger windows in the doors to enable better prisoner surveillance and each cell held one heavily pregnant woman. Every one of them was lying still on their bunk, holding their stomach and staring dreamily at the walls. I wondered if they had any understanding that the children they carried were less than human or that they would never have the chance to find out what it was like to be a mother.

I kept my head down and my pace slow so I didn't look like I was in a hurry to get out. Before long, I heard feet running back towards the centre of the prison to find out what had happened and get the escapees back in their cells. It wasn't much, but the thought of the chaos gave me the briefest moment of pleasure. It was the last bit of freedom those people would ever see.

Twenty-four

Outside the prison, the sun was high and the day was warming up. James would have been trying to find Perun and as a member of the ruling family, that meant finding their apartments. Back in the central square there'd been a large, markedly more ornate building than the others, several storeys high, with armed guards on the doors and it seemed a safe bet that it was Mandalina's residence. It didn't take long to get back there although I kept to the side alleys with a growing belief that my luck couldn't last much longer. A wide variety of people were going in and out of the enormous doors. Not all of them were Perelesnyk but everyone going through was well-presented and checked thoroughly by the guards. There was no way the travelling clothes were going to provide a good enough disguise so I followed the walls around the side of the building looking for an alternative entrance.

Sure enough, at the very back, I found a few steps leading down to a low door. There were no soldiers outside but I was sure there would be some form of security internally if the front was anything to judge by. When the door opened, a girl come out, notably shorter than the Perelesnyk, shorter than me even, and with much darker skin and hair. I couldn't see the detail of her face as she wore a hooded white tunic and walked with a stoop, face downcast. This had to be the servants' entrance. There was no way Mandalina or Perun would tolerate caring for themselves and I suspected they viewed their fellow tribe members as above performing domestic tasks. I watched the girl shuffle away then decided to go after her. My experience of serving staff was that they had little love for their masters and, knowing the people she served, I couldn't imagine her having any particular loyalty to them. A few streets away, where the lanes became less grand, she trudged into a set of small chambers. I

200

went in after her, running out of tolerance for the games I was having to play. I watched which door she entered inside and, hearing no lock click into place, I opened it and went straight in after her. She whirled around on the spot looking terrified then furious. For the first time I noticed her yellow, feline eyes and put my hands up in a gesture of surrender as she backed angrily into the far corner.

'I'm not here to hurt you,' I said. 'Please, listen.' She was cocking her head from side to side and I knew she could hear me but I wasn't speaking her language. The room itself was tiny, bare and had none of the beautiful finish of the outside world. This girl was living in a subclass, party to none of the idyllic lifestyle of her masters. She babbled at me in a continuous stream and I shook my head to show I didn't understand. I wanted her to calm down so that I could explain what I was doing, so I sat on the floor, keeping my hands high in the air, hoping she would feel less threatened. She seemed surprised that I had made myself so defenceless and lowered her voice although she didn't move any closer or sit down herself.

Studying me carefully, she gave a little upwards jerk of her head as if to say, come on then, tell me what you want. I showed her my boots, my wrist watch and my compass to prove that I wasn't from Manitu, that I wasn't one of them. She looked at the objects curiously and even held her hand out to take the lighter when it produced a flame. I talked as I showed her but she displayed no understanding of my words. Because Perun spoke English, I'd assumed they would use the same tongue in front of their servants. It occurred to me that perhaps having servants who were unable to repeat what they heard was a valuable thing. I waited until it was obvious that I wasn't there to hurt her and then said the one word I knew she'd understand.

'Perelesnyk,' I said and gestured with my pen knife across my throat. The corners of her mouth twitched upwards before she could stop herself but she moved straight for the door. At first, I thought she was going to leave but she locked it instead and came back to sit across the room, looking at me with new interest. I did my best to use simple language and hand gestures but we had no common ground so eventually I drew on the dusty floor, a child's line drawing of a big building with a tiny door at its base and a few steps down to it. I pointed at myself and mimed with my fingers going down those steps. She looked at me as if I were crazy, not unreasonably. She started shaking her head and I knew she was telling me I shouldn't or that it simply wasn't possible, or both.

I insisted, repeating the gestures and pointing at her clothing, motioning that I would put it on. She raised her shoulders at me, wanting to know why I would do such a stupid thing. I picked up the knife again and held it like a dagger.

'Perun,' I whispered. That was another word she recognised and when her eyes met mine I saw she knew exactly who he was and why I would want to kill him. She was completely still, contemplating. After a short while she looked at me sadly, shaking her head. She made the same gesture at her own throat. It would mean death for her, she was telling me. The risk was too great. If I'd had a choice I would have left it there, not tried to persuade her, but time was running out and I had no alternatives. I put my hands together and dipped my head towards her. She knew I was begging and looked at me with pity. I pointed to her and then her bed. You stay here, I was telling her. I grabbed at her clothes and then at me. They were all I need. She wouldn't have to go with me, just give me the disguise to get me through the outer door. I picked up the little metal lighter she'd admired and put it in her hand. It was only a trinket but she seemed to appreciate the gesture. She opened a drawer in a rickety chest and took out another tunic. She paused for a moment then gave it to me, looking uncomfortable but resigned to her decision.

I tried it on and it was obviously far too short for me. She pointed at my boots. I took them off and it made a small difference but not enough to cover the fact that I was never meant to be wearing those clothes. With a sigh and a shake of her head she pulled the white sheet off her bed and wrapped it around my waist to cover me to the floor. It meant that I could put my boots back on and would just have to stoop walking through the building so that I didn't stand out too much. Her generosity when she was so scared was extraordinary. I took off my precious gloves, stroking them lightly one last time and held them out to her. They were all I had left to give, my compass being the one thing I couldn't part with if I wanted to find my way back to civilization. She took them slowly, keeping hold of one of my hands as she did so. I looked in her eyes, oddly gentle now.

'Perun,' she said to me and pointed at my knife. She nodded to me and I knew that his death would be a welcome release to more people than just James and me. I had no way of finding out what other atrocities he'd committed here and maybe it was better I didn't know the details, but I felt comforted by her response.

'Thank you,' I whispered, laying my free hand on top of hers. She smiled at me and the differences between us vanished; language, race and geography. I pointed into my chest. 'Eve,' I said. She repeated the word back to me and I nodded.

She did the same to herself. 'Shelti,' she told me.

'Thank you, Shelti,' I said. I saw a small jug in the corner, pointed to it and she offered me water. I drank it gratefully then had a second and third cup. Seeing that I hadn't drunk for some time she opened a box and put bread and fruit on a plate. I shook my head, unwilling to take food from someone who had so little themselves but she insisted, pushing the plate back to me each time I shook my head. I gave in, starving at the sight of it and ate quickly, finishing every scrap. With that, I made sure my compass was still secured around my watch strap and tucked my penknife into my waist band, unlocked the door and left quickly without looking back. It was reassuring to know that in this strange and inhospitable place there was still some good to be found. I spent the brief walk back to Shelti's place of work practising my shuffle, making my knees bend painfully and trying to keep my back straight. I'd never make it if they stopped long enough to look at my face but all I needed was to get inside and then I could shed the tunic and take my chances.

At the back door I went straight in, knowing that if I waited around I would only attract attention. There was no-one immediately inside but I was in a long straight corridor with nowhere to hide. At the far end was another door and I could hear the hustle of a busy industrial kitchen behind it; fans whirring, pans clattering and the occasional shout of instructions that I couldn't understand. I opened the inner door more tentatively and peered through the crack. Others like Shelti were at stoves, cutting meat, washing crockery in steaming vats and running around collecting and delivering trays. I kept my head down, only raising my face enough to see where I was going. That meant making eye contact with one or two of them. Those who saw me looked startled but said nothing and I assumed they had no desire to get involved. When I passed the cook, though, he was unable to maintain a neutral face. His eyes shifted to an area ahead of me, his fingers became clumsy and the pan he'd been stirring crashed to the floor.

There was a hoarse yell from the far end of the kitchen and a gigantic caveman rose to his feet, striding through the kitchen, knocking the workers to either side as he came. I put a hand up to my face, considering whether to fight or flee. The half man, half brute was one of the tribesmen I'd last seen when Ellette was killed. She died fighting to free Zora and me when one of these brutish beings had taken her life. I knew what they were capable of and had witnessed their strength first hand but it bashed past me, picked up the cook by his collar and began to shake him violently. Suddenly I couldn't take any more, I had more than sufficient blood on my hands. Looking around I saw a whole tray of knives and picking up the largest meat cleaver, I swung it two-handed into the beast's back, hoping to sever its spine. I dealt it a serious wound, but not deep enough to kill or even floor it. I hadn't banked on the amount of natural body armour within its skeleton but at least it dropped the cook and swung for me instead. I had time to think how senseless it all was, the loss of loved ones and the sacrifices of strangers, only to end up bashed to pieces by some prehistoric throwback in a kitchen. He roared at me, spittle flying as its massive hand tightened round my throat. I kicked and thrashed at it with all my might but it was like a mouse trying to escape a rattle snake.

A cry from the back door stopped all the noise in an instant. As one, the heads of the workers turned towards the doorway then back to me. Like rats overpowering a large mammal, the caveman was attacked from all sides at once, with whatever they had in their hands at the time. When he dropped me, I ducked out of the way of frying pans, knives, ladles and hot fat. He protested and struck back but not for long and to no avail. Individually, they might be small and unimpressive but working together this was a lethal team. A hand reached out to pull me up and there was Shelti, shaking her head and talking to me rapidly as if I should be able to understand her, checking me over for injuries. She called a much older male forward who wouldn't even look me in the eye, but when Shelti gabbled at him he listened carefully and then spoke to me in broken English.

'She say you go, will die. Too much danger.' I looked straight at Shelti and shook my head but smiled and took her small hands in mine.

'I have to stay,' I said. 'I am looking for someone; a man. He escaped from the prison here. He is trying to get to Perun which is why I came here. You've done enough already and I am truly sorry I made you part of it.'

Shelti and the translator talked again and I noticed that others were already dragging the dead body to the back of the kitchen, stripping off his clothing and weapons.

'Vestas not afraid to kill. We must rid body. Not worry.' Between the mass of them, they managed to lift him onto a vast metal shelf. I flinched at the gruesome sounds when they began to hack at his body, but not one of them appeared bothered by the task. Gristle and hair flew everywhere and blood flowed down a drain at the end. These people were used to butchering meat and they were fast at it. When each limb was severed they stripped the meat and put it into a grinder, smashed the bones and tossed the fragments into a chute. I couldn't watch when they got to the head, the noise was all the detail I needed, but they just continued to chat amongst themselves as they worked.

'Will they not find the bones?' I asked.

'Bones go to Perelesnyk dogs down under. Nothing left. Weapons we sell, get gold. They think he lazy, drunk.' I nodded and was extremely glad I'd made friends with the Vestas instead of wandering in here as an enemy. A young girl, just half my height, came to Shelti's side and whispered to her. Shelti put a protective arm around her and patted the girl on the back as she went away. She gave slow and precise instructions to the man, who looked at me as if I'd taken leave of my senses and then spoke very softly as though we might be overheard at any moment.

'This man you search. Guards talk of noises in,' he pointed upwards, lost for the word. I looked above me.

'The roof?' I asked. 'The very top of the building?' He nodded enthusiastically.

'They think is belots.' I must have looked confused and he bared his teeth, making little claws with his hands and hissing. I guessed he was talking about the rodents I'd had such a close encounter with in the Moroi's body trench.

'I understand,' I told him.

'They not want go up. Girl say she see man, hide, when clean chambers. Not belots. Is your man?'

'Yes,' I said. 'I think it's my man.' I looked around until I made eye contact with the girl, smiled gently and said a silent thank you. An embarrassed curtsey told me she'd understood. 'How can I get up there? Can you take me?'

'Must go fast. Mandalina back from travel today. People come to speak her. No time.' So that's why James had been delaying his attack and hiding out. If they were on their way here, James wouldn't waste any more time.

'Take me up there, please,' I said. Shelti stepped forward, speaking with the man. He shook his head at her and they had a quiet, but unmistakable, difference of opinion. In the end Shelti won and I looked at her expectantly.

'Shelti take you. Will be danger. Not like,' he ended. I could do nothing but thank him and apologise for risking their safety but I had to get moving again. The kitchen was just about back to normal and the hub of activity at the ovens and chopping boards had resumed. Shelti pulled my hood up again. She motioned for me to walk behind her and I shuffled slowly out of the kitchen door into the hallways beyond which led to a variety of staff wash rooms, linen cupboards and stacks of cleaning equipment. Finally a carved wooden door was all that stood between us and the Perelesnyk's apartments. Shelti stuck her head out first to check for passers by and, satisfied that all was quiet, ushered me along.

Inside, the rooms were high ceilinged and ornate, sparsely furnished but luxurious. We walked softly and kept our heads down although the only people we passed were other domestic staff bustling away in preparation for the family's return. Here and there, louder voices boomed from side rooms but we walked through the ground floor without difficulty. On the second floor were a series of what seemed to be offices. We stuck to the stair case, using the main hallway to move to the far end of the building. It was vast, more palatial than it had looked from the outside and I would never have found my way around without help. Finally, at the top of the stairs, we reached the bedrooms from which I could access the roof space. I counted at least twenty suites. At the end door Shelti stopped. We listened carefully but heard nothing from within and even then Shelti took the precaution of knocking. When there was no answer she opened the door for me. Before I stepped inside she gripped my arm and I knew she was wishing me luck. Before I bade her a final farewell she pushed the gloves and lighter back into my hands. My eyes filled with tears and I lost my resolve to harden myself against such shows of emotion. The Vestas were extraordinary. They were kind, generous and brave and it was nothing short of a tragedy that they had ended up here serving this loathsome race. I took the objects, gratefully. They meant twice as much now as they had a few hours ago and I didn't argue with Shelti about it. Footsteps on the far staircase hurried us. She pushed me into the room, closed the door with a hushed click behind me and I listened as my new friend walked away.

These living quarters belonged to a female; they were beautifully kept with the additional touches of flowers round the room and silken rugs over the chairs with rich pink and orange colour schemes. It was a bit overpowering for my taste but the succubi were never ones to hold back. To my left was another door which should lead to the bedchamber. I opened it a fraction, checked that it was unoccupied and went in. The windowsill was high but reachable and above it I could see the ceiling panel to access the attic. I turned to use a chest of drawers as a step up onto the sill and there, crouching down, was a young man. I let out a shocked gasp when I saw him but my brain worked faster than my mouth and I already knew that he was just as worried about being caught as I. I took my foot off the chest and stayed still, unthreatening, exactly where I was.

By now the hood of my tunic was down and it was obvious I wasn't one of the Vesta staff but he had no idea who I really was. He recovered from the shock of being found and got up, quickly on the attack. Whatever I did, I had to stop him from raising the alarm. He was an incubus but young, perhaps a teenager by human standards, and he'd been caught red-handed. A thief was a thief in any culture. I looked at the delicate wooden box on the rug at his feet and the golden chains hanging from its hastily closed sides.

He tossed his head back haughtily and stared as if he were a king talking to a beggar.

'What are you doing in here?' he asked. 'You do not usually work here. Get out or I shall call the guards.' I took my time answering, keeping my voice soft so that he was in no doubt at all who had the upper hand.

'No, you won't,' I said. 'You won't call the guards because it's you who should not be in here. The jewels you were just hiding in your pockets do not belong to you and the person who loves them will not be pleased that you were here without her permission.'

'You're a servant,' he replied, sounding more panicked than haughty now and his voice was rising in pitch as he spoke. 'Why would they believe you?'

'They will believe me because you should never have been in this bedroom to have found me. Isn't that right? Now, you and I have done nothing more than end up in the wrong place at the wrong time.' I needed to get him on side before he bolted and I'd dealt with sufficient numbers of guilty young men to know how to do it. 'You have good reasons, no doubt, for doing this, as I have mine. I am not someone who wishes you ill and I think we are both old enough to keep a tiny, harmless secret. Let me help you and perhaps you can help me in return. Put the box back where you found it.' He looked wary and so I continued.

'Be careful. There are still chains hanging outside the edge. Make sure it is all exactly as you found it. The drawer should be shut just as it was. When you leave, look confident, don't appear as if you were doing anything other than making a planned visit. I will tell no-one that I saw you and if anyone is ever suspected of a theft then it will be the servants, not a member of the family. In return you will forget that I was here, yes?' I had talked him into submission, taking advantage of the eagerness of the young to have everything in life resolved quickly and easily. He pushed the box into the drawer and pushed it shut.

'No, careful,' I said. 'There's a scarf caught in the drawer. Be more gentle.' He looked at me and this time his face showed gratitude. When he slid the drawer shut and walked to the door he gazed at me for a moment. He wanted to ask who I was and what I was doing; those would have been the questions in my mind, anyway. I shook my head slightly to show we were done and he went. I cursed under my breath. The Perelesnyk had their own social problems and petty crime. In many ways it was reassuring, cracking the surface of this outwardly perfect tribe. It would have been better at any other time, though. I listened carefully to make sure he was gone and that there was no one else approaching. Satisfied with the silence, I got up onto the window sill, slid on the gloves that Shelti had returned to me and pushed open the panel above.

It was pitch black within and I realised that Shelti had given me the lighter back for a reason. This was the only way I'd be able to make my way around safely and avoid crashing down between rafters or through other ceiling panels. It took a huge effort to pull myself into the attic and, when I finally made it, my upper arms were burning with the effort. I had no desire to close the panel again but there was no choice. I needed both hands to do it as well, so striking the lighter would have to wait until it was done. I lowered the panel down and hated the few seconds of absolute dark that followed until the tiny flame sprang to life. Even with the light, my vision was limited to a radius of about two metres. The roof space was high enough that I could stand with a stooped head although the wooden beams were so thick with spiders' webs that I decided to crawl rather than get covered in them. It was dusty and dank. I fought the urge to sneeze, knowing that I had to keep silent, having no clue how much could be heard from the rooms below.

As I crawled, I found that old chests and boxes had been stored up here over many years. The attic space was divided into sections and in some places the path was blocked. I heard scratching ahead of me a few times but nothing approached except for an increasing feeling of claustrophobia as I found myself crawling on my belly in places, to get under supporting parts of the structure. As much as I wanted to shout James' name, it was too dangerous. If I were overheard, the guards would find a way up here in minutes. There was even a nagging suspicion in my mind that James would deliberately not respond, as determined as he was to end Perun's campaign of vengeance, and that was something I didn't want to contemplate, up here and alone in the dark.

A creature landed on my head and I dashed it off. It was heavy and scrabbled unpleasantly when I touched it. I willed myself to stay in control. There was no point coming this far then being scared by something so inconsequential. The next room was higher and I stood up, stretching my aching shoulders and back. A slithering movement around my ankle made me crash backwards against a wall and my face was instantly covered in a thick web, filling my mouth and nose, sticky to the point that it felt almost moist. I breathed in and gagged on the threads catching my tongue and throat. I clawed at my face, dropping the lighter. Then I felt the first bite on my hand like a bee sting. If this was a spider, it was bigger than any I'd ever seen and it wasn't going to be shaken off easily. I slapped at it but it was moving across me too quickly and I felt nauseous from the venom. I was coughing loudly, caution replaced by sheer terror then I felt a scuttling across the back of my neck and another bite. This time I screamed, the pain was awful and I didn't care who found me, I just wanted out. I was terrified, blind, in pain and retching with sickness. When something grabbed me from behind, I felt the spiralling of unconsciousness and sank to the ground, hoping that when I awoke I would be anywhere but here.

Twenty-five

I woke up on the floor in the dark again, with an aching head and a gag over my mouth. My hands and feet were tied together and I could feel a throbbing itch where I'd been bitten on my hand and neck. I started to kick out with my bound feet, trying to roll over and get up. Suddenly there were arms around me, pinning me down and a voice was shushing me. When a light flicked on I saw the face I'd pictured every time I shut my eyes for the last few months, full of concern, and telling me to keep still and quiet. When he pulled me into his chest, ripping the strips of cloth off my mouth and wrists, I was petrified that I was hallucinating from the spider bite and that if I shut my eyes again he would disappear.

'James, someone tied me up, they could come back any second. We have to get out of here.'

'It's all right,' he said. 'It was me. I'm sorry. I had to go back and find your lighter and I didn't want you waking up in a panic and running around. Are you alright? Are you hurt?'

I couldn't say a word. I just sat there staring at him in the wavering single flame, at last within touching distance and very much alive. He stroked a hand down the side of my face, pushing hair out of my eyes and then he smiled. 'Eve?' he said. I wanted to be angry with him, to tell him how much he'd hurt me and scared me. I was in the attic of an enemy who wanted me dead and that was if the rats and spiders didn't eat me first but at long last I was in the arms of the man I loved, and nothing else mattered in the world.

I leaned forward and kissed him, as if it were the first and last time I ever would. When we pulled apart for breath he laughed, holding my head in his hands and staying close enough that I could feel his lips moving against mine as he spoke.

'Well, that's an improvement on how I thought you'd greet me. The Eve I remember was more likely to slap me than kiss me.'

'And I'm not exactly used to you greeting me by tying me up and gagging me, so I guess we've both changed,' I said. He kissed me again and ran his fingers over the lump on the back of my neck.

'Is it bad?' he asked. 'The bites are nasty but I don't think they're dangerous. One got me as I was crawling in here.'

'I can cope,' I said. 'What I don't know is what you're planning on doing next. In case you hadn't worked it out yet, I'm here to stop you committing suicide.'

'Next, we move,' he said. 'The ceilings are thin and you made quite a noise. I cleared out a space when I knew I'd have to wait a couple of days for Perun to return. It's clean, compared to the rest of the attic and I have water and food. Follow me.' We crawled into the dark and he pushed a rope between my fingers. He'd left a trail for himself to follow and I marvelled at how stupid I'd been just blundering up here with no plan at all. We left the lighter off but nothing bothered us this time. James had obviously done a bit of wildlife management at this end of the building. He struck the light up again when we'd been moving slowly for about ten minutes. With it, he lit a rag stuffed into a bottle. It was wonderful to have a larger pool of light and the chance to see his face more clearly.

He looked thinner than I remembered him but still wiry and strong. His face hadn't changed although the shadows emphasized his cheekbones and eyebrows, making him seem sterner and more intense than the picture I'd carried in my mind. He handed me a flask of water and some flatbread. I ate a few mouthfuls but wasn't hungry, the spider venom still making me queasy. He had cleared out the little room we were in, even dusting the cobwebs and shifting the old furniture, spreading a tatty blanket over the floor and using some ageing cushions for pillows.

'It's not much,' he said, motioning around him, 'but it's better than the prison block.' I looked at him, lost for words. I'd pursued him across half the human world and through an enemy city in this one. Now, I had no idea what to say. He sat down next to me on the blanket and reached out a hand to hold mine, like teenagers on a date. 'I wish you hadn't come,' he said.

'But you knew I would. How could I not?' I picked up the hand holding mine and kissed the rough knuckles. 'Please don't do this. I know how far you've come and I understand why, but killing Perun and being killed in return isn't the answer.'

'You're right, it's not a resolution but it's a start. This is a race of cold-blooded murderers. They kill without remorse to get what they want or in anger when they don't. You must have seen what's happening outside the walls. They are literally feeding humans to those monsters that slaughtered Tim. I won't sit by and do nothing any more. It's what I did when they took Constance from me and I can't live with myself for it.'

'But before I got involved they were living more peacefully. They agreed not to bring humans here because they didn't need the Moroi for protection. It was only my taking the throne to protect Zora that tipped the balance. I know they took Constance from you and that individually they can be cruel and vicious, but surely it's better to create a lasting peace, minimise the damage.'

'If I thought that were possible I'd agree with you, whatever price I paid. But now that I've seen first hand what they're capable of, I have no faith at all that peace is what they want.' He laid my hand down on my lap and picked up the water, inspecting the red bite and cleaning the wound.

'Zora's dying,' I said. He stopped his ministration and looked up. 'She's close to death and there's nothing I can do to help. The Vilya are hiding in underground tunnels because they can't fight Perun with the army he's gathered. I left them with no ruler, no leadership, believing that Zora and my mother would step in and be able to control the chaos. I hadn't understood how powerful the Perelesnyk are, how destructive their hatred would be.'

'What's wrong with her?' James asked. He'd saved Zora's life before and I knew he'd be torn apart if anything happened to her now.

'Arsenic poisoning,' I said. 'They're having to drink water from an underground well. She's the only one there with human blood and so she's the only one reacting. There's no way of proving if the arsenic is coming from something natural in the rocks, or if the Perelesnyk are deliberately poisoning the water supply.'

'It's them,' he said, angrily. 'And you know it. Do they know where she is?' I paused. I wouldn't lie to him but I didn't want to add more fuel to the fire that was making him risk his life.

'They certainly have an idea where the Vilya are but their exact location, in a labyrinth of ancient lava tubes, is somewhere they'd never be able to navigate.'

'And you still think I shouldn't kill the bastard? Eve, nothing will stop him. No diplomacy, not the Council, half of which is undoubtedly under his control by now, and certainly not negotiations. The Perelesnyk have to be dealt a blow that shows them once and for all that they can't get away with this.' He stood up, unable to rein in his fury any longer.

'James, listen, I'm letting him have the rulership. I told Anousk that the only way to return peace to Manitu was to concede and she agreed. She's sending a delegation to convene the Council. I'm sure Perun knows by now what's happening, that's probably where he's been for the last couple of days. Once he gets what he wants, maybe he'll stop. He'll have the throne I deprived him of, he'll have recovered from the humiliation of the ascension ceremony and more importantly, he'll be publicly accountable for his acts. That means the Vilya can come out of hiding, get Zora some help, maybe I can even find a way to send medicine in to her.' I walked up behind him and put my arms around his waist, resting my head against his back. He didn't turn round although his voice was softer when he spoke again.

'They won't stop until she's dead. Even if they know you've ceded the crown to them, their hatred of Zora and the humanity she represents will keep them on their current course until they have purged this place of everything they can't control. Your mother and the rest of the Vilya will never be safe. There will be a constant threat, their lives will be eroded in a thousand unseen ways. Even with the Council there to stop him making

214

laws without their agreement, dictators find ways to make what they want happen and that's exactly what he'll be. You're deluded because you want so desperately for there to be a happy ending but real life doesn't work like that, Eve. This isn't something you can wish away.'

A younger me, and not so long ago at that, would have reacted to the slight, to the implication that I wasn't mature enough to see the world as it really was. I thought of the people suffering at the Perelesnyk's hands, of Constance and Tim, of precious, innocent Zora wasting away in the underground caverns and I understood James' frustration with me.

'Maybe you're right,' I said, pulling him round to face me. 'But one death won't fix it, in fact I believe it'll only make things worse. That's why I don't want you to do it. That and the fact there's no way you can possibly survive. Is it likely that more lives will be lost before there's a workable peace? Yes, of course. But an assassination; one more example that the Perelesnyk can use to show why humans are a lower life form; that's just playing right into their hands.' James rested his forehead against mine and sighed deeply. There was no answer and we both knew it. I felt his tension reduce and slid my arms around his neck.

'You've changed,' he said. I kissed him and this time it felt familiar and steadying.

'I came to terms with who I am,' I said. 'And I realised that I can't apply my rules to everyone else, whether I want to or not. It's been a tough lesson.'

'That's a shame,' he said. 'I liked the temperamental, impetuous you.' I pushed my body against his so that there was no space left between us at all.

'Oh, she's still here,' I whispered. 'You just caught me on a good day.' He ran his lips down from my cheek to my neck. 'No,' I said.

He pulled his face up, a flash of hurt showing as if he'd misread me. I stepped back so that I was at arm's length from him.

'Not until you promise me you'll stop. I have friends here now, the serving staff have no love for Perun. They'll help

215

us escape. I came here to get you out and I need your word that you'll come with me.'

I'd expected an argument. After everything he'd been through, I thought he'd try to fight his corner but he simply pulled me back into his arms.

'You walked into almost certain death for me. The second I heard you, screaming and almost bringing every guard in the place to where you were, I knew it would be impossible to say no to anything you asked. If that's what you want then so be it. But next time you pull away from me when I'm kissing you, I'll be less reasonable.'

'Really?' I asked, hardly daring to believe that I would have the opportunity to get us both out of here in one piece.

'I love you. As hard as I've tried not to, I love you. Thank you for saving me.'

'Don't thank me yet,' I said and the next time he put his lips against mine I opened my mouth and made sure he knew I had no intention of pushing him away again. Sudden noises below startled us, both fearful we'd been discovered but when we listened more carefully, we realised that the sounds were coming from at least two floors below and that a large number of people had suddenly entered a room. It seemed as if everyone there was talking at once although every now and then a single voice came through louder than the others.

'They're back,' James muttered and I nodded rather than speak out loud, although in the din we were less likely to have been heard than at any time before. Then the doors in the bedrooms below began to slam and the hallways echoed with footsteps as servants brought cases back into the living quarters. There was no way we were going anywhere right now.

'We'll have to be even quieter,' James said. The euphoria I'd felt when James said he was coming with me was quickly replaced by the prospect of trying to get out undetected. At least I had a reasonable idea of where I was going this time and if we could just make it back to the kitchens I knew Shelti and her friends would do their best to smuggle us out. 'No choice but to wait until they're asleep,' he whispered and this time when he spoke I saw the slight smile on his face, lifting his eyes and making him unbelievably handsome. We sat back down on the blanket, moving slowly and softly, lowering our bodies next to one another. 'Could be hours.' I slipped the Vesta tunic off and laid down.

'I missed you,' I told him and when he ran his hand over my belly I shut my eyes and imagined we were back at the ranch, lying outside on the grass with the sounds of the river nearby and the sun beating down upon us.

James unbuttoned the shirt I'd kept on beneath my servant's clothes and I traced the line of his jaw with my lips. He was like the mountains he loved so much, steady and unyielding. We'd had so little time together and yet he'd risked everything to save me once before. Whatever the cost, I would get him out of here alive. The world couldn't stand to lose any more good men.

When we made love it was as if we'd never been apart, eyes open, exploring one another and taking in every second, every movement, and we joined together as if trying to make sense of the horrific journey we'd undertaken. When he was naked I sat up to look at him, to absorb every detail of his body; the muscled chest, sinewy arms and the reddened skin from years of working outside. His body was a reflection of how he thought and spoke. There was no excess, nothing useless or pointless. His body was toughened by the life he'd lived and yet his hands were gentle and careful, never rushing or forcing. I was torn between wanting to abandon myself to the ecstasy of having him touch me after so long and not wanting to let the moment pass without committing every second to memory.

The need for silence made us both hold back for so long that by the time he finally entered me I was biting into his shoulder to stop from crying out loud. We rocked together, both intent on holding on to the anticipation as long as we could but in the end our bodies won and when I came with him inside me, I cried for all the hours I'd spent missing him, huddled at my window as if he would suddenly reappear. I wrapped my legs around him, knowing I loved him so much that I could never stand to see him hurt. I'd find a way to lift the curse that stopped us being together. When I opened my eyes I saw that he'd cried with me and I kissed his face, wiping away his tears with my tongue. We stayed like that, in perfect stillness, gazing at one another as if we could stop time. Eventually, in a haze of spent emotion and the warmth of one another's bodies we put our heads down to rest and wait for the Perelesnyk to do the same so that we could find a way out.

The makeshift candle had long since burnt out but this time I wasn't scared of the dark. James was with me and the world was as it should be. I felt his breathing slow and his hand relax its grip on mine. I thought of home, of the look on Sabina's face when I brought James back to her. I imagined Naomi cooking a meal to welcome us and Xander ready to greet us with his theatrics. We might still be a world away, but I'd make Bryn proud of me if it were the last thing I did. In the final moments before I, too, slipped into sleep, I thought I heard my mother's voice calling to me in the darkness and I told her it was alright now. Everything was going to be alright.

Twenty-six

We were so soundly asleep that we didn't hear the soldiers making their way up into the attic space and only when a sharp weapon poked me in the ribs did I come back to reality. They might be ignorant but they weren't stupid, having restrained James first so that my scream couldn't alert him to the attack. He was bound with his arms high behind his back and, judging by the size of the soldiers, escape was not an option. They were the same race as the guard in the kitchen, only better dressed and armed. No doubt these were Perun's personal guard. We must have made more noise than we'd imagined or perhaps they'd found the bones from the kitchen and made one of the Vestas talk. I prayed that Shelti hadn't been discovered; I didn't want her death to add to a growing list of regrets. It was odd but I wasn't particularly scared, more resigned to the fact that my happiness from the night before was an obvious precursor to this sort of ending. James turned to me before they began dragging him away and inclined his head with a wry look. Too late now. I smiled back and the remaining guard threw my clothes at me. At least I was going to be afforded the dignity of being dressed when Perun fed me to the Moroi.

We left the attic by a much larger panel which had the benefit of a permanent ladder attached to it in a hallway. At the base, more soldiers were waiting and I was promptly frog marched down two flights of stairs to what resembled a throne room with a central chair on which was sat an uncharacteristically nervous Mandalina. At a vast semicircular window, one of the main features of the building, was a man with his back to me. I choked back a laugh at the staged drama of the pose and Perun's pretended lack of concern at our presence and forced myself to play along, reminding myself that he was at his most dangerous when his pride was injured.

James was across the other side of the room on his knees. This wasn't going to be good. Mandalina wouldn't even look me straight in the eye. Perun waited until a servant brought him a parchment. He unrolled it, enjoying the uncomfortable silence until he was ready to show his hand.

'Eve of the Vilya, how lovely to have you as a guest in my house.' Mandalina looked slightly taken aback and I wondered how cowed she must be, not to have corrected him calling the palace his own. 'I have in my hands a petition, signed by your mother, stating that on full convention of the Council she will announce the abdication of her oldest child and pass the rulership to the Perelesnyk. The Council meets in just days.' He came to stand directly in front of me, a good head taller than I and with shoulders broad enough to make me look like a child before him. 'So what, after all my warnings, after the patience I have shown you, what were you doing hiding in my home?'

I kept my head down, anxious not to inflame him or seem challenging.

'You gave me fair warning not to come back, Perun and I heeded your words. I went so far as to instruct my mother to cede power to you. I came only to retrieve my friend who was brought into Manitu by a succubus. I heard he was here and knew he would need my help to get out. I have no business other than that. If you set us free we will leave straight away and never return.' I knew he would not. The sight of Mandalina with her face in her hands told me all I needed to know about Perun's mood.

'But your friend here is the same man whose company I have had on more than one occasion in the past. He didn't wander into Manitu under the thrall of a succubus, he's too well aware of who we are to allow that to happen. If he came to my citadel it was not by accident, now was it?' The guard holding James kicked him in the back of the legs and he raised his head towards Perun.

'I was drunk,' he said, softly enough. 'I wasn't in my right mind when she approached me or I wouldn't have gone with her. You're right, I should've known what she was.'

Perun strode over to him and reached a hand down to grab James by the jaw, made a fist and hit a crushing blow to the cheek. I heard the unmistakable crunch of a breaking bone. Blood flew from James' mouth and he landed on the floor half unconscious, unable to put his arms out to break the fall.

'Perun, stop it,' I said. He stalked back over to me, his temper wild, making him terrifyingly unpredictable. 'This war between us, it's over. You've won and you have the proof in your hands. He's nothing more than the tiniest irritation to you and you're beyond his reach. Why bother?'

'Why bother? It's an interesting question. In truth he doesn't bother me at all, but it does bother you, the sight of him being hurt at my hand. Has it not sunk in yet that I can and will destroy anything you love until you are no longer relevant? And it sets a good example to my people to see how I treat humans who come into our world to kill us. Did you really think I would fail to work it out? Hiding in the dark, waiting for our return, instead of fleeing the second he escaped from the prison. There is only one reason anyone would do such a foolish thing. Revenge is a powerful motivator. I found that myself in my dealings with you.'

'You've had your revenge,' James butted in. 'Zora's dying. You still want more?'

'Zora is human and her death is of no consequence,' Perun said. I forgot my earlier prudence, incensed by his malice.

'By your hand?' I asked.

'Is that what you want? To hear me confess? Very well, if it will make your death easier to know the truth then yes, she dies on my orders, as will you.' I shut my eyes, hoping my mother would never find out what was happening because the war that would follow would rage for a thousand years. Mandalina finally decided that Perun had said too much.

'Let us be done with this,' she said. 'Perun, we have other matters to attend to. There are arrangements to make for your ascension. Guards, take these two down to the cells.'

'What will happen to us?' I asked her, but it was Perun who answered.

'You are to be hung,' he said. 'You will be paraded through the streets and our allies will be invited to feast with us and celebrate the spectacle, so the world can see how we treat traitors and assassins.' Mandalina spoke before I could say anything.

'Perun, we agreed, you can kill the human but she is Vilya. You cannot be so outrageous in your dealings with her; we will all suffer.' When Perun replied, he spoke to her as if she were a servant and I saw that the balance of power had shifted. He was more dangerous than ever.

'This is no longer any of your concern, mother. When I ascend to power we can do as we please. I shall not be constrained by consequences any more. Eve has renounced her position in Manitu and she came here with her lover to kill us. The penalty is death. Do not argue with me again.' Mandalina swept out of the room, humiliated. I'd always understood that within each tribe the leadership was matriarchal. Perun had stepped beyond the normal boundaries and I wondered how long it would be tolerated.

'Take them down. Enjoy your last night together.'

The guards practically carried us into the cellars where we thrown into separate cells, around which were cages filled with wild dogs. It was dark, filthy and it stank. A small passageway was the only way in or out, with several guards sat at the far end. There was no prospect of escape or release. James and I sat on the dirt floor, fingers touching between the bars. There was nothing to say. We had both known this was the most likely end to our story. I only regretted dissuading James from doing what he'd planned when he came here. Perun could have been killed last night if I hadn't argued otherwise.

We sat like that for hours until a figure shuffled down the corridor towards us once the guards had checked what he was carrying. It was one of the Vestas with bread and water. When he raised his head I saw the man who had translated for me yesterday. He pushed the plates and cups through a small slit under the bars.

'Is Shelti safe?' I asked quietly, although the noise from the dogs covered our conversation. He nodded once.

'Was boy, Perelesnyk. He sell gold from bedroom. Got caught. Told Perun he see you.' I was glad the Vestas hadn't been implicated; they would have joined us at the end of the rope if Perun knew what they'd done. 'Shelti say sorry not help.'

'She helped a lot,' I said. 'Tell her thank you. Go now, keep your people safe.' He left without another word. There was no point taking any more risks. James and I ate and drank for something to do and considered what the next day would bring. I asked him about his travels and told him how Naomi and Sabina were doing. We made conversation as if we were friends catching up in a cafe after a few months apart. He told me how much he'd liked Patrick and I didn't have the heart to tell him that he and Bryn had lost their lives holding out the cabin while I came into Manitu.

We didn't really sleep that night, only dozing occasionally when we ran out of conversation, too exhausted to talk any more. I woke up every time James' fingers slipped from my own. By morning we were both freezing and stiff. We tried to move around in the confined space, to stretch our limbs and make some heat. I'd lost both my lighter and penknife when we were taken from the attic so only my gloves remained in my pockets with the compass still secured around my watch strap. The constant noise of footsteps above was testament to how busy the household was in preparation for the celebrations and their trip to the Rock of Ages for Perun's ascension. James had been right, he was a dictator in waiting. I didn't regret my decision to rescue James but it had been a fool's errand: the Vilya were no better off now than before. Perun would continue to use weaker races like the Vestas for his own purposes and terrorize those who dared stand up to him.

When the guards came to get us I began to shiver, the bravado of the last two days evaporating. James was pale and, when his hand was pulled from mine, I wanted nothing more than to be able to hold him one last time before we died. I was taken to a small room, given a red shift to wear and spears were pointed at my throat when I protested over it. James had been taken out of a different door and I had no idea what was happening to him. The guards bound my arms tightly behind my back with ropes that cut into my skin if I struggled. Once dressed, I was left tied to the wall, the guards grunting merrily outside the door. After a while I recognised a soft voice, the door opened and Shelti appeared carrying a flask of water. She gave me small sips until I'd had all I wanted. I tried not to cry when she looked at me so pityingly, but it was effort wasted. She reached up and wiped the tears away, her burning yellow eyes wet with her own. Someone hammered on the door to hurry her but before she left, she picked up James' gloves and gently slid them on my hands. They stopped the burning from the rope but, more than that, they gave me a little comfort. Shelti smoothed my hair and adjusted my clothes so that I looked less dishevelled, a simple act which gave me the courage to stand straight and hold my head up when the soldiers came for me. She hid her face in the hood of her tunic as I was taken away and I was glad not to see the sorrow in her eyes.

When we emerged from the cellar into the daylight I could barely see. It took a few minutes of squinting before I could make out the cart in the centre of the walled courtyard. Upon it was a crude gallows thoughtfully made for two. James was already being marched over, shirtless, for the audience to get a better view of the workings of the rope when he dropped. They stood him on the platform, put his head through the loop of rope but didn't secure him to anything else. His arms remained tied behind his back and the rope was just tight enough that it wouldn't slip off. I thought Perun would have prolonged the drama of putting our heads into the ropes but apparently he was keen to get on with it. I'd expected a huge crowd and was surprised that the only curious eyes were servants, guards and labourers. There were virtually no Perelesnyk in sight. Perhaps they didn't want to get their hands dirty but I couldn't imagine they were staying away from lack of appetite for our agonies.

I was soon stood next to James and I fought the urge to panic when the rope went over my head. The platform was uneven and insecure, and there was nothing to hold for balance.

'Look at me,' said James. 'Eve, concentrate on me.' I did as he said and steadied myself, staring into his eyes. He smiled at me. 'You look beautiful,' he told me. I laughed, startling myself and he joined in.

'Idiot,' I replied. Our sudden show of humour received strange looks from the soldiers but none dared berate us. I suspected there was something about people facing imminent death that made you keep your distance, as if it might be contagious.

'Bit of a poor turn out, given your celebrity status,' he went on. With that, a stable door opened at one side of the courtyard and two black stallions were led out to be reined to the front of the cart.

'I think we'll be making a bit of an entrance further down the line,' I replied. 'This may be the easy way out, anyway. To be honest things were getting complicated, you with that curse and me with my sworn enemies. I still hadn't figured out what to do about all that.'

James was serious for a moment and I knew for sure that this was the end. When he felt the need to express his feelings, it really was goodbye. 'I came here because I couldn't live without you. When I left California to travel I thought I could walk away, start a new life. Then they killed Tim and I had to do something. I pretended it was to get justice for Naomi and for Constance but the truth is I don't want to live without loving someone. Maybe other people can do it, just float from place to place, changing partners each time they cross a border, but that's not me. If I couldn't have the things I want; a wife, the intimacy of knowing someone completely, the prospect of children, then this seemed like a fitting end. For me, there's no point without all that. I just wish I hadn't dragged you here after me.'

'You didn't drag me anywhere, I came running and I'd do it all again. I never said thank you for my gloves. They're perfect.'

'I wanted to think of you riding. I was imagining you at the ranch, looking as terrified and exhilarated as you did the first time I gave you a lesson.' His eyes were full of tears and I carefully reached out one foot to touch my toes to his.

'No curse to worry about now so I can say anything I want,' I said. 'I love you. I tried to move on, to be angry with you, to persuade myself it wasn't real or that it wasn't meant to be but I never stopped believing we'd be together again one day and here we are.' The cart suddenly lurched into life and we both lost our footing on the platform. We shifted our feet left and right trying to stabilise but it was like ice skating in handcuffs. I bent my knees, making the rope even less comfortable but giving me more control over the movement and told James the one thing I needed him to hear before it was too late. 'I don't regret a single thing except that I couldn't save you,' I said. With that, the gates at the far end of the courtyard opened and suddenly the cart was moving through the streets, lined on either side with an audience shouting excitedly at the spectacle of the traitors strung up to die. We shuffled backwards and forwards on our ropes like marionettes, trying not to slip from the platform and bring the day to a much earlier conclusion than the one Perun had planned.

This was all part of the entertainment, of course, making us look desperate and ridiculous. One false step and the nooses would tighten around our necks, maybe not enough to kill us but sufficient to cause panic and pain while we got back onto the platform. We were travelling in a circle around the streets of the city so that the populace got a good look and the message was loud and clear: this is what happens to the enemies of the Perelesnyk, go out and tell everyone you meet. The Vilya ruler has been disgraced, do not make the mistake of underestimating the new regime. The route was thick with crowds of Perelesnyk and Moroi. Cavemen soldiers were situated at regular intervals along the streets although I was under no illusion that anyone was going to stop the cart's progress. Now and then there were Vestas and other underclass races who, I suspected, had been ordered to come out and watch. None of them met our eyes as we passed them and they looked uncomfortable and disconcerted.

It was tiring and humiliating, fighting for our lives as the onlookers clapped and cheered but it was no less than I'd expected. Perun had done his job well and the cart was even going to pass through part of the Moroi settlement. As we went through the gates and turned onto the steep, stony paths one of the horses turned an ankle. I wasn't ready for the movement and tripped, swinging out with my whole body weight on the rope. The noose tightened at once and I didn't even have time to take a breath. The crowd went wild as I kicked my legs madly as if pedalling some invisible bicycle. The pain around my throat was excruciating. My peripheral vision dimmed and coloured stars flashed across what sight I still had. I felt as if I were being dragged down and, just as I stopped thrashing and began to give in, I felt a hard impact to my front. James had turned himself sideways and kicked me so that I swung back towards him. He wrapped one leg around mine and leaned back against his own rope to hold me still. I knew it would be punishing him too, tightening the rope around his own neck as he used it for control but he waited until I was stable before thinking of himself.

I couldn't reverse the whole of the pressure on my neck from the fall but when I stood firm I got more oxygen again and over the next few minutes my vision and breathing became more normal. I looked at James, the fear still stamped on his face and knew I couldn't watch when he was finally pushed from the platform to choke to death. He'd saved my life one more time, ever optimistic that there was a reason to do so. For one self-pitying second I resented the thought that I would have to go through all that again when it could have been over already, I could be resting in my own private oblivion. Then I remembered that I don't want to die.

By the time I'd recovered, we were passing through another set of gates and back into the Perelesnyk's stronghold. This was the main square and there were thousands of incubi and succubi waiting here. Row upon row of tables were piled high with food and drink. At the top end of the square was a table on a dais and the cart came to rest before it. If nothing else, it was a relief when the horses finally stopped moving. I was exhausted and James looked the same way. I was past talking, the pain in my throat too great. The masses grew quiet and the banging of great drums in a slow rhythm heralded the entry of Mandalina, Perun and the other senior members of their family. The sun was not yet ready to disappear below the horizon and I realised their intention was for us to watch their celebrations before being put out of our misery. James reached one foot out tentatively as I had done before and we stood like that, toes touching, while they took their seats and the festivities commenced.

By the end of the next hour I was ready to drop. Each stumble was met by an increasingly loud roar from the crowd, now drunk as well as excited. I didn't look at Perun, determined not to give him the satisfaction of thinking I would plead for my life. The light was beginning to dim and it was as if a giant clock were ticking inside my head. Goosebumps spread over my arms and I couldn't respond to James when I heard him whisper hoarsely that he loved me. The drums silenced the crowd and Perun rose to address his tribe. It felt like a scene from an old movie; wooden and melodramatic. James cursed under his breath and if I'd had the strength I would have given him an ironic smile.

'The Perelesnyk family will not be tainted by the foul corruption of mankind,' he shouted, raising a goblet above his head. The audience reacted predictably and I raised my eyes to the sky. 'The false ruler, Eve of the Vilya, renounces her responsibility to Manitu and then comes here no more than an assassin, to slaughter the very people who would save our world from the war and decay she caused.' He was loving it and it occurred to me that if he'd been human he'd have been an ideal candidate for politics. From my elevated position, I could see a few heads turning away at the back of the arena. Perhaps he wasn't quite the mesmerising speaker he thought.

'In the days that follow we will take our rightful place leading the families of our land back to the old ways, when humans did our bidding and we were perceived as gods, not devils. I promise you this. When I am made King by the Council I will not be weak. I will not listen to one side while I whisper to the other. I shall take back the power we rightfully wielded generations ago,' he continued, but my attention was with the crowd at the far side. They were moving around now, their backs to Perun and the distraction was spreading. James had seen it too but Perun was oblivious in his self-importance.

'The new reign starts tonight with the destruction of all that is wrong here; this whore of the human world, who consorts with mortal men rather than rejoining her true family. And where have the Vilya been when Manitu needed them? They scuttled into the dark like insects, too scared to fight and too weak to lead.' James was on his toes now, straining to see what was happening. Half the people in the square were more interested in the agitation outside the gates than their leader's speech and others on the top table were becoming aware that something was happening. At last, I saw an incubus sneak behind Mandalina and tap her on the shoulder, clearly terrified that he would be struck down for interrupting such an important moment. Mandalina's eyes widened and she looked at me. I saw the confusion of hatred and relief as she calculated how best to get Perun's attention. He was talking to turned heads now and when his mother took his arm, his first reaction was to shake her off. It was enough to get his focus on the people around him, however, and when he heard what Mandalina was whispering his face turned to thunder.

As I watched, the bodies filling the arena parted to create a corridor. The enormous gates that had swung shut behind our cart opened once more and a woman on horse back, flanked by multiple guards on either side, entered. The intruders were in chain mail and had an almost medieval appearance. I had no idea who she was but given Perun's reaction to her entry I could only think that my enemy's enemy must be my friend. Perun's soldiers formed a barrier between the gallows cart and the newcomers and it was obvious that they had no intention of letting them near us. The woman walked her horse steadily forward and, when she was as close to the top table as she could get, she lifted the veil covering her face and looked straight at Mandalina.

She inclined her head, showing the proper manners to a matriarch and to my surprise I saw Mandalina rather stiffly do the same in response. Mandalina stood up, ignoring Perun's manic muttering and addressed her guest.

'Tetra of the Polevoi. You are welcome sister matriarch. Your presence is unannounced and you come to my gates with nothing less than an army. What is your purpose in my city?'

The woman on the horse was careful to keep a gentle smile on her face as she replied and I was struck by how serene she appeared in the midst of such hostility. Through the gates I could see a huge band of men, all on horseback, armed and ready for battle. Her force was vast but I doubted they were in a position to challenge both the Perelesnyk and the Moroi on their home ground. Still, there would be no clear winner once each side had suffered so many casualties. She'd come here to barter and this show of military strength was her way of opening negotiations.

Twenty-seven

'Mandalina, thank you for gracing me with entry. I come not with an army but supported by those who, like me, seek to understand how the ruler of Manitu appears roped as if preparing for death. The Perelesnyk and the Polevoi have shared these mountains since time beyond memory and we have lived peacefully side by side for many generations. I am here to talk, not fight.'

Perun rose to his feet and although Tetra's smile did not waver, she would not acknowledge him by looking away from Mandalina.

'The Perelesnyk do not need to explain ourselves to you. We have fought the...' Perun began to rant but Mandalina spoke over him, in public at least, maintaining her position as head of the family.

'I understand your concern Tetra, but Eve of the Vilya has renounced her position, I have it confirmed in writing by Anousk. She came here uninvited and secreted herself inside my house with this human, intending nothing less than to kill members of my family. The penalty for that is death as it would be had she treated the Polevoi with such disrespect.'

'Surely it should be the Council that decides her fate. I would be more than willing to have my men escort her and I give you my word she will be tried for her wrong doings.' I was holding my breath, the reprieve being exactly the thing I hadn't dared hope for. Mandalina glanced at Perun then back to Tetra.

'I appreciate your offer of help, sister, but this offence took place within my family's home and as such we choose to deal with it ourselves. I regret that you have had a wasted journey.' I waited for her to argue, for a show of strength. She could not have come so far to give up without more effort.

231

'I see you have built up your defences, the Moroi are powerful foot soldiers and it seems they are serving you well. I congratulate your son on his command. I had hoped that we could reach some accommodation but I will not put our families to war now I know that the Vilya plan to stand down. I look forward to joining you at Perun's ascension, Mandalina. Forgive me if I take my leave before you continue.' Mandalina bowed, gloating at her victory and Tetra pulled her horse's reins round to exit. That couldn't be it. There was an army outside the gates who had come to ask for mercy. This was my father's family. I tried to call out but my voice was too weak to make myself heard above the jeering of the crowd. James had his eyes firmly shut beside me, just as devastated as I to have had the prospect of freedom dangled so closely before us then whipped away. Tetra's guard had cleared her path and she was just about to disappear behind a sea of Perelesnyk, anxious to get their celebrations started now that the interlude was finished, when she pulled her horse to a halt, shrugged her shoulders as if irritated with herself and came back.

Mandalina looked strained but smiled at her again, as one would an annoying child.

'Forgive me, sister. I should have requested one small favour. I know that Anousk would like me to hear her daughter's last words. It is a courtesy always extended to the condemned and I know you will uphold the traditions of our land.' Perun stepped forward again, eager to offer his opinion but Mandalina held out her arm to signal him to stop.

'Of course,' she said. 'Perhaps it will make Anousk's burden easier to bear if she knows her daughter confessed her guilt before paying the price for it.'

One of Tetra's guards helped her from her horse. If I'd had the voice I would have shouted at her to leave, if that's all the good she could do. I would confess nothing and I certainly wasn't intending to pour out my heart to anyone so easily defeated. She was assisted up onto the cart and the smile vanished from her face as she neared me. I knew she could feel my seething anger and she met my stony glare with one of her own.

She drew down her veil, put her face cheek to cheek with mine, and spoke in a rapid, low hiss. 'Listen to me child and do as I say. I want you to start your lips moving right now as if you were talking to me and it were the last conversation you would ever have. Do not stop until I say you should.' It was not what I'd expected, but I had nothing to lose. An audience of thousands was watching and they had to believe it was me speaking, not her. I did as she told me, listening as she whispered into my hair, the veil camouflaging her conspiracy.

'You are still the ruler in Manitu, whatever your plans to cede the throne to the Perelesnyk, because until the Council of Families has ratified him, Perun has not taken your place. Do as I say and you will have a chance to plead your case. When I am back on my horse with my soldiers at the ready, you must call for the Judgment of the Overseers. Only the ruler can request such a hearing and it cannot be denied. I will do the rest. Beware, though, of what the consequences might be. There is a price to be paid for the justice they dispense and it may be greater than you imagine.'

'What do you mean?' I asked, but she had already pulled away, kissed me on both cheeks as if saying a final farewell, and held out her arms to be lifted down from the cart. As she mounted her horse, I swallowed hard and prepared to raise my voice above the noise of the crowd. I didn't care what her agenda was or who the Overseers were. Anything was better than swinging to my death at the end of this rope and watching the man I love die next to me. She took her time making her way to the edge of the arena and I saw her nod to one of her captains as she reached the gates. They were on their guard and ready for the consequences of what I had been told to do. Things were about to get ugly.

I put my head up, cleared my throat and shouted as loudly as I could. No sound came out, not a whisper. The damage the rope had done to my neck when I'd swung off the platform was too serious. I tried again but there was still nothing. James could see that I was making a huge effort to speak but he had no idea why, so quietly had Tetra been whispering in my ear. I stamped my foot on the ground in frustration. Tetra's soldiers were looking at me, concerned by my inaction. I kicked James' toes as hard as I could to get his attention.

'I need quiet,' I mouthed at him. He looked confused but wasted no time taking in a huge breath, then bellowed at the top of his lungs.

'Silence!' As one, every head turned and before Perun's soldiers could climb up and punish James for his impudence I made one last monumental effort.

'I call for the Judgment of the Overseers,' I said. My words were soft but unmistakable in the absolute stillness of the square. No one moved. I wondered if I'd said it wrong, if I'd misheard Tetra or if it had all been some cruel joke.

Mandalina's expression was one of utter incredulity. I could see from here that she was shaking as she spoke.

'Tetra, is this your doing? I thought we understood one another.' Perun flew from his seat, no longer under his mother's control, whatever traditions dictated.

'You fool, letting her up there. You allowed us to be played! Guards, close the gates. I'll show the Polevoi what happens when they intervene in matters that do not concern them.'

Tetra's guards raised multi-headed cross-bows. All around them, incubi started to back away, treading over one another in panic. Tetra held up one hand to command calm and when she spoke, it was with the absolute certainty that things would go her way.

'The Judgment of the Overseers has been called down, Perun. You can order your army to slaughter my men but you cannot change what is done. The ruler has the power to ask for their decision and none may stop it. My men fill the valley below and, whilst your army is strong, all we will do is wipe one another out.'

'What are the Overseers?' James asked me quietly, totally bewildered by the turn things were taking. I just shrugged, no wiser than he.

'You planned this all along,' shouted Perun at Tetra. 'That was exactly what you wanted. You are in league with the

Vilya and I will not be told what to do by you or anyone else who enters my city to overthrow my command.'

'Your mother is head of the Perelesnyk family, unless I am much mistaken. She has led this tribe for many generations. Have you asked her people if they are content for you to single-handedly alter the matriarchal system?' Tetra was on a knife-edge. She had no desire for conflict, that much was clear but I doubted she would ever bow down to Perun. A ripple of unrest went through the crowd and the succubi were noticeably disturbed. Perun had shown his hand too soon and Tetra struck exactly the right note. In his moment of hesitation, Mandalina reclaimed her place at the head of the tribe.

'The Overseers will come here, where they were called, only when it is fully dark. Their judgment upon Eve of the Vilya will be final. Will you stay to watch, Tetra, as it was you who orchestrated their calling?' Mandalina sounded stronger again after Tetra's speech.

'I will,' Tetra replied. 'I would be grateful if you would cut the ropes that bind Eve and her companion. The Overseers will have no need of them, after all. They cannot escape Manitu now, not before Judgment is passed.' I had the uncomfortable feeling that I'd been set adrift in the middle of the ocean and could only sit and wait until I was found, whether by friend or foe. The guards cut us down quickly, James and I rubbing at our sore hands and necks. My whole body was aching with the effort of staying on the platform and when we collapsed onto a wooden bench it felt like an armchair. James had stopped asking questions and I knew he was listening to the hushed conversations around us. Perun had disappeared completely and the crowd was starting to disperse. It wasn't long to wait until dark and I had absolutely no idea what would happen then.

Tetra's soldiers had closed off a small corner of the arena for her to sit and eat. Mandalina was surrounded by her closest family, huddled in conversation and one of Tetra's guards approached her to ask that we be taken to dine with the Polevoi matriarch. I was surprised when Mandalina granted the request although there was obviously no chance of anyone leaving here until this matter was settled. Tetra's guards walked us across the arena amidst much staring from the Perelesnyk, now able to get a closer look at us, but no-one dared jeer or hurl insults as if the mere mention of the Overseers had scared them into submission. Tetra stood when we approached and I bowed low before her, James following my lead. She motioned for us to sit next to her so that we could talk quietly. I sipped water, my throat too bruised to contemplate eating. When the crowd became bored of watching us, I leaned towards her.

'Thank you for risking so much to save us. I owe the Polevoi a great debt. Can you tell me how you knew we were here?'

She took her time answering, dipping some fruit in honey before she replied. 'A friend of yours spoke of your plans to Serenta. Upon hearing the news, Anousk sent word to me to help. Our citadel is across the other side of the Carpathian Mountains. We came as quickly as we could. I only wish it had been sooner so that a better outcome might have been possible.'

I'd asked Naomi not to tell Serenta where I was and I would be forever grateful that she had ignored me. How foolish I'd been to believe I could do this alone.

'And Zora?' I asked.

'She lives, although the poison has reduced her to a state of almost constant sleep. The knowledge of the poisoning helped and they have found another water supply. Still, it is unlikely she will survive much longer.'

'What have I done?' I asked, more to myself than her.

'You did what you thought was right. You took responsibility for the people you loved and you did not weaken. My nephew would have been proud of you.' Tetra passed me a cup of sweet, thick wine and I took a sip.

'Your nephew,' I said. 'Castevan?' She smiled at me and I understood why she had risked so much to come into the Perelesnyk's stronghold to stay my execution. 'So that would make you my great-aunt, right?' The phrase made her laugh.

'Humans are so particular about naming every pathway in their history. Your father's mother, Reema, was my sister. Although you look exactly like a Vilya, I can see Castevan in you; his fighting spirit, his temper.'

236

'I thought they kept it secret, who my father was, in case...' but she stopped me mid-sentence.

'Indeed, child, but there are things it is not safe to talk of with so many enemies listening. The daylight is fading and you should understand what is about to happen. Everything I say comes from the stories my mother told me. I have never witnessed the Overseers, nor has anyone here.'

'What are they?' asked James.

'They are the spirits of the first matriarchs, that is what the legends say. You, James, would call them ghosts but to us they are the embodiment of nature and they can be called down by the Ruler to reset the balance when an injustice or a wrong doing has occurred.'

'What will happen when they come?' I was feeling unsteady, whether from lack of food or my injuries, I didn't know.

'We must wait and see. But I warned you before; all they do is equal the scales. They can put right any harm that has been caused but they expect a settling up. They are not here to pass judgment on Perun and they are not here to rescue you. They will only do what is best for Manitu.'

The remaining light was just rays of red on the horizon and I could make out the first stars above us. I had one last question for her, not knowing what would happen after this.

'Tetra, is my father still alive?'

She gripped my hand hard with one of hers and with the other stroked my hair. 'We do not know,' she said. Her guards were waiting to escort us back to the centre of the square and many of the Perelesnyk had gathered again around the edges but there was no sense of celebration this time. Little groups huddled together as if unwilling to draw attention to themselves. Mandalina and Perun were back in their seats. James and I sat down on the bench where the cart had been, and waited. For a moment, I was transported back to an odd day at school when I'd been sent to the head teacher's office. I sat in a dark corridor, on a bench not dissimilar to this one and waited to find out what I'd done and what the punishment would be. I recalled the chill I felt, the trepidation, the mixed senses of awe and anxiety when I was finally called in to what seemed the grandest office in the world.

James slipped one large hand over mine. 'How about another riding lesson when we get home?' he said, with that amused expression I'd always been unable to resist. The sight of him then, ready for whatever the world had in store, was the most beautiful thing in the universe.

The sky was black and the stars above us were brighter and closer than I had ever seen before. As I watched, the golden lights in the sky seemed to shift, shooting downwards towards us. Muffled gasps echoed around the walls of the square and white beams of light flashed around James and me as we sat, transfixed. I had a sense of time stopping, of the air becoming completely still. James relaxed beside me and my heartbeat slowed. The beams of light began to intertwine, bending and plaiting together, forming shapes that wouldn't stay still but I could make out vague forms within them, human in size and shape but without solidity or detail. The Overseers were here.

Twenty-eight

'Eve of the Vilya, ruler of Manitu, stand and face us.' I didn't consciously move my legs and I don't think I could have done if I'd tried. Something else moved me, as if an invisible hand had lifted me out of my seat. I found myself upright and alone in the centre of the five Overseers, the lights shifting and twisting inside their outlines so brightly that I couldn't make out a single face in the crowd beyond. I wasn't even sure I was in the same place, so dense and unmoving was the atmosphere.

'What is the imbalance you have called us to right?' It was impossible to make out which of the shadowy figures spoke, the sound seemed to come from every side at once. I had addressed any number of courts in my life but I was unprepared for this. I wondered how much they knew or had seen, and I had no idea what to say. I stumbled over my words, trying to come out with something coherent, but it just didn't work.

A beam of light like a lash whipped my face, stinging and waking me from the daze I'd been in. I came to my senses and stopped looking at them, giving up trying to focus my eyes and simply stared down at my hands as I fought to speak aloud.

'I called upon the Judgment of the Overseers to plead for the life of my companion, James and myself. The Perelesnyk decided our fate without trial and we were to be hanged.' I had no idea if I was saying what they wanted to hear so I stopped and waited for guidance.

'And yet your companion came here to kill one of the incubi and you joined him willingly. That is no imbalance. We do not take sides. The Perelesnyk's laws are their own to make, trial or none.'

'But James was only here because they took the life of an innocent; a human, who had no dealings with this world. My friend was seeking justice for that and the murder of his own

239

wife, who died when a succubus was trying to lure him here. It is he who has been wronged.' I'd found my voice again and struggled to contain my emotions as I thought of Tim and Constance.

'We exist only to maintain the rule of nature within Manitu. Just or not, these affairs are beyond are knowledge and our boundaries. Do you say that no injustice has been committed within this world?' The pitch of the Overseers' voices was rising with irritation and I had to come up with something or this last chance to live would pass us by.

'Perun is poisoning the water that supplies the caves where my family, the Vilya, are hiding. Zora, my mother's ward, lays dying. They acted to break the will of the Vilya so that we would cede power and they could reign in my place.' There was a long period of silence and I convinced myself that it was over, then they spoke again, but not to me this time.

'Come to us, Perun of the Perelesnyk.' In seconds Perun appeared, as I had, almost as if he were being carried. 'Is this true? Have you poisoned the waters of Manitu?'

'I have not,' he said and before I could interrupt an outraged cry came from behind me.

'He admitted it!' James shouted and this time I was able to see what the Overseers did. When James appeared he was wrapped in tendrils of light, transported by the Overseers.

'I did no such thing,' said Perun haughtily. 'That creature has entirely human blood in him. He has no right to speak here; he shouldn't even be a witness to this.' A lash, like the one that had stung me into concentration, hit Perun markedly harder but this time across the shoulders.

'You lie,' the voices hissed and their tone was menacing. 'The lake's waters are tainted and the rocks are drenched with poison. But this man here, human or not, is accursed. He lives under a cloud cast upon him from this world and you cannot claim he has no right to speak here. One of your tribe, Perun, tied this human to the Perelesnyk forever. Who was it that imposed their will on this man and bound him to Manitu?'

A long way away, in the cover of the dark, a low female voice said, 'I did.' Into the circle she floated and I stared at her curiously, never thinking that James would have to face the succubus who caused the death of his wife. I saw him shaking but knew he couldn't move forwards; the Overseers were the only force in control here.

Perun, however, was not going to be cowed for long. He lifted his head up and spoke as if he were in charge. Part of me admired his guts. I felt so out of my depth that I would never have dared be so bold. 'Lantak is my mother's oldest female child and she will become matriarch in time. Whatever my sister did, it was in the course of our natural dealings with humans, the only way my people can reproduce. We cannot be held accountable for those things we have to do to survive. Zora is human also. She does not have the protection of the Overseers. She was brought here as part of a trade, nothing more. You cannot pass Judgment on me or my people for living to fulfill our potential, and ridding Manitu of such tainted blood simply helps return our world to its natural state.' So the succubus who was so proud that she cursed James for abandoning her, was Perun's flesh and blood. It made sense; that overwhelming ego and thirst for vengeance. James was going to lose his temper if I didn't take control of the situation first.

'Zora and I were changelings,' I responded. 'It is a practice that has been embraced in Manitu for centuries, if not longer. It is done sometimes to protect your kind in my world and sometimes to bring a treasured human into yours. Zora was accepted here until the ascension, no challenge was ever made to her being brought in. If you take nature into your own hands and kill her then you create an imbalance by failing to bring me back.'

'I asked you to come back,' Perun spat at me.

'You tried to trick me into coming back for your own purposes, so that you could control Manitu through me.' We had both gone too far and there was a deafening crack of thunder between us, stopping the argument before it could escalate further.

'Be still,' the Overseers warned us and I restrained my anger, trying to figure out where this was going. 'A war began at the ascension that has devastated Manitu and the damage threatens to leak out into the human world if there is no redress.

The Perelesnyk involved Eve of the Vilya, unwilling to let the changelings remain in the worlds where, as babies, they had been placed. It is our way, sometimes, to bring new blood into this place. It was not the Perelesnyk's right to reverse what was done. You seek redress and we accept that the scales need to be balanced once more. What is it you claim, Eve?'

I was ecstatic. Perun's evil had finally been recognised and I could undo some of the harm he had spewed out at the people I loved. The pain, the horrible things I'd seen, the sacrifices my friends had made; it was all going to be worthwhile.

'I ask that you restore Zora to full health and that James be returned to the human world with the curse lifted. I will go back with him and I agree, as I already have, not to come here again. I will leave the status quo as it originally was, with Zora here and me there.' I glanced over my shoulder at James who was staring at the movement of the Overseers, their light trails moving increasingly faster and more erratically. It seemed as if they were arguing amongst themselves until at last, they were ready to deliver their judgment and a safe passage home was just within our grasp.

'Eve of the Vilya, you manipulated the Council of Families, pretending you would take on the responsibilities of rulership when you had no intention of staying in Manitu.'

'No, that's not how it happened, I was just holding out until they found Zora.'

'You deceived the Council of your true intentions rather than speaking plainly about what you sought to achieve.' The Overseers were not backing down but I couldn't let this argument go.

'I would have had to accuse the Perelesnyk of taking Zora before I had proof, it would have started a war there and then,' I all but shouted.

'It did start a war.' That silenced me. Continuing my defence was only going to make things worse. I shut my mouth and listened. I may not like what they were saying but it was no worse than I'd thought a thousand times myself. I knew I was waiting for a sentence to be passed. The movement of the lights slowed to their earlier swishing and I calmed myself for Judgment.

'You are owed redress. Your anger, rightfully, at all that has been done to you and your people has caused a wound that will not heal unless we intervene. We can restore Zora so that she can live out her predestined life or we can lift the curse on your companion and return him to the human world alive. But not both. The Overseers decree that one life should be returned to you. The price you must pay for your part in this, is to choose which life is saved and which is forfeited.'

I shook my head back and forwards, as if I had misheard. They were asking me to condemn either James or Zora to death and this was their idea of dispensing justice.

'I won't do it,' I said. 'That's insane. How could I possibly choose either of them to die? I can't. It's not fair.'

'We are not here to satisfy you. We will give you back what you are owed and one life it is. More than that and the Perelesnyk will say you took no responsibility for your decisions. You have no option but to choose. You called down the Judgment of the Overseers. We do not appear here to do anyone's bidding. We are here to return Manitu's natural equilibrium so far as it is within our power.'

Tetra had warned me and yet I had no idea of just how high the price for their intervention would be. How could I let either Zora or James die? It was inconceivable. And yet if the Overseers left right now I knew Zora would die from the effects of the arsenic and the Perelesnyk would continue their original plan of hanging us both.

'What about my life?' I said. 'If I die, can they both live? Won't that be the balance you need to put things right?' I saw James try to move and speak but he was held fast by whatever unseen power the Overseers wielded.

'That will not right the imbalance. Your time in Manitu is not destined to end here. It will create a longer, deeper conflict if we take your life in exchange for the blood of two humans. This is not the answer.'

'I won't choose,' I screamed. 'I will not end the life of either of them. This is wrong, it is evil.'

243

'You called us, Eve of the Vilya. All will wait here until you have made your decision. All things in nature stand still until the Judgment of the Overseers has been implemented.' I thought furiously. No-one was getting out of this place, we were under the control of creatures I had no way to touch, let alone stop. My eyes met Perun's across the circle and I felt my loathing of him mushroom in my stomach. Everything that had happened here was because of him; his hatred of Zora's impure blood, his impatience to rule, his desire to dominate Manitu and turn it into his dictator's vision of perfection. If only I'd given in to him from the very start, ruled with him, let him have his moment of glory then not one single life would have been sacrificed. Perun just needed to be given what he wanted and the world could return to peace.

'I seek leave to speak with Perun, privately.' There was no real privacy here, of course, the Overseers saw and heard all things, everywhere.

'You have all the time in the world,' replied the Overseers and for the first time I caught the faintest mockery in their voices. This was what they had intended all along, of course. I'd seen judges do it so often that I was surprised how I been taken in. When you have two warring sides, you just need to create a mutual enemy and stakes that neither finds acceptable and suddenly they decide to negotiate. All I had to do was persuade Perun that I had something he wanted. I swallowed a significant amount of pride and approached him. He didn't move an inch, just lowered his face to mine and although his look was harsh, I could see the light of curiosity in his eyes.

'Truce,' I said. 'We both stand to lose more than we gain. I have a proposition for you. Will you put aside your hatred of me for a moment so that you can listen with your head clear?'

'What are you offering?' he asked. I fought the urge to slap him and walk away, remembering the price for it would be paid by the people I love.

'Marry me,' I said. 'A partnership, no tricks. We'll do it officially when the Council convenes. It will stop the war, you can rule a country reunited and I will persuade the Vilya to accept it. In return, Zora will remain living in Manitu with my mother and you will guarantee her safety. I will support you as you reign and I give you my word I will not leave or try to harm you in any way.' The words stuck in my throat but I continued. Perun, an enemy more vicious and despicable than any I could imagine, was my only hope.

My heart sank when he laughed out loud. He took his time but when he'd done mocking me he leaned down to whisper in my ear. 'You overestimate your own value, Eve. You have announced your abdication. I will rule Manitu without your help and those who do not like the way I use my authority can be put in their place easily enough. I do not have to tolerate Zora or your interference for another moment. The offer is too little, too late.'

'There's something else,' I said, putting my hand on his arm and pulling him to me. 'Something you don't know. The reason I was sent away and exchanged for Zora. Only half of my blood is Vilya. My father was Polevoi.' I saw the interest in his eyes before his guard could come down.

'The Polevoi are influential in Manitu but they have nothing I want, although I have to admit, the pleasure of seeing you begging is an unexpected benefit.' I took my hand off his arm.

'My father's mother was Polevoi too but she was impregnated by Gregor, a cambion. His father was an incubus and his mother was human.' He wasn't laughing now and I finally had his full attention. 'So you see, your family is also partly mine. And because I have some human genes I can also bear your child. I know how highly you value the offspring of cambions. It's why I was hidden from you for so long. But here I am and I stand by what I said. I give you my word, it is no trick. I want Zora and James both to live. I want your word that no harm will ever come to them by your hand. And I will be as faithful a wife as you could want.'

It was like offering a drug addict his fix. His pupils were dilated when he slid his hand round my neck, tilting my head back to look me in the eyes. 'You're telling the truth,' he said, but it was a statement rather than a question. 'Anousk was right then, sending you away like that. Do you know what you're capable of?' he asked. It was time to play nice.

'I'm sure you can show me,' I whispered. He nodded and the look of proprietary lust that came over his face sent a chill down my spine.

I gently freed myself from him and walked back into the centre of the circle, raising my voice and announcing my new proposal loud enough that no-one was left in any doubt about my commitment. 'We have reached an accord that will return peace to Manitu and settle both our debts with nature,' I announced, more sure of myself than before. 'I have agreed to marry Perun. I will stay here, as his wife. I have given my word that I will do him no harm, that I will not attempt to leave him, that I will be a fitting wife for a ruler. We will work together to mend the damage that our war has done. He has agreed that Zora can remain in Manitu, free from persecution and that James can leave with neither the taint of a curse or fear of pursuit.' I didn't look at James. I could sense his frustration but he couldn't help me now.

'If I do this, if I sacrifice my place in the human world, will you let them both go, restored to their former selves? Is that enough for the balance to be restored?'

There was a mad swirling within the lights. The circle went from bright to dim and for the first time I heard a clash of hissing voices as they were divided. Perun was agitated and I saw him making hard fists with his hands as he stood and waited for the Overseers to reach a decision. I held my breath.

'A life,' they said. 'A life to make you understand the value of all you have taken, sullied and destroyed. A life to make sure that you have sacrificed enough to stop you making the same mistakes twice.'

'No,' I hissed back at them. 'This is the only way I will do it. It is the only way to end the retribution forever.'

'Whose life?' Perun said. I whirled round to him.

'Perun, don't. Please!'

'The life of a loved one,' the Overseers called back and there was almost hysteria in their voices this time. I looked at James then pictured Zora in her bed the last time I'd seen her. It was impossible.

'Then I won't do it,' I told Perun. 'I won't let either of them die without killing myself too.' In a flash Perun pulled a ceremonial dagger from his belt. I ran towards James, putting my own body between him and Perun but I was going the wrong way.

By the time I turned round, Perun had grabbed his sister, Lantak, by the hair. In a single movement he sliced his dagger deep through her throat, holding her bleeding body up as if showing the Overseers exactly the extent of the sacrifice he was willing to make. It took just seconds for the life to fade out of her eyes and, with her final rasping breath, he let her slide to the floor in a crumpled heap.

A scream came from outside the circle, unmistakably Mandalina and it shocked me to feel her pain; the awful, shocked grief of losing a child. I heard her weeping and moaning but still Perun didn't flinch. The light from the Overseers was glowing different colours, blending into one another and hurting my eyes with its intensity.

'There you are,' said Perun. 'The life of a loved one. You have what you asked for. Now do your part.' I waited to see what would happen but the Overseers simply began whirling around us, saying nothing. The circle of light closed inwards, becoming brighter and more complete until there was no darkness left. Eventually there was just Perun and I inside it, staring at one another, both too perturbed to move or speak, wondering if it would ever end. When the lights wrapped around us I felt a surge of joy from the Vilya. I could almost reach out my mind to my mother and I knew that Zora had opened her eyes for the first time in days. The Overseers had done what they told me they could. They had cured her. Without thinking about it I reached a hand out to Perun to hold on to him.

'Thank you,' I said. Right then, whatever else happened, I meant it. Even if it was for his own selfish reasons and even if I had to give up everything to get what I wanted, he had helped me save her life. We stayed like that, with me holding onto him, until the lights vanished and all around me were the gasps and cries of the Perelesnyk and Polevoi, as the night returned to normal. The Overseers had disappeared. I let go of Perun and ran to James who was stood at the edge of the clearing with his back to me.

'James,' I said from behind him. 'It was the only way.'

'I'd rather you'd let me go. You know what these animals are capable of and now I have to go back there knowing they can keep you here forever. How is it you ever thought I would be able to do that?'

'You have to,' I said. 'I couldn't make a choice that would have meant death for you just as you wouldn't have done it to me. Please forgive me. At least this way you can go back, you can look after Sabina and Naomi, take care of the ranch. You can explain to them where I am and why, they'll understand. As long as I keep my promises, you and Zora and everyone else will be safe.'

'The price was too high,' he said and there was no point in disagreeing.

'I will ask the Polevoi to take you back into Slovakia, to a town where you can get help. Sabina will arrange to get you home.' I tried to keep my voice steady, let him see me strong and without regret but it was the worst of lies. 'This way you can have the life you've dreamed of. Find someone you can go home to every night, settle down, start a family. The curse is lifted, James. Make up for the time you've lost.'

'Knowing you're here, with him?' he motioned towards Perun. I steeled my heart for another goodbye, as unbearable as the first had been. There was no painless way of doing this.

'Yes,' I said. 'And you have to, because otherwise Tim, Patrick, Bryn and countless others will have given their lives for nothing.' I grabbed his shirt and pulled him towards me, holding him tight for a last few seconds. 'Go and live the life I wanted to live with you. Do it for me.'

I spun around and walked away, marching past Perun who had the sense not to try and stop me. I went to Tetra who was waiting calmly for me. 'Will your men take him back to his world?' I asked. 'He needs to find somewhere he can get shelter and call for help.'

'Of course,' she called to her soldiers and they immediately made their way over to James. I didn't look back, couldn't watch him go. I held my head up and let Tetra wrap a cloak round my shoulders as I held back the tears that I wouldn't give Perun the satisfaction of seeing fall.

'Come,' Tetra whispered to me. 'Perun's servants have shown my men where we can go to rest. I will stay with you a while.' She led me away and I tried to cling on to my last ounce of courage as I let go of all my dreams of home and happiness. I had saved the two most precious lives in return for my own. The price wasn't too high but then I hadn't really started paying for it yet.

Twenty-nine

Perun's personal guard escorted us back through the streets to the same building where I'd last been held as a prisoner in the underground cells. We were taken to apartments where I washed my face, carefully folding my precious gloves by the wash basin. Tetra was quiet as she waited for me to reappear.

I sat next to her on a long sofa, not knowing what to say in the circumstances.

'You had no choice,' she said. 'Your friend, James, will understand when the pain of his loss subsides. I think you were very brave.' I smiled at her, knowing that if I tried to speak I'd start crying and once that happened, stopping would be impossible.

'I shall send a messenger to Anousk to tell her what you did. I believe you can bring peace to Manitu, Eve. Your sacrifice, as great as it was, will not be for nothing. Perun knows how valuable you are to him and he will take no risks with your life. You will be safe with him.'

'Safe?' I said. 'With a man who slaughtered his own sister in cold blood, in front of his family, to secure his political position? He's a monster.'

'Give him what he wants and find ways to avoid him the rest of the time,' she said. 'Once you have won his trust, ask for the courtesy of having one of the Polevoi as your personal body guard. I shall send someone I trust completely, one of my own men, to look after you. Anything you need, he will get me word and I promise to come straight away. You are not so alone as you feel at this moment.'

'Do you think he'll let me see my mother? It's the one thing I have to gain from all this. Perhaps she and I can have some time together now.' Tetra held my hand and spoke to me softly.

'I think not, for a while. He will be too wary of the influence others might have over you. Speaking of mothers, take my advice child and stay away from Mandalina. The succubus Perun killed was her most favoured daughter. Lantak and Mandalina were inseparable. Her rage will not die quickly and she may behave unpredictably in her grief. At this moment she may be a worse enemy to you than your future husband.' A knock at the door disturbed us. Perun entered the room and I automatically got to my feet. Tetra stayed where she was, making it clear that she was still the more senior of the two but Perun's victory made him more gracious than I'd seen him before.

'Tetra, I am grateful to you for your care of Eve whilst I attended to arrangements. Your men are waiting to escort you back to your own citadel and I wish you safe passage. I am sure that we will see one another again soon. I must say, your intervention was welcome even if I did not show my thanks earlier. Perhaps we can reach an understanding now that our families are to be joined?'

'Indeed,' Tetra said as she allowed Perun to help her to her feet, kissing her hand deferentially as he did so. 'Treat her kindly, Perun. I want my family kept safe. Walk me to the door, child.' She took my arm and I went with her until we were just beyond the doorframe but still in Perun's sight. She let me go with a little wave back at him. I waited until she was at the far end of the corridor then went back into the suite.

'Sit down,' Perun said. 'You must be exhausted.' He was right and I did as he suggested. He watched me, assessing my mood although I was beyond playing games. 'You will want for nothing here. It was a fair compromise and I congratulate you on your resourcefulness. I admire you, Eve. It is not such a bad way to start a partnership.'

'I would have thought that slashing your own sister's throat might have given you more to worry about than me,' I replied.

'Do not concern yourself with Mandalina,' he said. 'My mother knows that she must do nothing to jeopardise our ascension now.'

'Do you really care so little for your own flesh and blood?' I asked, scared by how unmoved he was by the events of the past few hours.

'Would you rather I had taken the life of that male you seem so attached to?' I didn't answer. He could have killed him, I suppose; Zora would have been saved and I could have returned home never to trouble him again. He was obviously sure I had something he could use to increase his own power.

'You scare me,' I told him, brutally honest. I was all out of intrigue and had no defences left.

'I recall a time when I had a less chilling effect on you,' he countered and picked up my right hand. He began running his fingertips lightly up and down the sensitive skin of my inner arm between the wrist and elbow as I did my best not to squirm away. This was the existence I'd bargained for and it was too late for squeamishness. 'How did you find out that you have cambion blood in your veins?'

'Tetra,' I replied, not wanting him to try getting his hands on Adela's diaries when I'd read so little of them myself. 'I still don't understand it fully.'

He dropped my hand and leaned back, folding his arms behind his head in contemplation. He was different in his own surroundings, so at ease with himself, devoid of conscience and deep in thought. I could see the King he would become; self-assured and ruthless, charming and deadly. 'All of us are born of one human parent and an incubus or succubus, but cambions favour the physical nature of humans more whilst developing the non-physical traits of the incubi as they grow. They were often labelled witches or devils in your world. Why so many cambions choose to live there rather than with the Perelesnyk I shall never understand. It is only when cambion blood mixes with other races that we cannot predict what powers the child will have. You can heal and that comes from the Vilya. You can call down the storms and it is now clear that you have inherited that from us. Is there anything else changing in you?' I thought of the way I'd been able to view the scenes in other people's minds when they were recounting an event. At first I'd thought it was my overactive imagination but it was more than that. It was like seeing through someone else's eyes, completely voyeuristic.

'No,' I told him. 'Nothing new.' What was happening to me was my own business.

'There will be, I can feel you growing. Perhaps as you adapt to life here you will feel more sympathy for us. I will send a servant to feed and bathe you. I must attend to family matters but I shall return shortly. You have promises to keep.' He said it casually enough but the message was unmistakable. There were certain expectations of our relationship that I hadn't come to terms with yet.

'I, er, thought we would wait,' I stammered. 'Until our marriage is sanctioned by the Council.' He laughed aloud at that, genuinely amused.

'Oh, Eve, we are long acquainted now and I know that you have shown no such hesitation with other men. Let us not pretend that you are some shivering virgin. I want a child and you need to prove to me that your promises are real. I will be back soon and we can cement our agreement. You may not like me but that does not mean you will not like what I can do to you.'

He walked out and I stared at my reflection in the mirror on the back of the door. I was bruised and unkempt, my clothes shredded in places, with an angry wound on my face where I'd been struck by the light of the Overseers. I was in a beautiful prison with a barbarian for a fiancé. I had no way out and nothing to do. Before, there were always plans to make, the choice to fight or flee. Now there was only a frightened woman staring desperately at me from the glass as if I should have some magical solution up my sleeve. I grabbed the nearest heavy object and flung it at my reflection, shattering the glass on the door, shards flying out across the room. I was panting with the tension in my muscles and the adrenaline I couldn't release, when the door opened a crack. My face must have been the epitome of fury because the little eyes that peered in pulled back at first then, slowly the door opened wider to reveal Shelti, robes in one hand and a tray of food in the other. She surveyed the debris on the floor and began stepping carefully through it, avoiding the larger pieces with her thin shoes.

As she passed the door, she elbowed it shut behind her then reached out and clicked the little lock into place. She put down the things she'd been carrying and shyly held her arms open to me. I collapsed to my knees and buried my face in her chest, clinging on to her small body and crying uncontrollably as if she were my mother. She rocked me very gently and didn't let go until I'd recovered, speaking to me softly and continuously in a language I couldn't understand but they helped, those sounds of comfort. Eventually she took my hands and pulled me to my feet, settling me on the couch. She poured me water and gave me food. I did my best with it but had no appetite, unable to imagine ever wanting to eat again. Whilst I was playing with the morsels on my plate she went into another room and began running a bath.

I went through to where she was pouring oil into hot water and stripped off my filthy clothes. When I climbed into the bath, I felt the momentary relief of heat and weightlessness, shutting my eyes and pretending for a second that it would all turn out alright, that I could find a way to cope. I was deluded, of course. There was no escape from the demon waiting for me to show him how committed I was to the bargain I had just made. I opened my eyes when Shelti tapped my arm. She was holding a small, earthenware bottle on one hand and a goblet in the other. I raised my eyebrows at her, not knowing what she expected from me and she mimed pouring a little of whatever was in the bottle into the cup then closed her eyes, making a snoring noise.

I motioned at myself. For me? I was asking. She shook her head from side to side and then pointed out into the main suite. Knuckles began rapping hard at the other side of the door and Perun was suddenly bellowing to be let in. Shelti hid the small bottle in a chest of drawers, making sure I was watching as she did it, then went to open the door to Perun, pointing at the glass on the floor to explain why the door had been secured. I heard him call into the hallway for someone to clear it up. His footsteps moved into the room and then stopped. He must have sat down to wait as Shelti returned with a dress for me. I stepped out of the bath feeling a fraction of my former backbone return.

I slipped the pale green silken robe over my shoulders and Shelti brushed my hair. Whilst I was unused to having anyone fuss around me, it was reassuring to be looked after. She nodded at me in the mirror and patted me on the shoulders. I couldn't delay any more. Back in the main room, the glass had been brushed away and Perun had the courtesy not to comment on the incident. Before she left the room, Shelti slipped my gloves and watch into a drawer and inclined her head to me deferentially. As soon as the door closed, Perun walked to a side table.

'Wine?' he offered. I thanked him as he passed me a wooden goblet of the thick mead that Tetra had given me earlier. 'You look stunning,' he said.

'You don't need to bother with that,' I replied, more calmly than I felt. 'I gave you my word that I would play my part as your wife and I shall. You can save the compliments.'

'It is civility. You and I are capable of recognising that our life together will be all the better for it. Does it not make you feel happier, knowing that our marriage will be a matter of pride to me, not just an arrangement of convenience?'

'And yet you weren't the least bit interested until you found out exactly what I am,' I said.

'Is the thought of laying with me so terrible?' he asked. He undid his shirt as he spoke and I looked at the paradisiacal body beneath. His torso was tight with hard muscle and unblemished skin and he waited for my reaction.

'An hour ago we were enemies,' I said. 'Forgive me if I can't switch allegiance as easily as you.'

'Then let me help you,' he whispered as he walked over and pushed his fingers into my hair, leaning down to push the dress off one shoulder and run his lips over my neck. I steeled my heart, lifted my face up and when he pushed his tongue hard into my mouth I thought of riding out across the meadowlands at the ranch, imagined myself somewhere else, lost in the memories that would keep me sane. The only thing that would make this bearable was to get it over with as quickly as possible. I met his tongue with my own, pressing my body against his and running my nails down his back. He pulled my dress off the other shoulder and it fell to the floor. I was naked beneath and he took a step away to get a fuller picture of the asset he'd just acquired. As if I weighed nothing at all, he picked me up in his arms and walked into the adjoining room where an enormous bed waited. When he'd lowered me down, he kicked off his shoes and remaining clothing, and lay next to me naked. He ran one hand casually across my breasts and my skin crawled with revulsion. It was fortunate that he mistook my reaction for something much more carnal.

'You see,' he said. 'It is possible to overcome even the most impassioned of disputes. This is much better.' When he started to trail his fingers down my stomach I knew I couldn't take it any more. I pushed myself backwards off the bed, playing for time.

'I agree,' I said. 'Just one minute, though. I'll bring our wine in. There's no rush is there?' He raised his eyebrows at me but said nothing and I left the room, running my hands through my hair as I thought how I could stop this before it got ugly. I went into the bathroom to splash cold water on my face, trying to shock myself into a better state of mind and was stood in front of the chest where Shelti had hidden the bottle before I'd even realised what I was doing. I had no idea what the liquid inside was, if it would sedate him or kill him and the truth was, right then, I didn't care. I grabbed it and took out the stopper, sniffing cautiously at the contents. It was faintly floral with a bitter edge, but it would easily be masked by the sweet wine Perun had poured earlier. I took a deep breath, made up my mind that whatever happened I would know I did my best to stop it.

'Eve, are you waiting for me to come and find you? I am not in the mood for games.' Perun was calling from the bedroom. I forced my voice to sound carefree as I responded.

'Just another minute,' I replied, running with the bottle into the lounge. I picked up the two goblets and put a few drops of the clear liquid into Perun's cup then poured more wine over the top. As I waited I refilled my own. I may have no choice but to go through with this, but I didn't have to do it sober.

'Eve!' his voice rang out, louder this time. I would have to learn to live with his impatience. I grabbed the bottle and tucked it inside my gloves where Shelti had put them in the drawer. Forcing a look of serenity onto my face, I reappeared around the doorway to the bedroom.

'Here,' I said, offering him the cup and sitting back down on the bed. 'To a more peaceful future.' I raised my goblet and took a long draught of the wine, watching him do the same. I would have sat there longer, sipping away but he reached out and took mine from me, putting it down so that he could pull me back onto the bed.

'Come to me,' he whispered. I wound my arms round his neck and kissed his chest as he explored my body with his hands. When I closed my eyes I saw his dagger dripping blood, showing off his dying sister like a trophy. I felt his fingers push between my legs and tried to pretend it wasn't happening. I pressed my face into his neck so that he wouldn't hear me cry and in my head I began to count, hoping that if I could just focus on that one thing, counting to a high enough number and thinking of absolutely nothing else, soon it would be over. His hand fell away from my body as I worked to control the breathing that would give away my distress. Then the crushing strength of his arms relaxed and I felt his shoulders fall. I waited, almost not daring to hope, then lifted my head up slowly.

'Perun?' I said softly as I studied his face. His breathing was regular and deep, and his face had lost all emotion. I slid away, taking care not to disturb him, unsure how long his sleep would last. When I was safely off the bed I dressed again, not wanting to be naked in the same room as him. I turned off the lamps and pulled a cover across his body, doing all I could to make him warm and comfortable.

I went back to the drawer and took my gloves out, ensuring the bottle stopper was replaced securely. Whatever drug was in there wouldn't last forever and I knew this was just a stay of execution but at least for tonight, with James still so close and the blood of the day not yet dry on Perun's hands, I could keep him away from me. In the morning I would find out how much, if anything, he remembered. I washed the wine from the cups so that there would be no evidence of what I'd done and went to sit on the window sill, looking out across the skyline of the Perelesnyk's citadel.

It was stunning from here, lamp light shining across the facades of the marble buildings, everything orderly and neat, the distant walls keeping out enemies just as they would keep me in. I wondered how far it was to the Polevoi and knew it would do me no good to run. I'd given my word and perhaps, after all, this was justice. I had taken matters into my own hands before, thinking I could intervene and impose my own will on these people and now I was paying the price for it. I would stay with Perun, hope that he would grow bored of me, choose a different wife. When he ascended to power he'd have only a few years to reign until the next family in line would take over. Maybe then, when I could be of no more use, he might let me go.

Until that time I would have to do my best to please him and see if, in return, he would allow me contact with Tetra and my mother. I pictured Zora getting stronger, living freely and happily and knew that Adela would be looking down on me with gratitude. I would have to find a way to cope with Perun's demands. It was not such a big sacrifice in return for Zora's life. I wondered if James would ever forgive me. I knew he understood why I'd done it but that wasn't the same thing as coming to terms with my decision.

I needed to fill my time. I would do whatever I could to help the Vestas, to stop the abuse of the humans a stone's throw from my window. My life here didn't have to be wasted. From a far room I could hear muffled screeching and remembered Mandalina. It was little comfort to know that there was someone in even more pain than me, tonight. I pulled on James' gloves, stroking the soft leather and holding them to my face to breathe in the musty smell that would always remind me of the man I loved. After a few minutes I took them off again and slid them to the back of the drawer so they would not easily be discovered.

I put my head up and my shoulders back, not beaten into submission, not bettered by the monster whose bed and life I was destined to share. I thought of my friends; Naomi, Sabina, Xander, Daniel and wished them safe. James would look after them, now. I walked back into the bedroom and slid into bed next to my husband to be. I pulled one of his arms over me and curled up so that I was wrapped in his body. I told myself that this was not forever, that I would see the people I loved once more, that I would reclaim the life I longed for so much. This couldn't be an ending. I wasn't done fighting yet.

Acknowledgments

My grateful thanks to Dr. Christian Chilcott who provided not only his medical expertise but also a healthy dose of creative thinking. Any errors are mine alone. Thanks also to my friends and readers Emma Bulstrode, Andrea Gibson and Allison Spyer for giving up yet more of their precious time to lend support, critique and enthusiasm as needed. Prashant Singh, the cover designer, deserves a medal for his patience with me and also my gratitude for the finished article. Finally, to my family who have given me the space and encouragement to write, I can't thank you enough.

About The Author

Helen Fields spent thirteen years practising as a criminal and family law barrister. Since then she has worked as a producer/ script writer in a small media company. She lives in the south of England with her husband and three children, but San Francisco is her favourite city. She is the author of The Immolation of Eve, the first book in this series, and is currently writing her first legal novel. Eve will return to continue her journey with you in 2013.

Printed in Great Britain
by Amazon